LIVERPOOL LOYALTY

CAZ FINLAY

One More Chapter
a division of HarperCollins*Publishers* Ltd
1 London Bridge Street
London SE1 9GF
www.harpercollins.co.uk

This paperback edition 2021
First published in Great Britain in ebook format
by HarperCollins*Publishers* 2020

A catalogue record of this book
is available from the British Library

ISBN: 978-0-00-840511-3

This novel is entirely a work of fiction. The names, characters and
incidents portrayed in it are the work of the author's imagination. Any
resemblance to actual persons, living or dead, events or localities is
entirely coincidental.

Printed and bound in Great Britain by
CPI Group (UK) Ltd, Croydon CR0 4YY

For my husband, Eric. You truly are my other half.

And as always, for Finlay, Jude and James.

Chapter One

Grace Carter switched off the engine of her Range Rover and waited in the side street opposite St Anne's Street police station. She'd spent the best part of her day on the phone to various people, including her solicitor Faye Donovan, who had cut short her holiday to Monaco and caught the first flight home, heading straight to the police station when she'd landed at John Lennon Airport. Faye Donovan was the best solicitor that money could buy, and Grace paid her well to receive a priority service. Right now, her son Jake and stepson Connor were being interviewed by Merseyside's boys in blue, and Faye and her team were doing their best to stop any charges being brought against them.

Faye had assured Grace that she'd do her best to make sure the boys walked out of St Anne's that same day, and Grace believed her. If anyone could deliver on that promise, it was Faye. She was ruthless, and well known amongst her peers as being one of the most ferocious and relentless

1

opponents any of them had even encountered. It was rumoured that whenever her name came up on a trial docket, there was a collective groan from the CPS and the defence team. She'd worked her way up from a small criminal law firm based in Birkenhead to being the managing partner in Donovan, Haigh and Macaulay in Liverpool city centre. Faye only took on the most prestigious and highest paying clients, and Grace was her top priority. Over the years, Grace had practically bankrolled the setting up of the firm's new offices in Dale Street, but she considered Faye worth every penny she'd paid her. She'd kept Grace's, and later her husband Michael's, employees out of hot water on numerous occasions and in doing so had ensured that their operations continued to run smoothly.

Grace had left Michael with their two youngest children, Oscar and Belle, who were safely tucked up in bed, while she had driven into town so she could pick up Jake and Connor as soon as they were released. She'd had a text message from Faye a short while earlier to tell her that things were moving along, and she was hopeful that the boys would be released soon. Grace sat in her car, watching the rain running down the windscreen and hoped that Faye was right. The thought of Jake and Connor going to prison for murder made her feel like throwing up. From the limited information she'd been able to glean from DI Tony Webster, who was on Grace's payroll and had been the one to alert her to Jake and Connor's situation, the boys had been arrested for the murder of Billy Johnson, which had happened just over three months earlier.

Billy Johnson and his brothers had been a pain in the arse for Jake and Connor, but they'd never posed a credible threat to their business. At least, Grace had never figured them as one. There had been some rumours that the brothers had been involved in Grace's stepson Paul's murder, but there had been no credibility to them. Paul had been gunned down in broad daylight in the street outside the gym he frequented. It had been a professional hit, and both the hitman and the man responsible for ordering the job, Sol Shepherd, were now dead themselves. Shortly after Paul's death, the oldest Johnson brother, Bradley, had disappeared and Billy had been murdered. Grace suspected that Jake and Connor had been involved in Billy's death, but she'd never spoken to them about it. The aftermath of Paul's murder had been a difficult time for the whole family, and Jake and Connor had dealt with it in their own way. Grace had given little thought to the departed Johnson brothers since – she'd had much more pressing matters on her mind. No one else had seemed overly interested in them either – until now.

Grace was deep in thought when she saw movement from the corner of her eye. Looking up, she saw the unmistakeable figures of Jake and Connor approaching her Range Rover, with Faye Donovan following closely behind. Faye walked confidently, with a smile on her face as she flicked her long blonde hair over her shoulder with a toss of her head. Grace felt a huge sense of relief. Not only were the boys out of the station, but the look on Faye's face meant that it was good news.

Grace waited while Jake and Connor climbed into the back seat and Faye slid into the passenger seat beside her.

'So?' Grace asked.

'They've both been questioned in relation to Billy Johnson's murder, but the police don't have much to go on,' Faye answered in her usual calm and assured manner. 'No DNA at the scene. It's all circumstantial, which is why they've let the boys go pending further investigation. They don't have enough to charge, and in my opinion they've played their hand too soon. But that's to our advantage. Their whole case seems to rest on an eyewitness at the moment.'

'An eyewitness?' Grace replied.

Faye nodded.

Grace turned in her seat to face the boys. 'Is that possible?'

'Of course not,' Jake said.

'We're not that stupid,' Connor replied.

'Well, no. But there's still someone claiming that they saw you, isn't there?' she said with a sigh as she stared at her son and stepson in the back seat, looking to the outside world like the ruthless hard men they were, but to her like a pair of little boys who had just been sent to the Headmaster's office.

Faye cleared her throat and Grace was reminded she was still in the car.

'Sorry, Faye. You must be exhausted,' Grace said as she rested her hand on the other woman's arm. 'Thank you so much for rushing back for this. I can't thank you enough.'

'It's not a problem. Anything for you, Grace. You know that,' Faye replied with a smile.

Grace nodded. Faye had never once let her down in a crisis. 'Well, I appreciate it all the same.'

'The boys have told me everything I need to know. I'll let them fill you in, Grace. So, unless there's anything else you need me for, I'll be getting home for a shower and a large G and T,' Faye said as she rubbed the back of her neck.

'Of course. You get off home. I think you've earned that G and T,' Grace replied.

'Thanks. I'll call you tomorrow and we can discuss things further,' Faye said before turning to Jake and Connor. 'You two stay out of trouble, and call me if anything happens that you think I need to know about.'

Jake and Connor nodded. 'We will. Thanks, Faye,' they said in unison.

Grace watched Faye step gracefully out of the car before turning to give a final wave as she walked away. As Faye disappeared out of sight, Grace turned to the boys in the back seat. 'Ready to get out of here?'

They nodded.

'Too fucking right,' Connor said with a sigh. 'Is Jazz at home or is she at your place?'

'She's still at ours with your dad. She didn't want to be on her own, so we made up one of spare rooms for you both.'

'Sound. I'll come to yours then,' Connor replied.

'Jake?' Grace asked. 'Are you coming too? I've made up a room for you as well. Both have fresh bedding and I can promise a slap-up cooked breakfast in the morning.'

Jake shook his head. 'No. Take me to the club, please, Mum. I need a drink.'

'We've got all the drink you need at our house,' she reminded him. 'And it would give us all a chance to talk things through. Consider our next steps?'

'I just want a drink with the lads,' he snapped. 'We can talk tomorrow. I've been stuck in a sweaty interview room all day being talked at. The last thing I want to do now is talk some more.'

Grace frowned at him in the rear-view mirror and she saw Connor nudging him in the ribs.

Obviously remembering who he was talking to, Jake quickly added, 'Not tonight, eh, Mum? We can talk tomorrow.'

Grace sensed she wasn't going to change her son's mind, and as much as she wanted to have a good talk with him about everything that had happened that day, she let it go. 'Okay. I'll drop you at the club on our way home. You can still call in for a fry-up in the morning if you fancy.'

'I'll see,' he replied.

'We'll wait for you,' Connor added. 'We need to talk about today, and what we're going to do next, whether you feel like it or not.'

Jake sat back in the seat with a sigh. 'Fine. I'll be round for breakfast. Now can we go?'

Grace started the engine and resisted the urge to remind him that if it wasn't for her he'd still be sitting in that sweaty little interview room. She reasoned that he'd had a tough day, and he was entitled to go out and see his mates and let off some steam. It must be hard for him to see

Connor and his girlfriend Jasmine all loved up, especially when losing Paul was still so raw for him. It had been a shock for Grace to learn that Jake and her stepson, Paul had become much more than stepbrothers. They had been in an on/off relationship for years and had kept it a secret from almost everyone – for numerous reasons including the fact that Jake had been married at the time and also firmly in the closet. Grace had learned about their relationship shortly beforehand, but it was only after Paul was shot and killed that she discovered just how much her son had loved the other man. His death had hit them all hard, but Jake seemed to be unable to pull himself out of the pit of despair he'd been wallowing in. She knew that despite having his family around, all of whom adored him, he still felt alone. He and Connor were like brothers, and, being Paul's twin, Connor had been hit harder by Paul's death than anyone. But Connor had Jasmine and their unborn baby to focus on and give him a reason to go on living. Michael had, understandably, been floored by the murder of his son. But he had Grace to keep him warm at night and his other children to think of. Jake had his daughter Isla, of course, but he didn't see her as much now that Siobhan had moved to Lytham. His contact had been reduced to one weekend a fortnight, but that was at Jake's own request. Grace wondered what on earth she could do to try and make him see how much he still had to be grateful for.

Chapter Two

D I Leigh Moss stormed through the open-plan office of St Anne's Street police station with a face like thunder. Walking into her office, she sat down on her chair and threw the manila folder she was carrying onto her desk.

DS Nick Bryce followed her inside, closing the door behind him.

'Damn Faye bloody Donovan,' Leigh snapped. 'She is a pain in my sodding arse.'

'She's stopped more people going down than herpes,' Nick said with a laugh.

'How the hell does she sleep at night?' Leigh asked in exasperation.

'On a gold plated four-poster bed, probably. But to be fair to her, I'm not sure we'd have got a word out of Conlon or Carter even if she wasn't their brief.'

'You're probably right, but nobody can put the shits up an interviewing officer like she can. I should have interviewed them both myself.'

'With respect, Ma'am, you can't be in two places at once, and you were needed in court last minute.'

'Yes, I was, wasn't I? And don't tell me there wasn't something fishy about that. I finally lift two of the biggest villains in Liverpool and all of a sudden my witness testimony in the O'Keefe trial is needed a day earlier than expected. You think that's just a coincidence?'

'You know how trials are. Besides, do you really think Conlon and Carter have that much clout that they can influence trials?'

'No. But Grace Carter does. All it would take is a word in the right judge's ear, and I'll bet my life on the fact that she's got at least a couple of them in her pockets.'

Nick sucked the air through his teeth and shook his head. 'I think you're being paranoid, Leigh,' he said, breaking rank and using her first name in the safe confines of her office.

'Then you obviously don't know Grace Carter very well.' Leigh glared at him.

'And you do?' he asked with a raise of his eyebrow.

'Of course,' she snapped. 'It's my job to know. Now, how about you make yourself useful and use your considerable charm to get Forensics to put a rush on those fingerprints. If Conlon or Carter touched anything at that crime scene, I want to know.'

'Of course, Ma'am,' he replied before walking out of her office.

Leigh sat back in her leather chair with a sigh. She'd snapped at Nick unnecessarily, and now he was pissed off with her. He was so bloody sensitive sometimes. She wondered at times like these whether it was sensible to have him in her team, given their relationship. They had been good mates for years, and friends with benefits for most of that time. But lately it had been turning into something more. They'd agreed to keep their relationship secret until they figured out whether they had any real future together. No point in screwing up their working relationship unnecessarily. The truth was that he'd hit a nerve with his quip about Grace Carter. What Nick, or any of her colleagues, didn't know was that in another life Leigh had known Grace well. They were what some people might consider friends. But that had all been before Leigh had joined the police force and Grace had become the queen of the Liverpool underworld. It was amazing to Leigh that they had taken such different paths in life. Once allies, they were now on opposite sides of the fence.

Leigh shuddered when she thought about how her life could have turned out so differently. What would have become of her if she hadn't aborted Nathan Conlon's child? If he'd divorced Grace and married her instead, as she had once begged him to do? Would it be her sitting in a mansion in South Liverpool? She had to believe that she would have never have sunk so low, but who knew? She had been an entirely different person back then. She smiled at the irony of it all. If it wasn't for Grace Carter, she'd have been left for dead in an alleyway. Grace had saved her life, and given her the chance to become who she was today. And it would be Grace who'd try to stand in her way when she finally brought the Conlon–Carter empire down. Leigh would do it though. Even if that meant bringing Grace down too.

Chapter Three

Michael was waiting at the open front door by the time Grace and Connor arrived home at a quarter past midnight. Connor walked up the path first and Michael pulled his son into a hug before ushering him inside.

'I told you I'd bring them home,' Grace said with a smile as she reached him.

He put an arm around her. 'I never doubted you for a second,' he replied. 'Where's Jake?'

'Gone to his club. Said he needed a drink and didn't want to talk about anything. Not yet anyway.'

Michael didn't respond as they walked into the house together and Grace suspected he was resisting the urge to say something she might not appreciate. She was well aware that she had overlooked too much of Jake's selfish behaviour recently, but what choice did she have? He was her son and he was in pain. So even if, on this occasion, she might agree with whatever Michael had to say, she was still grateful that he chose not to say it.

Walking into the living room, Grace saw Connor and his heavily pregnant girlfriend Jasmine locked in an embrace. Jasmine was holding onto him as though she might never let him go and Grace could hear her gentle sobbing.

Seeing them walk into the room, Connor gently pulled away from her. 'I'm not going anywhere, babe. I promise,' he assured her, before turning his attention to Grace and Michael.

Jasmine turned to look at them too and Grace noticed how tired she looked. At eight months pregnant, and after the day they'd all had, she had every reason to be.

'I'm sorry, I must like a right mess,' Jasmine said as she wiped the tears from her face. 'Pregnancy hormones?' she added with a slight shrug.

Grace walked over to her and gave her a hug. 'Well, either that or this one and my son almost giving us all a heart attack,' she said as she pulled away and nodded towards Connor.

Jasmine laughed and gave Connor a playful shove. 'Oh yeah, and that.'

Connor held his hands up in mock surrender. 'Don't blame me. I didn't plan to be arrested for murder when I got out of bed this morning.'

A silence fell across the room and nobody spoke for a moment, not wanting to think about the potential implications of that statement.

'Why don't you head off to bed, babe? You look shattered,' Connor said to Jasmine.

'Yes, I think I will,' she said. 'I'll see you all in the morning. Goodnight.'

'Goodnight, Jazz,' Grace and Michael said.

'I'll be up soon, babe,' Connor said as he gave her a kiss on the cheek.

'Brandy?' Michael asked as Jasmine left the room.

'Yep, and make it a large one,' Connor replied.

'Just a small one for me,' Grace added.

Connor knocked his drink back straightaway and Michael quickly poured him another.

When the three of them each had a drink in hand and were sitting comfortably, Grace was finally able to ask the question she was sure she knew the answer to, but had to ask anyway.

'So, did you and Jake do it?'

Connor nodded and sat back against the sofa with a sigh. 'We hadn't planned to, but it just got out of hand. Neither of us were thinking straight. We just wanted … for Paul…'

Michael placed a reassuring hand on his son's shoulder. 'We know, son.'

Grace appreciated that it was painful talking about what happened, but now wasn't the time to let emotions run away with them. She had to know what happened and whether the police would find any further evidence, or, more importantly, whether there was anything she could do to prevent that from happening. 'Faye said the police didn't seem to have much to go on. That it was all circumstantial?'

'Yeah. Seemed to be. They have our car driving into the street around the time of the murder, but thanks to the building works at the end of the road, no CCTV of us leaving the same road. They took our fingerprints and DNA samples, but we both wore gloves, so it's not likely we'd have left any of our DNA on the body. We weren't cut or anything.'

'Did you use any weapons?'

Connor shook his head.

'Well, at least there won't be a weapon to be found, or any fragments on the body that could have your DNA on,' she said as she sat forward. 'But Faye mentioned they had an eyewitness?'

'Yes. She told us that. But there were no witnesses, I told you that.'

'How are you so sure no one could have seen you? It could have been a neighbour who saw you go in the house.'

'That street's half empty. Most of the houses are boarded up. And the people who do live there don't talk to the filth. None of them saw us, but even if they did, they wouldn't have talked. I guarantee it.'

'Was there anyone else in the house?' Grace asked.

'No. We checked.'

'But Billy lived with his youngest brother Scott. So maybe he was there and you didn't find him?' she said, aware that after a day of being interviewed, the last thing Connor probably wanted to do was answer more questions, but it was important that she knew everything that there was to know. She had to think of every angle, just as the police would.

'He may have been there before we arrived, but he definitely wasn't there afterwards – we checked. And if he'd been there and seen his brother getting the shit kicked out of him, he'd have phoned the bizzies, wouldn't he?'

Grace nodded and sat back in her chair, deep in thought. 'Faye said that it was Scott and Craig who found the body. I think maybe Scott was at the house before you got in, and he went to get his brother.'

'You're probably right,' Michael said.

'So, you think Scott's the witness then? But he must have lied and told them he saw us going into the house,' Connor said.

'How else would he be an eyewitness? He would have to have seen you, and if you're sure he didn't, then he must have lied,' Grace replied.

'But why is he just coming forward now?' Michael asked.

'Maybe he's not. Faye mentioned she thought the police had revealed their hand too soon. Maybe they've been trying to put together an investigation for a while but this is all they've come up with?'

'Or maybe he's only just plucked up the nerve?' Michael added.

'Whatever the reason, I think Scott Johnson may be the key to all of this,' Grace said.

'Well, let's just see if Faye can work her magic first, eh?' Michael said as he downed his brandy.

'Either way, the Johnson brothers are going to need managing,' Connor reminded them.

Grace nodded but she saw the hint of a scowl flicker across Michael's face. He'd been getting increasingly restless lately. Talking about moving out to the suburbs and selling the security business. He seemed to want to turn his back on everything they had built. She knew it was because of Paul's death. He wanted better for their remaining children, but he didn't understand that they couldn't just walk away and leave Connor and Jake to handle things. Not until the boys had proved they were capable of doing so, at least. And so far, they hadn't. What Michael didn't seem to realise was that leaving this life behind them might protect Belle and Oscar, but it would be tantamount to throwing Jake and Connor to the lions. Grace couldn't bear to think what might happen if both she and Michael took their eye off the ball. They both wanted to protect their family, but they both had different ideas about how to go about it. It was a strange feeling when he wasn't on the same page as her, and one she wasn't used to. He'd always had her back. He had always trusted her judgement. Perhaps he still did, but she wasn't so sure…

'Any chance of a refill?' Connor asked as he held up his empty glass.

'Of course,' Michael said, standing up and taking the glass from his son's outstretched hand.

'I think I'll head to bed and leave you two boys to it,' Grace said as she stood up too. 'It's been a long day.'

'I'll be up soon, love,' Michael said, giving her a kiss on the cheek.

Grace slipped out of the room and left them to it.

Grace looked up from her phone to see Michael entering the bedroom. He walked towards her as she sat on the bed, placed his hands on her shoulders and kissed the top of her head.

'Has Connor gone to bed?' she asked him.

'Yeah. That last glass of brandy sent him over the edge. I practically had to carry him upstairs.'

'It's been a tough day,' Grace said.

'For everyone,' Michael replied as he sat on the bed beside her.

Grace placed her hand on his. 'How are you feeling?'

Michael shrugged. 'Better now that Connor and Jake have been released. But this isn't going away, is it?'

Grace shook her head. 'Not for a while,' she replied with a sigh. 'But Faye is the best. And if she can't fix it, we always have other means at our disposal.'

'Well, let's hope it doesn't come to that.'

Grace nodded. Although she hoped so too, there was nothing she wouldn't do to prevent Jake and Connor going to prison for murder and if what Connor had told her about that night was true, then she was in no doubt that the police's eyewitness was the youngest Johnson brother, Scott. It would be easy enough to get to him, but if she got to him now, it might look too suspicious and make the police even more determined. However, if she left it too late, the police could build a stronger case. Without knowing exactly what the police had, it was hard to determine what to do for the best. Grace was sure that her meeting with Faye the following day would give her some answers. For now, all she could do was wait.

'What time are you meeting with Faye tomorrow?' Michael asked as if reading her thoughts.

'We didn't agree a time. I'll probably go over in the afternoon. You coming with me?'

'Yeah. It will be good to hear what she has to say. Then we can plan our next move.'

'That's exactly what I was thinking,' Grace said as she turned to look at him. The day had taken its toll on him. In the past, he'd have taken something like this in his stride, but since Paul's murder he'd lost something of himself – he'd once had a belief that things would always work out in the end. Understandably, he no longer viewed the world in quite the same way.

'You didn't know I could read your mind, did you?' Michael said with a faint laugh.

'Well, you must know what I'm thinking now then?' she said as she turned her body and wrapped her arms around his neck.

'I think I have a pretty good idea,' he answered with a grin before pushing her back onto the bed and smothering her with a kiss.

Chapter Four

Grace looked around Faye Donovan's beautifully furnished office while she and Michael waited for her to arrive. She'd been delayed at court and was running late, which wasn't unusual for her. Grace had first met Faye ten years earlier when Michael's father, Patrick, had found himself in a spot of bother with the police while doing some business for her. Even back then, before she'd married Michael, Patrick had been like a father to her, so she'd looked around for the best solicitor she could find and had stumbled upon Faye.

Faye Donovan was a formidable opponent and a formidable woman. She was only a few years older than Grace, and the two of them had hit it off straightaway. Grace had been impressed by Faye's commitment and her willingness to do whatever it took to get the job done. Grace supposed they were alike in many ways, and the two women had worked together ever since.

Glancing across at Michael, who was sitting beside her

nursing the now lukewarm coffee Faye's assistant had brought them ten minutes earlier, she wondered just how much longer Faye was going to keep them waiting. Michael looked up at her and was about to speak when the large wooden office door swung open and a breathless Faye walked through it. Grace had always marvelled at how quickly Faye could walk in five-inch heels.

She smiled at the two of them as she brushed her long blonde hair back from her face. 'I'm so sorry to keep you both waiting,' she said as she walked past and took a seat opposite them. 'I just couldn't get away this morning.'

'No problem. Beth made us a coffee while we waited,' Grace answered with a smile.

Michael nodded and downed the last of his, before placing his cup on the desk.

Faye nodded and leaned forward in her chair. The smile slipped from her face and her carefully composed and cool façade took its place, signalling that the pleasantries were over with.

'Your boys have got themselves into a bit of a mess with his one. I've told them they'll need to be careful from now on and expect every move they make to be under scrutiny. They could well be under surveillance. That new DI, Leigh Moss, is on a crusade. She's determined to make them go down for this. But that could also be the very thing that tips the scales in our favour.'

'Oh? How so?' Grace asked as Michael placed his warm hand over hers and gave it a reassuring squeeze.

'I think DI Moss may have jumped the gun arresting them when she did. She could have taken the time to build a better case in my opinion, but she obviously thought what she had was enough.'

'And is it?' Grace asked.

Faye gave a slight shrug of her shoulders. 'There's an eyewitness – apparently. Not enough to charge them with yesterday, but who knows what will happen in the future?'

'Maybe she didn't have anything else to build a case with? Maybe this eyewitness is all she's got?'

'It was certainly all she had, but now she has the boys' prints and their DNA…'

Michael nodded. 'That's why she pulled them in then.'

'If they left any prints at the scene…' Faye started, not needing to finish her sentence.

'They said they wore gloves,' Grace replied.

'Let's hope so. Limits the chance of any DNA being left behind too.'

'So who is this eyewitness?' Grace asked.

Faye shook her head. 'They haven't disclosed yet. But I'm working on it.'

'I have a feeling it's Scott Johnson,' Grace said. 'He lived with Billy. He's the only one who could have seen anything, and he's probably the only one green enough to go to the police about it if he did.'

'From what the boys told me, they're sure there was no one else around, but you never know,' Faye added with a raise of her eyebrows.

'What do you think the chances are that they'll go down for this?' Michael asked as he leaned forward in his chair.

Faye looked at him, as though giving serious thought to his question. 'If you want my honest answer, in a murder trial it could go either way. If this witness is credible, and he really did see something, he could be the key to the whole thing...'

'But?' Michael asked, as though he was waiting for her to finish her sentence.

'But if anyone can discredit a witness, to gain the sympathies of a jury, then it's Faye,' Grace replied for her.

Faye gave a faint smile. 'I've certainly beaten worse odds before.'

'But there's a chance they'll go down for life if this ever goes to trial?' Michael snapped.

Faye nodded. 'There's always a chance if it goes to trial. But I'll do my best to make sure that never happens. I promise.'

'And so will we,' Grace said as she looked at her husband.

Michael sat back in his chair, his shoulders slumped as though in defeat. 'We'll fix this,' Grace said to him as she placed a hand on his arm. He looked at her and nodded but Grace saw no conviction in his eyes.

Grace leaned back in her seat as Michael pulled the car away from the kerb and began the drive home from the city centre to their home in Mossley Hill.

'Are you still going into the office?' Grace asked.

'Yeah. I need to sort some stuff out. I won't be too long though.'

'No problem. I have to take the kids to that party anyway.'

They drove in silence for a few moments before Michael spoke again. 'So, what are we going to do about Scott Johnson?' Michael asked.

Grace closed her eyes. 'I don't know yet. We need to be careful. If we approach him, we need to be one hundred per cent certain that he'll co-operate. Or...'

'Or we need to make sure that he doesn't have the chance to co-operate with anyone?' Michael finished her sentence for her.

'Exactly,' Grace replied.

She heard a soft sigh and out of the corner of her eye saw Michael shaking his head.

'What?' she asked him. While they might be effectively discussing the elimination of Scott Johnson, it was nothing they hadn't done before to protect their family.

'Nothing,' he replied.

'Don't lie to me. What's going on with you?'

Michael turned to face her as they stopped at the traffic lights on Edge Lane. 'Our kids might go down for murder, Grace. That's what's going on with me,' he snapped at her.

'Don't you think I know that? Isn't that precisely what we're talking about here?'

'I know, Grace. I know,' he replied, his tone much softer now. 'I'm just worried about them. I can't lose another son.'

Grace placed a hand on his arm. 'You won't,' she said, trying to convince herself as much as him.

'I hope you're right.'

'I am.'

'When this is all over, we need to seriously consider leaving all of this behind us,' he said as he continued driving, his eyes fixed on the road ahead.

'We will,' she replied with little conviction. How could they possibly walk away and leave Jake and Connor in charge?

Chapter Five

Michael Carter sat back in the leather chair of the office he shared with Grace and his brother Sean in their flagship restaurant and bar, Sophia's Kitchen. It was situated in Liverpool's Albert Dock and was considered one of the finest eateries and meeting places in the wider Merseyside area. Grace and Sean had always used the restaurant as a base, while Michael had favoured their office at Cartel Securities, the security company that he and Grace owned. More recently Grace had been spending a lot of time setting up their new wine bar in Lytham and Michael had felt the need to distance himself from the security side of their business as much as he could, and so he'd taken to working in the place too. Ever since Paul had been killed eight months earlier, he couldn't stand to be around all of the lads who'd known his son so well. He realised that some people might have found it comforting, but for him it was a daily reminder that his son was no longer with him.

The office in Sophia's Kitchen was big enough for him,

Grace and Sean to occupy comfortably, although it was very rare the three of them would be in there at the same time, and today Michael was glad he was there alone. Connor and Jake's arrest had him rattled and he wanted time away from anyone involved in it. Grace was doing her best to convince him that everything would be okay, but he no longer trusted that it would. Since he was avoiding the offices of Cartel Securities, his head bouncer and trusted right-hand man, Jack Murphy, or Murf, as he was commonly known, would often call in to Sophia's Kitchen to keep Michael apprised of any developments, or just to sit and talk. Today was one such afternoon and Murf popped his head in through the open door.

'All right, Boss?' he asked.

'Yeah, come on in, Murf,' Michael replied with a wave of his hand.

Murf took a seat opposite, his heavy frame filling the chair. 'I heard what happened with Connor and Jake,' he said. 'Everything okay?'

Michael shook his head and sighed. 'Fuck knows, Murf. They've been released without charge for now. But they're still under investigation for murder.'

Murf shook his head. 'Fuck!' he breathed.

'Tell me about it.'

Murf leaned forward in his chair. 'I'm sure Grace will sort everything out though?' he said with a smile that didn't quite reach his eyes.

'Well, she thinks so too…'

'But?' Murf prompted him.

'But what if she can't this time, Murf?'

'She's Grace Carter. She will.'

'If they're both charged with murder, and there's enough evidence, then I'm not sure there's anything Grace can do about it. As good as she is, she's not a fucking magician.'

Murf frowned at him and Michael sensed his friend's discomfort at the direction the conversation was going in. They were rescued from any further awkwardness by a knock at the door.

Both men looked up to see Sophia's Kitchen's newest waitress and barmaid, Lena, standing in the doorway with a tray in her hand.

'The drink you ordered, Boss,' she said as she smiled sweetly and sashayed into the office with a swish of her long, flaming red hair. Michael could see Murf staring at her – unapologetically so. It was something Michael assumed she was used to as she seemed to have that effect on almost every man she came into contact with. She was one of those women that turned heads when she entered a room and she had been a massive hit with the customers – both male and female. He'd noticed that when she spoke to people she had a way of making them feel like they were the only person in the room. Bending over his desk, she placed the large mug of coffee in front of him. 'Hot and sweet. Just how you like it,' she said with a laugh and a lick of her lips. Then she spun around and faced Murf, giving her behind a little wiggle in the process. 'Would you like something nice and hot yourself? Or would you prefer something cold?' she purred.

'A Coke would be great,' Murf stammered as he pulled at the collar of his shirt with his index finger.

'Coming right up,' she said before turning to Michael again. 'Anything else I can get you. Boss? Anything at all?'

'No. I'm fine, thanks, Lena,' he replied.

'Jesus Christ,' Murf said with a sharp intake of breath after Lena had left. 'Who the fuck was that?'

'She's our new waitress, Lena. Grace hired her a few weeks back. The customers love her.'

'I can see why,' Murf said with a laugh.

'You're old enough to be her dad, you perv,' Michael said with a smile.

Murf shook his head. 'She's got her eye on you, Boss. How the fuck do you work around her all day and get anything done?'

'I'm too busy to be perving over the staff, Murf. And besides, have you met my wife?' he said with a raised eyebrow.

Murf chuckled good-naturedly and turned his attention to their earlier conversation. 'Speaking of your wife, I'm sure she'll straighten this whole mess out, Michael. Has she ever let you down before? And this is her son we're talking about. And Connor. Do you honestly think she'd let them go down for murder?'

Michael stared at Murf. There was a time when he would have wholeheartedly agreed with him. But that was before Paul was murdered. Before everything had changed. 'We can't always protect the people we love though, Murf. No matter how much we want to.'

Murf considered him for a few seconds before giving a brief nod. 'I suppose you're right,' he replied with a shrug. 'But I wouldn't underestimate Grace.'

'I never do,' Michael snapped at him, conscious that the conversation was becoming far too personal. Murf had been a good and loyal friend to him over the years, but he was still an employee. He worked for Grace as much as for Michael, and for that reason Michael felt some guilt for talking about her in such a way. But mostly he was annoyed that Murf had the nerve to suggest that Michael would ever underestimate Grace – as though somehow Murf knew her better than he did.

'Okay, Boss,' Murf said, raising his hands in surrender. 'I was just saying.'

'What did you come over here to see me about anyway?' Michael asked.

Murf shuffled in his seat. 'Nothing in particular. Just wanted to see how things were and catch up, you know? I heard about the lads and just wondered if you were all okay? Or if there is anything I can do?'

Michael looked at Murf and felt a pang of guilt. He knew that the worry over Connor and Jake was clouding his judgement and he was being unfair in taking some of his anger out on Murf. But some days he felt angry at the whole world.

'Thanks, Murf. I appreciate it, but there's nothing you can do right now.'

'No problem, Boss,' he said as he stood up and straightened his jacket. 'I'll leave you to it then.'

Just as he was turning to leave, Lena returned with his drink. 'Here you go, that should cool you right down,' she said with a flutter of her eyelashes and a grin at Michael.

'Thank you,' Murf replied as he took the proffered drink and watched her disappear out of the doorway again.

Murf took a long swig of the Coke and placed his almost empty glass on Michael's desk. 'You'd better watch yourself with that one,' he said with a grin. 'She's dangerous.'

Michael smiled. 'I think I can handle her.'

'I'd certainly like to,' Murf said.

Michael shook his head as Murf walked out of his office.

Lena Munro leaned on the bar and watched as the stocky, bald-headed man she now knew as Murf walked out of the restaurant. He turned and winked at her and she giggled in response. She'd seen the way his eyes had glazed over when she'd walked into Michael's office earlier. She always had that effect on men. It was laughable really how easily she could get them to do her bidding. A winning smile and a flutter of her eyelashes and she had men like Murf eating out of the palm of her hand. Not that she had any interest in Murf. He wasn't her type at all. But Michael Carter – now there was a man she'd like on her arm, and in her bed. Big and brooding. And with all that money and power. Lena felt the butterflies in her stomach just thinking about him. So far, he had resisted all of her subtle advances and she feared he was one of those men who just didn't have a clue when a woman was flirting with him. She would have to ramp up her efforts, because she couldn't stop thinking about him. He was the hottest man she had ever encountered in her life, and if she didn't get him into bed soon, she might just implode.

'Haven't you got some customers to serve?' Lena's colleague and friend Jamie came up behind her and whispered in her ear.

'I'm going,' she said with a sigh as she straightened up. 'Just having a quick daydream.'

'Not about *him* again?' Jamie said with a roll of his eyes.

'You're just jealous,' she replied, giving him a playful shove.

'Yeah, right,' Jamie snorted. 'You honestly think you have a chance with him?'

'Of course I do,' she snapped at him. 'Just you wait and see. Give me a few more weeks and he'll be begging for me.'

'Seriously, Lena. You need to be careful,' Jamie warned her. 'This is Grace Carter's husband you're talking about here.'

Lena shrugged. 'Isn't she his third wife? Obviously, he doesn't like to stay married for long, does he? I'm sure it won't be the first time he's cheated, but it will be the last,' she said with a wink.

'Oh, you think you might be the next Mrs Carter, do you?' Jamie said with a shake of his head. 'You're deluded, babe.'

'We'll see, Jamie. We'll see,' she said as she picked up her notepad and made her way over the group of men in suits who'd just been seated in her section. She winked at Carlos, the maitre d', as she passed him. He always gave her the best customers.

Chapter Six

Grace sat at one of the tables outside All Bar One in Victoria Square and sipped her lime and soda. She'd chosen the perfect spot with an unhindered view of the entrance and exit of Liverpool Crown Court. It was a sunny day and she pondered how little time she had these days to sit and relax. Her life felt like a constant whirlwind where she lurched from one crisis to another. Everyone was always looking to her to solve their problems. But wasn't that exactly how she liked it? That was what Michael would say anyway. He thought that she craved the adrenaline, that she thrived on it, but Grace wasn't sure if she did or not. She sometimes thought about the brief time she'd spent in the little village of Harewood near Leeds. She'd moved there just after her ex-husband Nathan was killed, and just before she'd found out she was pregnant with Belle. She had spent a blissful eighteen months there before she'd had to return to Liverpool – to her old life. And while she didn't regret her decision for a moment, she did sometimes miss those quiet, carefree days.

Michael was keen to move away from the city now, although not too far away, and she would like that too, but it wasn't so easy just to up and walk away. They both had responsibilities. Grace didn't always enjoy being the one who made the decisions, but the truth was she was good at it. The few times she had left other people to take up the reins, it had ended in disaster.

A flash of a bright red coat caught Grace's eye and she recognised DI Leigh Moss leaving the court. Grace stood up and walked towards her. Just like Grace, Leigh was a difficult woman to get time alone with. But Grace had plenty of contacts within the court who had alerted her to Leigh's presence there today.

Leigh saw Grace approaching and frowned. Grace reached her and fell into step beside her and they walked through the crowded square towards James Street.

'What do you want, Grace?' Leigh asked.

'I want to know what the hell you're playing at arresting my son and Connor,' Grace replied.

Leigh gave a brief shake of her head. 'My job!'

'Your job? But he's my son, Leigh.'

'What difference does that make?'

'Are you kidding me?' Grace snapped. 'It makes every difference.' She grabbed hold of Leigh's arm and the two women turned to face each other.

'Look,' Leigh said through gritted teeth. 'I know you're upset about this, but this is my job, Grace. I don't have a choice.'

'Of course you do!'

'What? And be like Webster and whoever else you have in your pocket? Just turn a blind eye?' Leigh hissed.

'If you have to,' Grace hissed back.

'I would never do that. You know I wouldn't. I thought you understood that?'

'Jake and Connor are off limits. I thought you understood that?' Grace snapped.

Leigh shook her head. 'Nobody is off limits, Grace. Not even you.'

Grace glared at her. The woman standing before her might think she was a million miles away from the stripper whom Grace had once had to rescue from being murdered in a grubby alleyway, but Grace knew differently. 'Don't threaten me, Leigh.'

'It's not a threat. If you stand in my way, I will take you down too.'

'I'd like to see you try,' Grace said quietly, to ensure that no passers-by would overhear. 'Be careful, Leigh. You don't want to make an enemy of me.'

'Ma'am,' someone called and both women looked up to see a uniformed officer standing near a squad car.

'There's my lift. I need to go,' Leigh said with a smile before walking away.

Grace watched her climb into the front seat of the police car and frowned. She had known that Leigh wouldn't budge. Despite her past, she was straight now that she was a police officer. But Grace had wanted to look her in the eye and remind her of who she was – of who they both were. And on that score at least – mission accomplished.

'Everything okay, Ma'am?' Constable Barrett asked as Leigh climbed into the patrol car.

'Yes, why?' she asked, sure that the constable from Traffic wouldn't have recognised Grace Carter.

'You just look a bit flushed. Was that woman bothering you?'

'No. She asked me if I knew where Ted Baker was. I told her I didn't have a clue but I don't think she believed me.'

'Oh, okay,' he said with a smile as he pulled away from the kerb.

'Thanks for the lift,' Leigh said. 'I didn't fancy walking after all.'

'Not a problem, Ma'am, I was in town anyway when the boss asked if anyone was free. I'll drop you back at St Anne's Street and then I've got some paperwork to catch up on.'

Leigh nodded and settled back in her seat. Her meeting with Grace had her rattled. Despite her assertion that she would take Grace down if she had to, she didn't feel quite as confident as she'd sounded. It was one thing talking about bringing down Grace Carter – actually doing it was a whole other matter entirely.

Chapter Seven

Craig Johnson sat at his usual table in The Grapes, sipping his pint and waiting for two of his brothers, Ged and Scott, to meet him. Since their eldest brother Bradley had disappeared four months earlier, things hadn't been going very well for the Johnson brothers. Craig had once worshipped the ground that Bradley walked on, but now he realised that his former hero was a coward and a backstabbing cunt. Not only had Bradley left them all in the shit and disappeared with over two hundred grand of Alastair McGrath's money, but his big mouth had also ended up getting their younger brother Billy killed. Bradley had been stupid enough to insinuate that they had been responsible for Paul Carter's murder, and poor Billy had paid the ultimate price. Craig took a swig of his pint and continued watching the door for Ged and Scott. He had to give his older brother, Ged, credit – he'd always known that Bradley was a bad apple, but Craig and the rest of the family had put it down to Ged having a massive chip on his shoulder because he wasn't the oldest and therefore hadn't become the head of the family when their father died. Now, Craig knew that Ged's instincts had been spot on all along. For the moment, at least, Ged seemed to be happy to look to Craig to tell him what to do next.

It was Craig who'd scored them the contract with Alastair McGrath. Alastair was a Scot who had married into a well-connected Essex family and was now one of the biggest gangsters in England. Alastair had trusted Craig to start growing his business up north and the plan was for the Johnson brothers to finally become a firm to be reckoned with. But for some reason Craig still couldn't fathom, Bradley had fucked them all over and done a runner with all of Alastair's money. Since then, it had been a constant game of cat and mouse, trying to convince Alastair that nothing was wrong, while sending him dribs and drabs of money in an attempt to cover the fact that they had lost a shitload of his cash. But there was only so long that someone like Alastair could be fobbed off before he stopped asking questions and instead started dismembering limbs and burying people in deep, unmarked graves.

Craig was about to order himself another pint when he noticed his two brothers walking through the door. They came straight over to him and took seats at the table.

'How's things, bro?' Ged asked.

'Not good,' Craig replied with a shake of his head. 'Alastair's goons are still breathing down my neck. I'm not sure how much longer I can hold them off for. If we don't get Alastair his money soon, we're fucking toast, lads.'

'What are we gonna do then?' Ged asked.

'We need to pull off a big job,' Craig replied.

'What? Like nicking someone's drugs?' Ged asked.

Craig shook his head. 'There's no time for that, now. We need to nick the money from somewhere – or someone.'

'Do you have any ideas where we could get our hands on that kind of money?' Ged said.

Craig nodded and leaned forward so only his brothers could hear him when he answered quietly, 'Nipper Jackson.'

Even Ged, who was usually game for anything, flinched at the name. 'You mean Jake Conlon and Connor Carter's counter?' Ged whispered. 'Are you mental, Craig? You want to steal their money? After everything that's happened?'

'I don't see what other choice we have, lads,' Craig replied. 'I know it's a risk, but so is Alastair McGrath finding out we've lost two hundred grand of his money. Besides, we owe those pair of bastards after what they did to Billy.'

Scott shook his head while Ged stared at Craig in disbelief.

'Look, I've got a plan. And there's every chance that if we do things right, Carter and Conlon will never have an inkling that we had anything to do with it.' Craig said.

'They might have their hands full with other things by then anyway,' Scott, who had been completely silent until this point, piped up.

'What are you on about?' Craig scowled at him.

'I've sorted it. Jake and Connor will be out of the way for a long time,' Scott replied with a smile.

'What have you done, Scott?' Ged snapped.

'They were arrested for Billy's murder yesterday afternoon,' Scott answered.

'What? How did that happen?' Craig said.

Scott sat back in his chair with a smug grin on his face and Craig resisted the urge to shake him. 'What the fuck did you do, Scott?' he hissed.

'I told the police what they did to Billy,' he replied.

'You stupid fucking bastard!' Ged said before Craig had a chance to.

'What?' Scott asked as he looked between his two older brothers. 'They've been arrested. I told the police I saw them do it.'

'But you didn't!' Ged said.

'So? We know they did it,' Scott replied with a shrug.

'That's the least of our fucking worries, to be honest,' Craig snapped. 'You've gone and signed your own death warrant, Scott.'

Scott stared at them both as the colour slowly started to drain from his face and Craig was reminded how young and naïve his baby brother was. He'd been coddled by their mother all of his young life and it showed.

'What do you mean? I told you they've been arrested,' he stammered.

'And you think they're not going to walk out of that police station today? If they haven't already.'

'But I told the police I saw them do it. I spoke to the DI from the organised crime task force and she told me that she'd make sure they went down.'

42

Ged started to laugh and Craig shot him a withering look, causing him to stop.

'You know, for someone with an IQ worthy of Mensa, you're as thick as pig-shit sometimes, Scott. Do you have any idea of the connections that Jake Conlon and the Carters have? They have half of the fucking city on their payroll. Not to mention a fucking shit hot legal team. They will be walking out of that police station without so much as a parking fine and they will find out that it was you who fingered them for murder.'

Scott shook his head. 'They won't. They're not going to find out it was me. That DI said—'

'Never mind what she said. She'd tell you the sky was green if she thought it would help her put those two away. You're living in cloud cuckoo land. That's not how the real world works, lad. I'm off to get some fucking drinks,' Ged said as he stood up and stomped towards the bar.

'Do you really think they'll walk?' Scott asked Craig once Ged had left the table.

'Yes, mate,' he said with a nod. 'I really do.'

'But they were arrested,' Scott persisted.

'Scott! We're not talking about your average Joe here. You have grassed on the two most powerful men in Liverpool.'

'Well, you wanted to nick their money,' Scott offered in protest.

'Yeah. Because we're fucking desperate and there was a chance we could pull it off and not get caught. But what you've done is completely different.'

'But why?'

'Where do I even start? Firstly, you do not grass people up to the filth. That is the surest way of making sure you'll either end up dead or at the very least you'll never make any half decent money ever again. And if that wasn't bad enough, you fucking lied about what you saw, and we all know you don't do well under pressure. If it ever did get to trial, which I highly fucking doubt, you'd fall to fucking pieces. But all of that doesn't mean shit really when you consider that you have just tried to stitch up two men who have the means, and quite probably the inclination, to wipe you, me and our Ged off the face of the earth and not lose a wink of sleep about it.'

Scott stared at his older brother, his bright blue eyes blinking as beads of perspiration started to form on his forehead. 'They won't know it was me though, will they?' he repeated.

Craig considered his younger brother and felt a twinge of sympathy. Scott was as green as freshly laid AstroTurf and he had never been cut out for the family business. Bradley should have let him fuck off to university like he'd wanted to, but instead their eldest brother had insisted Scott follow in his older brothers' footsteps. Scott was a fucking liability – but he was also his baby brother. 'Maybe not,' Craig lied, knowing full well that Grace Carter alone had the means to find out anything she wanted to. 'But you just keep your head down from now on.'

Scott nodded. 'I'll go and speak to that DI, and ask her to put me in witness protection or something. They haven't got a case without me.'

Craig almost spat out the mouthful of lager he'd just gulped. 'What?' he snapped. 'And just leave me and Ged to take the fall instead?'

'Maybe they'd put us all in witness protection?' Scott offered, confirming to Craig that he just didn't get it at all.

'I'd rather take my chances with Conlon and the Carters than collude with the filth, you stupid little prick!' Craig snarled. 'You stay the fuck away from the police. Next time that DI comes sniffing around you, tell her to fucking do one. And if you dare disappear and leave me and Ged to deal with this on our own, then I'll find come and find you my fucking self.' Then, shaking his head in disgust, he stomped off towards the bar to stand with Ged.

————————

Scott watched at his older brother walked away from him with a face like thunder and sipped his pint as he tried to ease the queasy feeling in the pit of his stomach and mulled over their recent exchange. He knew Craig and Ged didn't like the police, but he hadn't expected that kind of response from them. If they could only see past their hatred of coppers, then they would recognise that what he was doing was right. So what, he hadn't actually seen Jake Conlon and Connor Carter murder Billy? He was sure that they were guilty and the only way Scott knew to make them pay for what they did was for them to be sentenced for Billy's murder. Craig and Ged, however, seemed unwilling to do anything about the fact that the two men who had beaten their brother to death were carrying on with their lives as though nothing had happened. And if Craig and Ged wouldn't do something to rectify that, then he would.

Scott was starting to feel a little better. Surely Craig was exaggerating – trying to scare him off? Scott knew that his brothers thought he was stupid, but he was far from it, and there was no way that he was going to let the men responsible for Billy's murder get away with it.

Craig walked over to the bar and stood next to Ged, who was drinking his pint.

'That stupid little bastard is gonna get us all killed,' Ged said as he placed his glass on the bar.

'I've told him to fuck that DI off if she comes asking again. Hopefully we can undo any damage before this goes too far.'

'You think?' Ged scoffed.

'Yes, I do think, Ged,' Craig snapped. 'Which is more than I can say for you or knobhead over there.'

'And what the fuck's that supposed to mean?' Ged shouted.

'It means that I don't see either of you trying to sort out the situation with Alastair. You're either out on the pull or just pissed. And Scott – well, the least said about him, the better.'

Ged turned to Craig with a scowl on his face. 'You're a cheeky fucker, Craig. So, you think you're the boss now, do you? Think you're clever, eh?'

'Well, I think you've proven that you're not up to the job!'

'Really? I was the only one who saw through your precious Bradley though, wasn't I?'

'Oh, fuck off. You couldn't see through a window, you thick bastard. You just hated the fact that you were always second to him,' Craig snapped. He knew that wasn't true but he was angry and he needed to take it out on someone.

Ged frowned. 'And now I'm supposed to play second to you too, am I? I'm the oldest after Brad. That means I'm in charge.'

Craig placed a hand on Ged's shoulder. 'Tell that to Alastair McGrath, or any other face round here. You're not a leader, Ged. You're the muscle. You always have been. So, you just do what you do best and leave the thinking to me.'

'Fuck you,' Ged growled before turning back to his pint.

Craig ordered himself a drink from the blonde barmaid who was his Friday night bit on the side. Ged was understandably pissed off, but deep down he had to know that Craig was right. Craig was the boss now, and their brief but loaded exchange meant that Ged had finally accepted that.

Craig sat on the bar stool and ran a hand through his hair in exasperation. Bradley had well and truly left them all in the shit. Alastair McGrath was breathing down their necks for his money and there was only so much longer that Craig could keep fobbing him off. While Craig understood Scott's desire for revenge – he was devastated by Billy's death too – there was a time and a place for everything. But now Scott had gone rogue, making the Johnson brothers an even bigger enemy of the Carters than they already were. Who in their right mind would want to be responsible for leading this shower of fuck-nuggets? Picking up the whisky chaser he'd ordered and downing it in one, Craig realised with despair that he was the only man for the job.

Chapter Eight

DI Leigh Moss watched as her sergeant, Nick Bryce, strode across her living room with a plate of curry in his outstretched hand.

'Lamb Rogan Josh, Ma'am,' he said as he handed her the plate.

She took the plate from him before picking up the cushion beside her and throwing it at him. 'Don't be a smart-arse,' she said with a laugh.

Nick ducked and the cushion missed him. 'Smart-arse? Me?' he replied with a grin as he walked back out into the kitchen. He returned a few seconds later, shirtless this time, and with his own plate of curry in his hand. Leigh raised an eyebrow at him and he looked down at his naked chest. 'What? I didn't want to get curry on my T-shirt.'

'Yeah, right,' she said before tucking into her dinner.

Nick sat on the sofa beside her and they fell into their usual evening routine of eating dinner in her lounge before chatting about their day and watching a film – usually a cheesy superhero one that Nick chose.

Leigh and Nick had been good mates and on-and-off lovers for the past four years. They had made a promise that they would never get too serious about each other, which had suited them both down to the ground. They were both too committed to their work to commit to another person as well. But despite that, they had been spending more and more time together over the past few months, and although neither of them was prepared to admit it, they were a couple in every sense of the word. Leigh looked across at him. Nick kept himself fit. He was good-looking in an understated way. But, more importantly, he was funny, and kind, and he was a man of principle. She knew that the more time they spent together, the harder it would be to stop whatever this thing was they had going on. She loved him. But was love enough? She thought about the ribbing he would get from the other lads at the station if they found out. Most of them thought she was a dragon. *A jobsworth with a stick up her arse* was how she'd overheard one of the constables describe her once. Not that she cared what other people thought of her. Leigh was comfortable in her own skin and happy with the person she had chosen to be. But she did worry about Nick. The job was his life too, but in a different way. His colleagues were his family, and like family, he cared more than he should about what they thought of him.

Leigh's thoughts were interrupted by the ringing of her mobile phone. Picking it up, she saw Scott Johnson's name flashing across the screen and her heart started pounding. This couldn't possibly be a good development, could it?

'Hi, Scott,' she answered, trying to sound as casual as possible.

'DI Moss,' he answered breathlessly, as though he'd been running. 'How likely is it that Jake Conlon and Connor Carter are going to find out that I'm the key witness in this investigation?'

Leigh swallowed. 'Well, they won't find that out from me or my team, I promise you that,' she replied.

'That really doesn't answer my question though, does it? Will they find out some other way?'

Leigh looked across at Nick, hoping illogically for some help, despite knowing that he could only hear her side of the conversation. 'I suppose they might put two and two together and think it was you. You did live with Billy after all.'

'Shit!'

'If you're worried about that then let me bring you in. We can offer you witness protection—'

'No, I can't do that,' he interrupted her. 'Who knows when or if I'd ever be able to come back to Liverpool, and I can't just leave my brothers in the lurch like that. I've already lost two brothers, I couldn't handle the possibility of never seeing Craig and Ged again too. Besides, you said they wouldn't find out,' he said and Leigh could hear the edge of desperation creeping into his voice.

'I have never told you that, Scott.'

'Okay, but you implied it. You would have said anything to get my testimony though, wouldn't you?'

'That's not true,' Leigh said, trying to maintain her temper and speak calmly. 'I have never lied to you about the possible implications. But it's true that we have no case without you, Scott. Without your testimony, the men who murdered your brother will never see the inside of a courtroom, let alone a prison.'

'I know.'

'Let us protect you,' she insisted.

'No! Look, I know they'll figure out it was me if they haven't already. But they'd be stupid to take out the key witness, wouldn't they? Surely that would prove their guilt?'

'Perhaps,' Leigh answered, thinking that Scott had watched far too many cop dramas on television.

'Then I'm going to go and stay with an old friend of mine from school for a bit. No one knows where she lives, or knows we've stayed in touch. She lives in Widnes, and I'll be safe there. I'm going to ditch my phone, but I'll text you my new number as soon as I get it.'

'Okay. And if you see anything suspicious, or feel like you're in any danger at all, phone 999 before you call me. Okay?'

'Okay. I will. I'll speak to you in a few days.'

'Bye, Scott.'

Leigh put her phone down on the coffee table and sat back with a sigh.

'What was that about?' Nick asked.

'Scott Johnson getting twitchy about the investigation.'

'Understandable,' Nick replied, putting his plate down on the floor beside him. 'You think he's going to back out?'

'No. He's scared, but he still seems determined to go ahead with it. I'd feel better if he agreed to go into witness protection though. At least then, we could keep an eye on him for the duration of the investigation.'

'I do too, but we've had that conversation with him before, and it didn't seem like he was willing to budge.'

Leigh nodded in agreement. 'I know. He's going to stay with a friend of his in Widnes for a while. Apparently no one knows about her. But I don't think he appreciates the reach the Carters have.'

'I know what you mean. He's a bright lad, seems quite clever actually, but no common sense at all. Can you imagine him growing up with the rest of the Johnson lot? He must have stuck out like a sore thumb.'

Leigh smiled. 'Would you really want to blend in with them though?'

Nick laughed. 'Suppose not.'

'The best thing we can do for Scott is arrest Jake and Connor as soon as possible. I'm going to speak to the CPS tomorrow and see if there's any progress on being able to proceed with a charge.'

'Let's hope Forensics come back with something.'

'I know,' Leigh replied with a frown. 'Even a fingerprint or a shred of DNA would give us something to tie them to the scene. Without that all we have is Scott's testimony.'

Nick winced. 'And even that is iffy. He saw them going in, but didn't see the murder. Faye Donovan will tear him to shreds on the stand.'

Leigh nodded. 'I know. But we'll just have to prep him

to hold his nerve. I believe he's telling the truth, and I just hope that a jury would be able to see that too.'

'The truth? Whoever cared about the truth? Grace Carter and her bloody family walk around this city believing they're invincible. But one day we will have them banged to rights, and I for one can't wait.'

Leigh nodded at him again. 'Me too,' she said although with less conviction.

Nick held up his arm and Leigh leaned against him on the sofa, inhaling the clean, soapy smell of his freshly showered body. Nick was right, of course, and she wanted the streets of Liverpool to be safe again as much as he did. Bringing down the Carter family would be an epic feat and one that would cement her career in the police force. But that would mean bringing down Grace too, and although she was prepared to do that, it wouldn't be as easy for her.

'What do you fancy watching?' Nick asked.

'You choose,' she replied and she watched as Nick flicked through the channels. She thought about Grace Carter: the women they had both become, and the women they had once been.

Leigh Moss had been nineteen years old when she'd applied for a job as a barmaid at The Blue Rooms. She'd been studying law at Liverpool University and had wanted a decent-paying job to help her keep on top of her bills. She had been raised in one of the roughest and poorest neighbourhoods in Manchester and her parents didn't have any spare cash to help her out if she was ever in a jam. In fact, they'd been pretty annoyed that she'd decided to 'flounce' off to university instead of getting a job in the local supermarket or claiming the dole so she could start finally bringing some money into the house. She could still hear her mother's words now – *If it was good enough for me and your father, why do you think you're any better than the rest of us round 'ere?*

Leigh couldn't wait to get out of the house she'd grown up in – she'd never felt comfortable enough in the place to call it home. She was raised by a mother who was a spiteful bully, seemed to resent Leigh's youth and intelligence and belittled her every chance she got, and a father who was only interested in where his next six-pack of Skol was coming from.

That had all changed when Leigh had moved to Liverpool and she had finally been allowed opinions and friends of her own. One such friend had told her that she could make a few hundred quid in tips alone working at The Blue Rooms. So, she'd walked in there that evening, in her sexiest little black dress, to ask for a job behind the bar. On her way to the bar, she'd been stopped in her tracks by the most gorgeous man she had ever seen. Then he'd smiled at her and she'd almost passed out with lust. Her heart still thumped in her chest when she remembered her first encounter with Nathan Conlon. He'd told her he was the club owner and twenty minutes later they were drinking Cristal champagne in one of the Club's private booths.

Nathan Conlon had swept her off her feet, showering her with gifts and attention. She hadn't cared at the time that he was married with a child, that was his wife's problem and not hers. Besides, Nathan had told her that he didn't love his wife any longer. She had trapped him in a marriage he didn't want by getting pregnant. They never had sex. He didn't love her, but *it was complicated*. Leigh shuddered inwardly as she thought about the naïve little girl she'd been back then. Nathan had promised her the world and she'd believed him. But after a few months her fantasy had started to turn into a nightmare and it had all happened so slowly that she hadn't even realised it. Nathan had told her that her incredible body was wasted behind the bar and that she should become a dancer instead. But such was his charisma and charm, he'd sold it to her in a way that she had believed it was her own decision. He was a master manipulator. Soon, she was dancing five nights a week, had dropped out of university and was doing coke and ecstasy just to get through the day. But even then, she'd thought it was all worth it just to have Nathan on her arm. He'd strung her along for almost a year. Soon his attention had turned to the other dancers, but he always had a few crumbs for Leigh, or Candy Malone, as she had called herself in an attempt to disguise her identity, and she, like the pathetic excuse for a woman she'd become, would lap them up. All he had to do was smile at her, give her a few quid to buy herself something pretty and promise her that she was still his girl, and she forgot about it all. God, what a narcissistic prick he was.

So Candy had gone on hanging around, waiting for any scraps he would throw her and hoping that one day he would realise how much he loved her. But that had all changed when she'd found out she was pregnant. In her drug-addled brain, she had thought that the baby would be the thing that would make Nathan finally realise how much he loved her. How wrong she was. He had demanded that she *get rid of it*, and when she'd refused, he had promised her that he would leave his wife and son if she aborted their baby. He didn't want any more children, he'd told her. He wanted a nice easy life – just the two of them. And he'd made it sound so plausible that she'd believed him. Then, after she told him she'd had aborted their child – her one and only chance to have a child, she'd later discover – he had laughed in her face and told her she was a deluded cow. She had sunk to her knees, sobbing and begging him to love her and he had pushed her away and told her that he had never loved her at all. He adored his wife and she, Candy, had only ever been a good fuck. That had all been bad enough, but then she had decided to confront his wife.

Leigh's cheeks burned with shame and anger whenever she thought about that night – something she tried to do as little as possible.

It had been a freezing Christmas Eve when Candy had stormed into Grace and Nathan's pub, The Rose and Crown, to tell everyone who cared to listen that she had been screwing Nathan for the past year. That she had aborted their baby because he had promised to leave his dried-up shrew of a wife for her. At the time, she had paid little attention to Grace's reaction, but now she could recall it in great detail. How this beautiful and broken woman had stood there, in her own pub, while this crazed loon told all of her customers in graphic detail about the intimate details of her affair with her husband. Grace had looked just like Leigh had felt – defeated and completely worn down.

Nathan on the other hand had been incandescent with rage and had frog-marched her out of the pub. Then he had raped her, and tried to kill her, before Grace had intervened. Grace Carter had saved Leigh's life and Leigh knew that she would always owe her for that. No matter how different their lives had become, Grace had done that for her. She had put her own life in danger for a woman she barely knew, and who she had just found out had been sleeping with her husband. And despite who she had turned into, that was the kind of woman Grace was.

Leigh could only ever wonder at the years of abuse and torment that Nathan had put Grace through. Grace had hinted at it afterwards, when the two women had become friends for a short time. They had been married young and he had controlled every aspect of Grace's life. All the things he had ever done to Candy paled into insignificance compared to the years of torture that Grace had endured. Yet she had come out on the other side of it with compassion and humanity. Leigh often wondered whether she would have had the strength to do the same and she was ashamed to admit that she wasn't sure if she would. At least, not back then. In her darkest times, Leigh still thought about what might have become of her if she hadn't aborted Nathan's child, or if he had left Grace for her. Would she have had the strength to endure? And if she had, would she have blood on her hands too? Would it be her, fighting to protect her child from going to prison? What was it her old nan used to say? *There but for the grace of God go I.* Leigh closed her eyes as she thought about how true that was.

Chapter Nine

G race poured two mugs of coffee and handed one to Michael as he sat at their kitchen table with their one-year-old son Oscar, who was noisily enjoying his lunch.

'Can you pick Belle up from school at three?' she asked Michael. 'I was hoping to go to the wine bar and go through some final invoices with Siobhan, and then I can hand it over to her.'

Michael raised an eyebrow at her and smiled.

'What?' she asked him.

'You're going to hand Carter's over, are you? Just like that?'

Carter's Wine Bar in Lytham was their newest venture and therefore Grace's latest project. She'd been heavily involved from the outset. Choosing the new premises and almost every piece of décor, as well as choosing the menu. She loved the excitement of setting up a new business. Her soon to be ex-daughter-in-law Siobhan Davies was managing the place for them and Grace considered her a competent and trustworthy appointment.

Siobhan had been married to Jake for two years, and together they had a daughter, Isla, who was almost two years old. The previous year, just before Paul had been murdered, Siobhan had dropped the bombshell that Connor could be Isla's father, and understandably all hell had broken loose. It was only then that Grace had learned Jake was gay. It had caused a huge family rift and there was a time when Grace had wondered how they would all find their way back together again. Then Paul had been murdered and the tragedy of his death had bound them all together. Jake and Siobhan were in the process of divorcing, but Grace hadn't been able to cut ties with her daughter-in-law entirely. The truth was she had come to love Siobhan, and the troubles within her and Jake's marriage – of which there were many – were really none of Grace's business. Siobhan had mended some fences with Connor and Jake too, but she was keen to make a fresh start for herself. That was when Grace had come up with the idea of Siobhan running the wine bar for them. It would mean she could start anew in Lytham, which wasn't too far away from Liverpool, and Grace would have someone she knew and trusted managing the place.

'Of course I'm going to hand it over,' she said to Michael. 'What's so funny?'

'It's just that you have trouble handing anything over, Grace. You can't help yourself. Some people might say you're a control freak.'

'Well, it's still our wine bar,' she said as she walked over to him. 'Of course I'll be involved. But I'll step back from it. I promise.'

'Good,' he said with a smile as he put his free arm around her waist. 'It will be nice to have you back at Sophia's again.'

Grace nodded. 'It will be nice to see more of everyone. I feel like I've neglected the place. But I know you and Sean are more than capable of handling the place without me.' She planted a kiss on the top of his head and sat down at the table with him and Oscar. 'You haven't been at the Cartel offices for a few weeks. Is everything okay?' she asked, knowing that since Paul's murder Michael had distanced himself from their security business.

'Everything's fine,' he replied. 'It's just nicer working at the restaurant, that's all.'

'Do you need me to do anything? I can work there for a while. Make sure everything is ticking over?'

'Murf has got it all under control. There's nothing to worry about. Besides, I was looking forward to having you around Sophia's a little bit more.'

'Okay,' Grace said, taking a sip of her coffee. She sensed that this was all part of Michael's long-term plan to have them take a back seat in the more dangerous aspects of their business and focus on their bars and restaurants.

'I've asked Webster to brief us on what the police have got so far. He said he'll meet us at the usual place at half past one, he can't chance coming here with so much spotlight on the family. Is that okay?'

DI Tony Webster was a police officer whom Grace had known, and paid off, for many years. Along with a few of his colleagues, he was paid a considerable amount of money to look the other way wherever possible, and provide crucial information when needed. Michael hated Webster, and although Grace wasn't his biggest fan, she had to admit that he sometimes had his uses.

Michael nodded. 'I'll ask my dad to watch Oscar for an hour.'

———————

An hour later and Grace and Michael had dropped Oscar off with his grandparents, Pat and Sue, and were walking into a small café in Everton.

'Do you actually think he'll have anything worth telling us?' Michael asked as he held the door open for Grace.

'Who knows? But I like to remind him who he's working for at times like these.'

Walking into the café, they spotted Webster sitting in the table furthest from the entrance, and they made their way over to him.

Webster nodded as they approached. 'I got you both a coffee,' he said indicating the mugs on the table.

'Thanks,' Grace said as she and Michael sat opposite him.

'So, what can you tell us about the investigation?' Michael asked as he picked up his mug and blew lightly onto the steaming liquid.

'Not a lot, I'm afraid,' Webster said as he sucked air through his teeth. 'The DI in charge of the investigation is a right jobsworth. Got a stick so far up her arse it's a wonder she can walk.' He laughed at his own joke.

'What evidence does she have on Jake and Connor?' Grace asked.

'I don't know,' he said with a shake of his head.

'You're fucking useless,' Michael spat.

'Look, you don't understand the way this DI works. She's a rottweiler, and she's playing this one really close to her chest. She won't let anyone not directly involved with the case within a sniff of it. I'm doing my best, but it's not easy. And for some reason, DI Moss seems to have taken a bit of a dislike to me—'

'I can't think why,' Michael interrupted.

'So, there's nothing of any relevance you can tell us?' Grace asked with a sigh.

'Only that Leigh Moss is on some sort of one-woman mission to clean the streets of Liverpool. I think she sees herself as some sort of fucking saviour. She's not even from Liverpool, she's from Manchester,' he sneered, his disdain for his colleague blatantly obvious.

'Is that why she's arrested the boys? Has she got it in for them?' Michael asked.

Webster nodded. 'Them and every other gangster in Liverpool.'

Grace felt Michael bristle beside her and she placed a hand on his leg. 'Do you know what her next move is?'

'No. But she would have charged them if she could have. I swear this woman is like a dog with a bone. She won't let this go. If she doesn't get them for this, she'll be looking for something else. You should tell the boys to be careful.'

'Are they under surveillance?' Grace asked.

'Not yet. At least I don't think so. I spoke to my mate in Intel. But, as I said, Moss is playing this one very close to her chest. If she's got them under surveillance it's all being kept top secret. But approving an operation like that would need approval from the top. You know the assistant Chief Con is a golf buddy of mine?'

Grace nodded. 'Keep us posted on any developments, will you?'

Webster downed the last of his coffee. 'Will do,' he said before standing up and walking out of the café without a backwards glance.

'That man has a face that's just begging to be punched,' Michael said as he drank his coffee.

Grace smiled at him in response.

'This DI sounds like bad news though,' he said.

'Hmm,' Grace agreed. She'd been wondering whether to tell Michael about her history with Leigh. Although she hated keeping secrets from him, she'd decided that telling him about that now would only cause more problems and she would have to explain why she hadn't told him before. How could she possibly explain that even after everything that had happened, she felt some sort of loyalty to Leigh Moss? Grace had once made Leigh a promise that she would never reveal the secrets of her past, and Grace was a woman who kept her word. Besides, keeping that word, and the fact that Grace had once saved her life, meant that Leigh was indebted to Grace – whether she admitted that to herself or not. That was a more powerful tool in her arsenal and while Grace knew there was no way she could coerce Leigh into dropping the investigation into Billy's murder, perhaps she might be able to convince her that someone else was responsible for the crime?

'How about I take you out somewhere nice for dinner tonight?' Michael asked, interrupting Grace's thoughts. 'We haven't been out, just you and me, for ages.'

'That would be lovely,' Grace replied. 'I'll be back from seeing Siobhan about six. But would you mind if we went to Sophia's? Steph told me she's put some new dishes on the menu and I'm desperate to try that chocolate and hazelnut soufflé she's been going on about. Please?' she said with a smile and a squeeze of his arm.

'We can go wherever you want,' he said before leaning in to give her a kiss.

'Great. It will give me a chance to catch up with Steph too. I haven't seen her for a few weeks.'

Michael rolled his eyes. Steph was Sean's daughter and their niece. At the age of thirty, she was the eldest of the next generation of Carters and she and Grace had become good friends years earlier.

'I'll only speak to her for a few minutes. She'll be working anyway.' Grace laughed. 'For the rest of the evening, I'll be entirely yours.'

'I'll hold you to that,' he replied.

She placed her hand over his. They had both been so busy lately, it would be nice to spend some time alone together.

Chapter Ten

G race walked through Carter's and admired the tasteful décor. The place had opened a few weeks earlier and was already doing better than they'd hoped. It catered for an eclectic mix of customers, from the super-rich who had made the seaside town of Lytham their home to the holiday makers, young, old and everywhere in between – everyone was welcome and it worked. Grace had to admit that Siobhan Davies had played a big part in making the place a success. Although Siobhan was in the process of divorcing Jake, she would always be family to Grace. She was the mother of her beautiful granddaughter for a start, and despite the fact that less than a year earlier she had thrown a hand grenade into the Carter family by revealing that Connor could be Isla's father, after the two of them had had a one-night stand, Grace couldn't help but love the girl. She was feisty and intelligent and she didn't take shit from anyone. She reminded Grace of herself when she was younger.

Siobhan had wanted to get away from Liverpool after the whole paternity issue had been resolved, and Grace couldn't blame her – hadn't she done the very same thing herself a few years earlier when she was pregnant with Belle? But Grace couldn't bear to be too far away from Isla, and she had also needed someone she could trust to manage Carter's, so offering Siobhan the job had seemed like the perfect solution. It meant that both Siobhan and Isla were only an hour's drive from Liverpool, and Grace still got to see her granddaughter at least once a week.

Grace was walking towards the bar when she saw Siobhan walking out of the back room. Her beautiful auburn hair was hanging loose and she was wearing a fitted green dress which complemented her skin tone perfectly. She looked every inch the professional woman and Grace felt a surge of pride.

'Hey, Grace,' Siobhan said with a smile as she looked up.

Grace sat on one of the stools. 'Hi, Siobhan.'

'Can I get you a drink?'

'A coffee would be great.'

'You said you wanted to go over some paperwork?' Siobhan said as she made Grace's coffee.

'Yes. I wanted to make sure you had everything you need before I hand the place over.'

'Hand it over?' Siobhan said in surprise.

Grace nodded. 'I think it's about time I let you get on with managing the place, don't you?'

Siobhan smiled in return. 'Well, only if you're sure?'

'I am. The place is doing amazing. I don't think there's

anything else I can do but leave the place in your very capable hands.'

Siobhan placed Grace's coffee on the bar. 'Thank you,' she said softly. 'I really appreciate everything you've done for me, Grace.'

'I know. Now don't have me getting all emotional,' Grace said with a wave of her hand. 'You've earned this chance, Siobhan. I wouldn't leave you in charge of my wine bar if I didn't believe you were capable of it.'

'Well, thank you anyway. After everything that's happened…'

'Forget about that now. Is Jake having Isla this weekend?'

Siobhan looked down. 'I'm not sure, to be honest.'

'Oh? Why not? Is this about the other day?'

Siobhan's head snapped back up. 'Why? What happened the other day?'

'He was arrested. Him and Connor. Didn't he tell you?' Grace asked although the look of shock on Siobhan's face answered the question.

'What were they arrested for?'

'They were released the same day,' Grace replied.

'But what were they arrested for?'

'Murder,' Grace said quietly. 'But they weren't charged.'

'Bloody hell,' Siobhan said as she leaned against the bar. 'Will they be charged?'

'No,' Grace replied quickly, trying to convince herself as much as Siobhan. 'It will be fine.'

Siobhan shook her head. 'Will it though?'

Grace studied the younger woman's face. 'Is there something else going on, Siobhan?'

'I'm not sure I should say,' Siobhan said.

'Well, you'll have to now. What's going on, Siobhan?'

'Last week when I picked Isla up from Jake's place, he was…'

'What?' Grace asked, although she was afraid she already knew the answer.

'He seemed like he was on something. I could smell he'd been drinking too, although he said he'd only had a couple. He looked different, and he was acting really weird. I know him so well, Grace, I knew he'd had something more than a few drinks. I'm no angel, Grace, and Jake can do what he likes in his free time, but he was looking after our two-year-old daughter, for Christ's sake. Anything could have happened to her,' Siobhan said with a shake of her head.

Grace frowned. She'd seen the change in Jake for herself. It had started shortly after Paul's murder and initially Grace had accepted that it was her son's way of dealing with his grief. But it had been over eight months now and Jake seemed to be getting worse rather than improving. He was moody, prickly with almost everyone. He picked fights constantly and more than once the bouncers who worked for her and Michael had had to intervene on his behalf. He was drinking every day despite the fact that he'd never been much of a drinker in the past, and although he would deny it until he was blue in the face, she knew he was using coke too. It was a slippery slope when suppliers started taking their own product; Grace knew it, and so did Connor, but Jake didn't seem willing to listen to anyone. There had been a time when Grace could always get through to him, but now she wasn't so sure. She saw so much of Nathan in him that it terrified her. Jake could be charming and charismatic when he wanted to be, when he wanted something from someone, and then in a split second his whole demeanour could change. Just like his father. And now he was drinking and taking drugs when he was looking after Isla too. Even his beautiful daughter wasn't enough to keep him on the straight and narrow.

'I don't think I can trust him to look after Isla on his own after that, Grace. I know you might not agree with that—'

'I don't blame you, Siobhan,' Grace interrupted her. 'He can't be getting wasted while he's in charge of a child. I can't believe he'd stoop so bloody low,' she said with a sigh. She sipped her coffee before looking up at Siobhan. 'I thought I raised him better than this, you know?'

Siobhan placed a warm hand over Grace's. 'You did,' she assured her. 'He's just lost right now. He'll find his way back.'

'You have a lot of compassion for a man who lied to you for your whole marriage,' Grace smiled.

'Well, I wasn't exactly a saint, was I?' she replied with a laugh.

'I see so much of his father in him, it scares the living daylights out of me, Siobhan,' Grace said suddenly, surprising even herself with her candour. While she had her concerns about Jake, she never criticised him openly. He was her son and she was loyal to him, but something had to give. If he carried on down the path he was currently on, she was sure that she'd end up visiting him in jail, or, even worse, at his graveside.

'He's your son, Grace. He'll see sense soon. Just give him time,' Siobhan said. 'But until he does, I can't have Isla staying with him. I just can't trust him.'

Grace nodded. 'Why not let Isla stay at our house for the weekend? That way you still get a bit of time to yourself and we'll all get to see her – Jake too. I'll suggest it to him if you like. With everything he's got going on, it won't sound too suspicious that I'd offer to have her stay with us instead.'

'That would be great.' Siobhan smiled. 'I wasn't looking forward to having that conversation with him to be honest, so the longer I can put it off, the better. Maybe he'll even sort himself out before I have to?'

'Well, that would be good, wouldn't it? If incredibly unlikely.'

Siobhan nodded. 'Wishful thinking?'

'I'll speak to him later and let you know what he says. I shouldn't see it being a problem though. Anyway, shall we go through this paperwork then? I have to get back soon, I'm off out and I need to get ready.'

'Oh? Anywhere nice?'

'Just for a meal with Michael. It feels like we haven't been out, just the two of us, for ages.'

'Well, let's get this paperwork sorted then so you can get ready for your hot date,' Siobhan replied with a grin.

Chapter Eleven

'Come on, Grace,' Michael shouted up the stairs as he fiddled with his cufflinks. 'We'll be late.'

'We own the restaurant. They're hardly going to give our table away,' she said as she walked down the stairs, fixing her earrings in place.

'You look gorgeous,' he said as she walked towards him. 'I think I've changed my mind about going out. Is there any chance I can take you back upstairs and relieve you of that dress?'

She smiled and ran a perfectly manicured fingernail down his chest. 'You've just been telling me to hurry up, and now you want to delay us further. Come on, handsome. Let's go.'

Grace walked through the open door of Sophia's Kitchen with Michael's hand on the small of her back. She smiled at the bouncers as she passed, all of whom nodded to her and Michael in greeting.

'I've kept you the best table,' Carlos the maitre d' said as he ushered them towards the table near the window. 'Lena will be your waitress,' he added as he handed them a menu each.

Grace sat on the chair that Carlos pulled out for her and smiled across the table at her husband. A few moments later, Lena walked over to them, flashing her megawatt killer smile.

'Good evening, Grace, Michael,' she said. Grace noted the change in Lena's voice when she addressed Michael but quickly dismissed it. She trusted her husband implicitly. Grace had hired Lena a few weeks before after a particularly memorable interview during which Lena had impressed Grace with her wit and charm. The fact that she was stunningly beautiful to boot was a bonus, and she had been an immediate hit with the customers.

'A bottle of Barolo, and some water for the table,' Michael answered.

'Coming right up,' Lena said with a smile.

'She's turned out to be a good fit, hasn't she?' Grace said as she watched Lena disappear through the crowded restaurant.

'Hmm. The customers like her,' Michael replied as he opened the menu and started to read.

'Well, yeah. And the fact that she's absolutely stunning doesn't hurt,' Grace said.

Michael looked up from his menu. 'I can't say I've noticed, love,' he replied with a twinkle in his eye.

'Liar,' she said, and laughed.

Grace was just tucking into her puttanesca when she heard her mobile phone ringing. Taking it from her handbag she saw John Brennan's name flashing on the screen. Grace's history with John was a long and complicated one. He had once been Nathan Conlon's right-hand man – but now he was hers. She answered it with a frown. Why was he calling her when he knew she was out with Michael?

'What is it, John?' she asked, and noticed how Michael scowled when she said John's name.

'I need to speak to you, Boss.'

'About what?'

'I'd rather not say over the phone.'

'Why? What's going on?'

'I've found something out that I think you should know about.'

'John, please just tell me what's going on?'

'It's about that DI who's investigating Jake and Connor. I know her, Grace.'

Grace swallowed. Of course John would recognise Leigh if he got close enough to her. He had been almost constantly at Nathan's side, back in the day, and must have met her on dozens of occasions.

'Where are you?' Grace asked, at which point Michael put his knife and fork down on the table.

'The Blue Rooms,' John answered.

'I'll be there in half an hour,' Grace replied before ending the call.

'What's going on? Where are you going?' Michael asked.

'I need to speak to John about something. I'm sorry but I'll have to go.'

'Can't it wait?' he snapped.

'Not really,' she replied. 'It's important.'

'For fuck's sake, Grace. What's so important that you're going to walk out of here in the middle of our dinner? Is it the boys?'

Grace shook her head. 'No. Look, can I tell you later? I need to go.'

'Well, I'll come with you then,' he offered.

'It's fine. You stay and finish your meal. Sean said he was calling in tonight. Why don't you have a drink with him and I'll see you at home in few hours.'

'Are you fucking kidding me?'

She stood up. 'I need to go. I'll explain later,' she said with a sigh. She would have to tell him about her connection with Leigh, she knew that, and she didn't fancy doing it right there in the middle of their busy restaurant. He would feel like she'd deliberately kept it from him. Perhaps she had. But it had been such a long time ago. It wasn't like she'd lied to him, she just hadn't given him full disclosure. And how could she? When Leigh had come back into her life, Michael had been dealing with the murder of his son. It had just never seemed like the right time. Besides, it pissed her off that he seemed to have an issue with her and John, despite never having been given a reason to.

'Fine,' he replied.

Lena watched as Grace Carter walked out of the restaurant, leaving her handsome husband sitting alone. From the look on Michael's face they'd had some sort of row. Lena smiled to herself. If she was Grace, she'd never let Michael out of her sight, least of all abandon him in the middle of dinner – in their own restaurant! How embarrassing for him! Well, Lena would make sure he wasn't left alone for too long. Taking a bottle of the best scotch from behind the bar, she poured him a glass.

Walking over, she placed it on the table in front of him and sat down in Grace's now unoccupied seat. 'I thought you could do with a drink, Boss,' she said, flashing him her best smile and leaning forward just enough to give him the perfect view of her cleavage.

He looked at the glass in front of him. 'I don't drink scotch.'

'Oh? You look like a man who appreciates a fine whisky,' she said.

He stared at the glass for a few seconds. 'Actually, I do,' he said as he picked it and downed the drink in one before slamming the glass down on the table.

'Can I get you another?' she asked.

He looked at her, his brown eyes burning into hers. For a second she thought that this might be the turning point in their relationship. Maybe he would stay behind and have a few more whiskies? They would talk and she'd make him laugh so much that he'd forget about his frigid cow of a wife. Then perhaps he'd finally take her home and fuck her. Her insides trembled just thinking about it.

'No thanks,' he said and for a second she wondered if she'd said those things out loud, but then he stood up and handed her his glass and she realised he was talking about the offer of another drink.

'Okay. Maybe next time?' she said, hopeful that he would change his mind and kiss her right there in the middle of the restaurant.

He smiled at her. 'Goodnight, Lena,' he said before walking away.

Lena watched him leave and smiled. He was going to be hers soon enough.

Grace walked through the crowd of clubbers to the office at the back of her son Jake's club, The Blue Rooms, where John Brennan was waiting for her. Pushing open the door, she went inside and saw him sitting on the small sofa in the office. To her relief, Jake and Connor weren't there. She hoped that John hadn't disclosed Leigh's true identity to anyone else yet.

John looked up as she walked into the room. 'Thanks for coming so quickly, Grace. I know you were out with Michael, but this can't wait,' he said as he ran a hand over his face.

'Well, Michael's not very happy that I've just walked out on him in the middle of dinner, but I know you wouldn't ask me here unnecessarily. So, what is it?'

John nodded and started talking. 'I was meeting the lads earlier. You know they're trying to keep their noses clean at the minute so they've been asking me to sort out a few bits out for them. They also asked me if I'd look into this DI who seems to have it in for them.' He paused and looked at her. She hadn't sanctioned any such operation, but she supposed they were all grown men, and while John worked for her, that also meant he sometimes worked for the boys.

'Okay,' Grace said, with the sinking feeling that she knew exactly where the conversation was heading.

'Well, I spoke to Webster about her. I got the impression she's not his biggest fan, and he fucking hates her. Anyway, he had no qualms in telling me where she lived.'

'What the hell, John? We don't go around stalking the bloody police!' she snapped. 'What if someone had seen you?'

'I wasn't stalking her, Grace. I just had a little drive past her house. I waited outside for a few minutes and saw her parking up and going inside and then I left. I was on my way to our Kelly's and I promised to take the kids a pizza and there was a little takeaway on the end of her road. So, I stopped in. I figured she has no idea who I am so there was no problem with me going there just the once. But as I was coming out, she came in. She was looking at her phone and I had an armful of pizzas. She walked right into me. Then she looked up from her phone and said sorry. And I think she recognised me—'

'But you said she wouldn't know you?'

'Well, DI Leigh Moss wouldn't. But Candy fucking

Malone would. I recognised her too. And there's something you should know about Detective Moss.'

Grace sat down on the chair.

'I already know, John,' she said.

He stared at her. 'What?'

'I already know that she used to go by the name of Candy, and she worked here.'

'What? But how? And since when?'

'Since I found out she'd been having an affair with Nathan and aborted his child.'

John shook his head in apparent disbelief. 'So you knew her before she even started looking into Jake and Connor?'

'I've known she was in the police since she joined up. Our paths used to cross occasionally, but I hadn't seen her for years. I saw her again just after Paul was killed. She helped me out.'

'Fucking hell. I thought I'd stumbled on the perfect way to get the lads out of bother – but you already knew?'

Grace nodded. 'Yep. And I can't use it. I've thought about it. But what would I say? The fact that she once screwed the father of one of her main suspects, albeit a lifetime ago, might get her thrown off the case, but it wouldn't stop the investigation. And who could prove it? Mine and your word against that of a highly decorated DI? Besides, you know what Nathan was like better than most people, John. You know how he operated. How he treated women. He almost ruined her life, and she pulled herself up by her bootstraps and made something of herself. If she can do that then I'm sure she could brazen out a bit of a scandal. Don't you?'

'Probably. She was tough as old boots back then as I recall. And as mad as a fucking box of frogs too. I could hardly believe it was her when I saw her looking all professional and respectable. The last time I saw her she was wearing a thong and shaking her arse in Nathan's face,' he said.

Grace closed her eyes and leaned back in the chair with a sigh.

'Sorry,' John said. 'I forgot who I was talking to for a minute then.'

'Don't worry about it,' Grace replied. 'If I got upset every time one of Nathan's ex-conquests was mentioned, I'd have to avoid half of Liverpool.'

John laughed. 'I'm surprised you didn't murder him before you did to be honest, Grace.'

'Well, it wasn't for want of trying, John,' she said, grinning at him.

'Still, I can't believe that Candy Malone is a copper. She's changed her hair and she looks different, but I would never forget that face.'

'Can you do me a favour and keep this to yourself for now?' Grace asked.

'Of course. If that's what you want,' he assured her and Grace had no reason to doubt him. He was a loyal soldier.

'Thank you, John,' she said as she stood up. Walking over to him, she placed a hand on his shoulder. 'I'd better get home before Michael sends out a search party. I'll catch up with you tomorrow.'

'Night, Boss.'

Grace noticed that the living-room light was on as she pulled into the driveway, signalling Michael was already home and was waiting up for her. That would mean he'd be waiting for answers. What would she tell him though? The truth, of course. It was now or never. They had promised never to lie to each other, and while she hadn't lied, she had kept the truth from him, and she knew from experience that was just as bad. She only hoped that Michael was more forgiving than she had been when he'd kept the possibility of Connor being Isla's father from her the previous year.

As Grace pushed open the living-room door she almost collided with Michael on his way out.

'I thought I saw your car pulling in,' he said and she caught the smell of whisky on his breath. It knocked her and she took a step back from him.

'Have you been drinking scotch?' she asked.

He nodded. 'Just the one. Lena brought it over after you left.'

Grace walked past him to their drinks cabinet and poured herself a brandy. Michael never drank whisky as a rule. She hated the stuff. It reminded her of her ex-husband, and even all of these years later the smell still made her nauseous. She'd never asked Michael not to drink it, but he usually didn't. She wondered if his decision tonight had anything to do with her leaving to meet with John.

'Want one?' she asked him.

He nodded and she poured him a glass and handed it to him.

'So what was so important that you had to leave to meet John Brennan in the middle of our dinner?' he asked.

'He found out some information about that DI who's investigating the boys,' she answered.

'Oh? What?'

Grace sighed. It was one thing not telling him about Leigh, but blatantly lying about it was a whole different matter and she couldn't do it. 'He found out that she used to be a stripper at The Blue Rooms. And as well as that she was also one of Nathan's many conquests.'

'What? She was a stripper?'

'Well, she would have called herself a dancer, I suppose, but she worked at a lap-dancing bar and took her clothes off for money.'

'And she was screwing your ex-husband?' he asked, his mouth open in shock.

Grace nodded.

'Well, fuck me!' He whistled. 'This is good news though.'

'Why?'

'Because the DI who is trying to pin a murder on our kids is an ex-stripper—'

'It's not a crime to be a stripper.'

'She was also shagging the biggest gangster in Liverpool! I'm pretty sure she wouldn't want her bosses finding out about that.'

'So, you're suggesting we blackmail her?'

'Yes. And I can't believe you're not,' he snapped.

Grace shook her head. 'It wouldn't work. She's too straight.'

'But if she knew that we knew—'

'She does know,' Grace interrupted him.

'What?'

'She already knows. Well, that I do, at least. I know her, Michael. I knew who Leigh was all along.'

He frowned at her. 'You knew? So why didn't you tell me? Why didn't you say something as soon as the lads were arrested? Or when Paul was killed?'

'It's a long story,' she replied with a sigh.

Michael sat down on the sofa. 'Well, I've nowhere sodding else to be. Do you?'

Grace sat down beside him. 'I met her years ago. In another lifetime, or at least that's what it feels like. It was the Christmas Eve just before Nathan went to prison. Leigh, or Candy as she was known back then, turned up at the pub demanding to see Nathan and screaming the place down about how she'd got rid of their baby for him.'

Grace took a sip of her brandy. The memory of that night was still a painful one for her. Taking a deep breath, she went on. 'Nathan threw her out, and he told me she was crazy. He said that she was some dancer from the club who was besotted with him. But I knew he was lying. Anyway, after he and Leigh had caused such a scene, I couldn't face the customers, so I went upstairs to the flat and that's when I heard her screaming again. But this time it was different. He was hurting her. At first I was just worried that Jake would hear or the police would come, and our Christmas would be ruined. He was only five.'

Michael said nothing and continued to stare at her.

'I went outside to the alleyway behind the pub and

found them there. Leigh was half naked, he'd ripped most of her clothes off – he got off on that – and he was strangling her. I could see her lips turning blue. She was looking at me. Silently pleading with me to help her. So I grabbed hold of him and tried to pull him off her. It distracted him long enough for her to wriggle free.' She picked up her drink and knocked the rest of it back. A tear she hadn't even known was there rolled down her cheek.

Michael placed his hand over hers. 'What happened after that?'

Grace wiped the tear away with the back of her hand. 'Nathan turned on me instead and Leigh ran away.'

Michael swallowed. 'So you saved her life? And she just fucked off and left you to fend for yourself?'

Grace nodded. 'She was terrified, and I was used to fending for myself. She came back a year later when he was in prison and apologised. She thanked me for helping her turn her life around. We stayed in touch for a while, until it became clear we were two very different people with very different outlooks on life.'

'But you saved her life, Grace. She owes you.'

'I've already called in the favour, I'm afraid.'

'When?'

'It was Leigh who gave me Solomon Shepherd's name. And I'm not sure we would have ever found out he was behind Paul's murder if she hadn't.'

He shook his head. 'So you got that information from the woman who's now trying to put two of our other children away for life? Talk about fucked up!'

'I know.'

'She still owes you though,' he added.

'We have other means at our disposal first,' she said to him.

He downed the last of his brandy. 'You should have told me.'

She nodded. 'I know.'

He turned to face her then, all traces of anger gone. Reaching out his hand, he brushed her hair from her face. 'I wish I had known you when you were married to that bastard. I would never have let him hurt you,' he said.

Grace nodded. 'I know,' she lied. Because she wasn't sure that anyone could have saved her from Nathan – anyone but herself. 'I'm sorry I left you in the middle of our romantic evening out.'

'Well, it wasn't exactly the night I had planned. But I'll get over it,' he said with a smile.

'Well, the night is still young. And the kids are at your dad's,' she said as she stood up and took hold of his hand, pulling him up from the sofa.

'Oh. What do you have in mind?'

'What do you think?' she teased.

He pulled her towards him and pressed his body into hers. 'I've been thinking about getting you out of this dress all night,' he whispered in her ear as he started to undo the long zip up the back.

Grace leaned her head back as Michael trailed hot kisses along her neck and jawline. Being wrapped in Michael's arms was the best way in the world to purge any thoughts of her psychopathic ex-husband.

Chapter Twelve

Alastair McGrath glared at his right-hand man Jock Stewart and scowled. 'How long has it been since we've had some decent wedge from those fucking Johnson brothers now?' he barked. 'It must be at least six weeks? Or more?'

'I reckon more, Boss. Last time I went up there I met with Craig and he only gave me eight grand. Gave me some cock and bull about waiting for payments and problems with the supply chain, but if you ask me, something fishy is going on up there in Liverpool.'

'What else have you heard?' Alastair asked.

'Not much, except no one has seen the older brother for a few months. He was supposed to be running their little outfit, but my sources tell me he's disappeared.'

'Sounds fucking well dodgy to me. But from what you told me, he was a knobhead anyway, wasn't he? If it's got anything to do with my money or my drugs though, I want to fucking know about it.'

Jock nodded. In his opinion, the Johnson brothers were prize idiots to follow their eldest brother the way they did. It was clear that Craig was the only one who had any real nous about him and the rest of them shared a brain cell between them. It was Craig whom Alastair had met in Frankland when they were banged up together, and Craig who had convinced his boss that he and his brothers were the men to expand their business up north. Jock didn't agree with that at all. He knew that Jake Conlon and the Carters had the whole of Merseyside sewn up, and that the Johnsons were small fry in comparison. The Carter twins had done some work for some associates of Jock's a few years back and they had always impressed anyone they worked with. They were clean, ruthless and professional. Jock had been shocked and saddened to learn of Paul's untimely demise, but he supposed that was to be expected in their chosen profession. You live by the sword and all that. If Jock had been making the decisions, it would have been the Carters that they'd have gone into business with, not the Johnsons. But he didn't make the decisions, and no one, not even Jock Stewart, who was as hard as they came, questioned Alastair McGrath.

'I think it's about time a few of the lads took another visit up north, Jock. And this time, tell them not to come back without my money, my drugs or one of the Johnsons' heads on a spike.'

Jock nodded. 'Of course, Boss. I'll go, and I'll take Nev and Finn with me.'

'Not you. I need you here. I've got something more

urgent I need you to sort out for me. The Russians are breathing down my neck and I need you to speak to your contacts in the West End to find out what went wrong with their deal last month.'

'Okay. I'll get on it. And I'll send Jerry with the lads. He'll make sure they don't cause too much mayhem while they're there.

'I don't care if they cause fucking mayhem. In fact, let them wreak fucking havoc for all I care. Tell them I want answers, Jock. I was supposed to have my feet well and truly under the table up there by now. So, what the fuck is going on?'

'They'll get to the bottom of it, Boss,' Jock replied. 'I have a few contacts up there I can call on. I'll put the lads in touch with them.'

'Good,' Alastair said, smiling for the first time since their meeting started. 'Fancy a smoke?' he asked as he opened the ornate wooden box where he kept his finest Cuban cigars.

'I wouldn't say no,' Jock replied as he took one from the box. Taking his cigarette lighter from his pocket, he lit Alastair's cigar and then his own. He sat on one of the stiff leather chairs in Alastair's lounge and took a long drag of the cigar. There was no way he'd be telling Nev and Finn to cause mayhem in Liverpool, and he would keep to his original plan of having Jerry keep an eye on them. The last thing they needed was a war with the Carters. Especially when they had Alexei Ivanov and his gang of Russian mobsters to contend with. In Jock's opinion, they needed allies, not more enemies. He'd have a discreet word with Jerry and make sure he knew the score before he and the lads set off for Liverpool. What Alastair didn't know wouldn't hurt him.

Chapter Thirteen

Craig Johnson was making himself a couple of slices of toast when he heard the hammering on the front door. Assuming it was his eldest daughter Cheyenne forgetting her key again – she had just turned thirteen and at the same time had become the teenager from hell – he slammed the butter knife onto the kitchen worktop and stomped down the hallway, swearing under his breath. The last thing he needed tonight was a run-in with Cheyenne. His wife Gemma was out at her mum's with their other daughter, Sasha, and she was always able to handle their wayward older daughter much better than he was.

Opening the door, he was about to launch into a rant when a large hand pushed him back inside the house. He staggered backwards as he watched the three unknown men barge into his hallway.

'Who the fuck are you?' Craig shouted, immediately regretting going to the door without something to defend himself. Even the butter knife was looking like a good option right now as the biggest of the three men came bearing down on him.

'We're friends of Mr McGrath,' the one at the back replied just as a large fist connected with Craig's jaw.

A few moments later Craig had been manhandled into the kitchen and onto one of the wooden chairs. He looked at the three men who had forced their way into his house and felt a sickening feeling building in the pit of his stomach. Bile rose in his throat and he swallowed it down. Two of them were about his age, early thirties, and built like tanks. All muscle and shaved heads. The third man was obviously in charge because the other two looked to him the way his brothers usually looked to Craig – waiting for orders on what to do next. The third man was older, dark-skinned and with a thick head of grey hair. He reminded Craig of his old woodwork teacher in school.

'Where is Mr McGrath's money?' the older man asked.

'It's in a safe place. I can get it for you tomorrow,' Craig lied, trying to buy himself some time.

The bald men laughed and their boss frowned at them. 'You expect me to believe that? Do I look like a cunt?' he snarled, his attention now directed back to Craig.

Craig nodded and licked his lips. 'I've got it, I swear. I'll get it to you tomorrow.'

The old man smiled. 'Oh, I know you'll get it to me, you little prick. Because if you don't, I'll have to settle for your head instead.' He pulled out a flick knife from his pocket and held it to Craig's throat.

'I'll get it,' Craig stammered.

The old man nodded. 'Mr McGrath will need something

for his trouble too. You've kept him waiting for far too long, and you know he's not a man to be kept waiting?'

He moved his hand and held the knife directly under Craig's eye. Craig felt like he was going to shit his pants as he realised who was standing in his kitchen holding a knife to his eye. When he'd met Alastair in prison, he'd told him numerous stories about Jerry the Jamaican, who was fond of popping out an eye and offering it to his boss as a souvenir. Alastair McGrath had talked of how much he loved Jerry's party trick, and he had laughed every time he told the story. Craig had laughed along too – never for a moment imagining that he might be on the receiving end. He squirmed under the pressure of the knife and one of the bald men came behind him, pinning his shoulders down so he could barely move. Craig grimaced and instinct made him struggle, even though he knew there was no escape. The man holding him down was freakishly strong, and he knew he was going nowhere.

A trickle of sweat ran down his back as he felt the tip of the knife pierce his skin. Then suddenly the front door slammed. 'I'm home, Dad,' came his daughter's voice from the hallway. Her footsteps were coming towards the kitchen and Craig swallowed. God, he couldn't let them hurt his daughter.

Suddenly, Jerry had pocketed his knife in one swift move. 'Not in front of a kid,' he mumbled to the man who was holding Craig down. Then Craig felt sweet relief as he was released from the man's grip just before Cheyenne breezed into the kitchen in her crop top and garish makeup.

She barely batted an eyelid at the three intruders in the

kitchen. She was used to different people visiting the house all hours of the day and night.

'Can I have that toast, Dad? I'm starving,' she asked, spying Craig's discarded supper on the worktop.

'Yeah, of course, love,' he replied.

'We'll call back tomorrow for our money,' Jerry said with a smile. 'Two hundred and fifty.'

Craig swallowed. They'd only lost two hundred grand of Alastair's money and they'd paid back at least twenty already.

'Interest,' Jerry said as though reading his mind. 'Enjoy your toast, darling,' he said to Cheyenne.

Then the three of them walked out of the kitchen as quickly as they'd came in.

Craig stood up on shaky legs and walked towards his daughter, before giving her a hug, thankful that she'd come home when she did, and that neither he or she had been harmed. At least not tonight. But Jerry and his two henchmen would be back, of that he had no doubt.

'Urgh, gerroff, Dad, what are you doing?' Cheyenne said as she pushed him away from her.

'Oh, stop being a moody cow for a change, Chey, and give your dad a frigging hug,' he said.

She looked up at him and her face softened. Maybe she saw the lingering terror there. 'Oh, all right,' she said with a grin and she gave him a brief squeeze. Then she picked up the plate of toast and flounced out of the kitchen in a cloud of Body Shop perfume, leaving Craig to wonder just exactly how he was going to find two hundred and fifty grand in less than twenty-four hours.

Jeremiah 'Jerry' Smith stood by the open window of his hotel suite and lit himself a cigarette. He blew a smoke ring and watched it drift off through the night air towards the twinkling lights of the Liverpool skyline. He could hear the laughter of Finn and Neville coming from the interconnecting room next door. They were in high spirits and getting ready for a night out on the town. A rare chance to let their hair down and sample the legendary Liverpool night life. Their encounter with Craig Johnson hadn't quite gone to plan after his teenage daughter had arrived home and spoiled their fun. Jerry shook his head in disbelief. What teenager in their right mind came home at eight o'clock at night? He took another long drag of his cigarette. There was no harm done. Craig Johnson would repay his debt to Mr McGrath before the week was out – one way or another.

Jerry knew that Craig Johnson actually having that cash was about as likely as Jerry being granted an audience with the Pope, but if Craig didn't have the money, Jerry would make sure that he paid in other ways instead. Craig and his wife owned their little terraced house, and while it wouldn't cover the money owed, it would be a start. Mr McGrath had dozens of properties all over the UK, some of which he'd bought as an investment, and some of which he'd been 'gifted' when his debtors couldn't pay up. Mr McGrath would be kind enough to let Craig and his family keep living there – so long as they paid him a substantial monthly rent, at least.

'We're heading off, Jerry,' Finn shouted as they walked through the open door. 'You sure you don't fancy it?'

Jerry shook his head. 'I'm too old for clubbing now. I'm going to have myself a nice drink in the bar downstairs. A good steak in the restaurant and then it's a film and bed for me,' he replied with a grin.

Finn smiled back. 'Don't expect us back until tomorrow. I'm sure we'll pull some fit Scouse birds,' he said with a wink.

Jerry laughed. 'I'm sure you will.' He flicked his cigarette butt out of the window and walked back into the centre of the room, which now reeked of expensive aftershave. 'But listen to me, you two,' he said sternly. 'Don't you be causing any shit tonight, do you hear me? This is not our city, so fucking behave yourselves.'

'But Alastair said we should stir things up a bit?' Nev protested.

'And we will. But with those idiot Johnson brothers, and no one else. I told you what Jock said. We are not to go making any more enemies while we're up here. Understand?'

The boys nodded at him and he waved his hand at them to leave. They bolted for the door like a pair of kids running to the ice-cream van and he sat on the bed with a sigh. Nev and Finn would be spoiling for a fight after they'd been interrupted at Craig's house earlier. He just hoped they didn't pick a fight with the wrong person.

_____

Chapter Fourteen

Connor Carter walked through The Blue Rooms, nodding to the bouncers as he passed. It was technically Jake's club, having been left to him by his father. But he and Connor were business partners in numerous ventures and they used the club as the base of their operations, where they oversaw the day-to-day running of their considerable empire. As he made his way towards the back office, which he shared with Jake, he wondered at the state he'd find his business partner and best mate in this evening. If he thought about it, it was becoming a rare event to see a sober Jake Conlon. With each passing week, Jake seemed to be sinking deeper and deeper into a pit of self-loathing and substance abuse. Of course, he brushed it off whenever Connor tried to broach the subject with him, claiming that he was just having some fun, and who could deny him some fun after the year he'd had – the year they'd both had? Paul's murder eight months earlier had hit them both hard. There wasn't a day that passed when Connor didn't think of his twin almost every moment. Sometimes, if he thought about his brother too much, he felt like his grief would swallow him whole, so he tried not to dwell on how much he missed him – preferring instead to remember happier times and Paul's sense of humour, rather than spend long periods thinking about how much his life had changed, and how he would never see his brother again.

Connor knew that Jasmine and their unborn baby were also a big factor in keeping him on the straight and narrow. He sometimes wondered what he would do without them to keep him grounded. Would he have ended up like Jake too? Seeking comfort in the bottom of a whisky bottle or a bag of white powder? Who could tell? He understood how hard it was for Jake to deal with losing Paul. He had loved Paul too, albeit in a very different way. Jake and Paul had been attracted to each other like magnets, unable to stay away from each other, despite the potential ramifications of their being together. But sometimes Connor felt like he'd lost Jake as well as Paul. He missed the sharp, sober Jake, who was always on the ball. The man who was funny and charming, and had a great head for business. The man he would trust his life with.

He reached the office and paused to collect his thoughts. The Jake sitting on the other side of that door was only a shadow of the man he really knew, and if he didn't do something to snap himself out of the self-destructive mode he was in, Connor didn't know what he would do. He felt like he was keeping things afloat on his own, and he didn't know how much longer he could do that, especially now that the police were sniffing around them. Connor needed a partner with a clear, level head, not one who didn't know what day of the week it was.

Taking a deep breath, he pushed open the door. Immediately he wished he'd knocked when he saw Jake and a topless barman snorting coke off the desk.

'For fuck's sake,' Connor shouted across the office. 'The police could walk in here any minute. Could you be a little bit more fucking discreet?'

Jake looked up, bleary-eyed, and frowned. 'Con. What are you on about? The door was fucking shut. Not like they can just barge in here without a warrant, is it?' he snapped.

The barman gave a wan smile as he wiped the traces of powder from his nose.

'Fuck off,' Connor barked at him as he nodded towards the open door. Picking up his shirt from the floor, Jake's latest conquest made a hasty retreat.

'You two weren't fucking in here, were you?' Connor said, his nose wrinkled in disgust.

'So what if we were?' Jake replied with a shrug.

'God, we'll need to bleach this fucking desk then,' he said as he sat down. 'Can't you keep your dick in your pants for a few hours? You were supposed to be sorting out the Blackpool job. Have you?'

Jake nodded before wiping his nose with the back of his hand. 'It's all sorted, mate. It won't be a problem.'

Connor eyed him suspiciously. They couldn't afford any slip-ups with the police breathing down their necks. He wasn't sure if he could trust Jake to handle anything any more, but what choice did he have? He couldn't manage everything on his own. The Blackpool job should be straightforward enough. A shipment of their finest Colombian marching powder to be delivered straight from the docks and up the M6 to their dealers. It was a smooth operation ordinarily, and one of many, but a firm in Blackpool had tried to chance their arm and nick the last shipment. They had all ended up getting the shit kicked out of them for their trouble, but Connor wanted to make sure that something similar didn't happen again, so they were going to send reinforcements.

'I said it's sorted,' Jake snapped.

'Okay. Keep your fucking hair on.'

'Well, stop looking at me like I'm a fucking idiot then.'

Connor shook his head. 'I'm not. You're no idiot, Jake...'

'But?'

'But you're fucking wasted again. We can't afford to have any cock-ups. We need to be more careful than ever after we got pulled in for Billy's murder.'

'Oh, relax. They've got fuck all on us,' Jake replied dismissively. 'And they can follow us around all they like, but they won't get anything on us. Murf sweeps this place for bugs every other day. No one would dare breathe a word to the filth about what we get up to. We're untouchable, mate.'

'But someone has breathed a word, haven't they? The police have a witness.'

Jake shrugged. 'They've got nothing.'

Connor shook his head. There was no getting through to Jake when he was on coke. He thought he was made of titanium.

'We need to go and check on Nipper and make sure he

knows who he's paying what to over the next few weeks. We can't be driving around with bags full of dough any more. The plod will be looking for any reason to pull us over and nick us, so let's not give them any more than we already have, eh?' Connor said.

Nipper Jackson was their counter. He handled all of the cash they had coming in from their various ventures. He sorted, counted and stored it, but now he would be responsible for paying everyone who needed to be paid too. He was a crucial cog in their well-oiled machine and they paid him very well for his trouble. But Connor had come to value Nipper's work ethic over the years, and more importantly, his discretion. As far as Connor was concerned, Nipper was worth every penny they paid him.

Jake stood up and took his jacket from the back of his chair. 'Come on then, lad. Let's go and see our Nipper then.'

———————————

Connor and Jake left the club by the back door, oblivious to the carnage that was starting to unfold at the main entrance. Jack Murphy –Murf – had just taken a sucker punch from a burly skinhead with a southern accent. It wasn't often that Murf was caught off guard, but he'd been coming out of the gents and was still zipping up his fly when he'd been punched in the gut. He looked up to see another fucker coming at him with a machete. Despite being out of breath, Murf dropped to his knees and the sword struck the wooden doorframe instead, lodging itself there. Soon the club's foyer was filled with the sound of a woman's screams as blood from one of the bouncer's noses spattered across her white mini dress. Murf looked up to see the bald man who'd punched him and another man with tattoos on his face wielding baseball bats and swinging them with abandon, not caring who or what they hit with them. Murf staggered to his feet. It was a Wednesday night, the day before the start of the Grand National, so he'd given his most experienced bouncers the night off, knowing they'd be working all hours for the next four days. Still, the lads he had with him were no mugs and there was no way they should be getting their arses handed to them by a pair of southern twats.

Murf straightened up and ran towards the melée. 'Come on, let's scarper,' the bald-headed one said to his mate. Before Murf could reach either of them, they had bolted for the door. Still winded, and with at least twenty years on them, Murf didn't have the energy to chase them. Instead he looked around the foyer and surveyed the damage. One of the large glass doors was smashed, along with a few mirrors, and would need replacing. There was a machete wedged into the toilet door frame. Three of his bouncers were on the floor bleeding, and one was out cold. The two who were inside the club, watching the room, came running into the foyer.

'Too fucking late, lads. Where were you?' Murf snapped as he walked over to the unconscious doorman and tried to rouse him.

'We only just heard, Boss. They were in and out,' Carl, the youngest one, answered.

'Call a fucking ambulance for him, will ya?' he ordered. 'Are Jake and Connor still here?'

Carl shook his head. 'They're not in their office.'

Murf frowned. He hadn't seen them leave. They could have gone while he was having a piss, although more often than not they slipped out of the back door these days. How was he supposed to keep a bloody eye on them if they didn't tell him where they were going? Not that Jake and Connor knew he was keeping an eye on them; they'd have a bloody canary fit if they found out. But he'd made a promise to Grace and Michael that he would look out for them. He sighed as he realised he'd have to phone one of them and tell them about tonight's little adventure. It could have been nothing, just some scallys looking for a fight. Or it could mean something much more.

After making sure the injured bouncers were okay, Murf went to the back office for some privacy. He wondered whether to phone Grace or Michael and decided on the latter. Both of them would be pissed off about what had happened, but as big and hard as he was, the truth was Grace scared the shit out of Murf when she was angry.

He dialled Michael's number and waited for him to answer.

'All right, Murf?' Michael answered.

'Not exactly, Boss,' Murf said.

'What the fuck has happened now?'

'We've had some trouble at the club—'

'Are the boys okay?' he interrupted.

'Yeah. They weren't even here. Look, it might be nothing. It could just have been some lads looking for a scrap...'

'But?'

'But they were all tooled up. They were good. And they were from down south.'

'Down south? Like London?'

'Maybe? I don't know. They all sound the fucking same to me. But it makes me wonder if it was a deliberate attack. They were in and out pretty fast. Smashed the place up a bit. Gave some of the lads a good walloping. Put me on my arse as well. Then they left.'

'Did anyone recognise them?' Michael asked.

'Nope. Like I said, they weren't from round here, Boss.'

'Was the CCTV working?'

'Of course,' Murf replied, slightly offended by the question. He always made sure it was – unless it was in the best interests of the boys for it not to be.

'Send it over to me, Murf. I want to see what went on.'

'I'll email it over, Boss.'

'Thanks.'

'Let me know if you recognise them, or if there's anything you need me to do.'

'Will do.'

Murf hung up the phone and turned on the computer to upload the CCTV to email over to Michael. He found the right section on the video and watched while he waited for the file to upload. Murf felt a twinge of embarrassment as he watched his bouncers, and then him, easily bested by the two intruders. It wasn't an experience he was used to, nor one he wished to repeat any time soon. He made a mental note to review the rotas for the next few weeks and make sure he always had at least some of his most experienced bouncers on with him in future.

Chapter Fifteen

Connor turned off the engine as they parked outside Nipper Jackson's house in West Derby. He looked across at Jake and noticed his best mate was getting twitchy and agitated. The coke was obviously wearing off.

'Why don't you have a line before we go in?' Connor asked with a sigh. At least then Jake would be sharp and not sitting fidgeting like a crackhead in Nipper's kitchen.

'Yeah, I will,' he replied as he took a small silver bullet-shaped cylinder out of his jacket pocket. 'Want some?' he asked Connor.

'No,' Connor snapped. 'You know I don't touch that shit. But at the moment, you're more use to me on it than coming down off it.'

Jake tipped some of the white powder onto his hand before sniffing it up into his nostril. 'That's better,' he said as he wiped his nose with his finger and thumb. 'Ready?'

Connor nodded. 'Come on.'

Nipper had opened the door before Connor had a

chance to knock. They had phoned him en route so he was expecting them.

'Come in, gents,' Nipper said with a smile as he opened the door wider. 'I've put the kettle on.'

Soon the three men were sitting in Nipper's kitchen drinking tea. 'So, what's the score, lads? Do you need cash?' Nipper asked.

'You hear about us getting lifted the other day?' Connor asked, ignoring the question.

'Yeah, I did, and it's good to see you both out and about again so soon.'

'Yeah, well, we're under investigation for murder in the meantime, so we need to lie low for a while.'

'Fuck,' Nipper said with a whistle. 'A murder charge? Well, that will cramp your style, lads. What do you need me to do?'

'We can't be driving around with any cash on us, so, until this thing blows over, you'll be dealing with some of our employees rather than us, Gary Mac and his sons will be looking after the money drops. You might have a few extra people dropping by but Gary will let you know in advance who will be turning up and how much they need paying,' Connor answered.

'Not a problem. I'll make sure everything runs like clockwork.'

Connor nodded. 'Nice one.'

'So, who are you supposed to have murdered then?' Nipper asked.

'Billy Johnson,' Jake growled.

'Oh?' Nipper replied as he sipped his tea, not probing

any further. Connor knew that Nipper was very much of the what he didn't know couldn't hurt him persuasion. While he was very good at his job, he was a bean counter – an accountant by trade, he stayed away from the other side of the business.

'Don't you want to know if we did it?' Jake snarled, his lip curled up like an angry dog.

Nipper shook his head furiously. 'Nope. It's no business of mine, Jake.'

'Jake!' Connor snapped at him. 'Come on, it's time we left.'

'Why did he ask who we murdered if he didn't want to know if we did it?' Jake shouted as he stood up suddenly, his chair falling to the floor with a clatter. He stalked across the kitchen towards Nipper. 'Do you know something you're not telling us?' Jake said as he edged closed to a now terrified Nipper who was physically shaking in his seat.

'No,' Nipper mumbled.

'For fuck's sake,' Connor barked as he grabbed Jake by the arm and steered him towards the door. 'Leave him the fuck alone, will you?'

'What if he knows something?' Jake asked, his eyes wide as he stared at Connor, who suddenly realised that that last line of coke was one too many and had pushed Jake over the edge.

'Sorry, Nipper,' Connor said as he guided Jake out of the door. 'Gary Mac will be in touch.'

'No problem, Connor,' Nipper replied shakily.

Jake shrugged Connor's arm off him and tried to run back into the kitchen but Connor stopped him. He was bigger and stronger than Jake, and even a coked-up Jake was no match for him. 'Get the fuck out of here and into the car,' Connor hissed through clenched teeth. 'Before I knock you the fuck out.'

Jake backed off and stormed out of the house towards the car, rambling incoherently to himself as he did.

Connor drove Jake home in silence. Jake had made a complete tit of himself at Nipper's house. Nipper was a good soldier and he was discreet too, but if word started getting out that Jake was unhinged, then it was only a matter of time before someone tried to take advantage of that. It was at times like these that Connor missed Paul more than ever. He would give anything to have his twin back by his side.

As they pulled up outside Jake's apartment block on the waterfront, Jake opened the door and almost fell out of the car. Connor pressed the button to lower the passenger window and leaned over so that Jake could hear him. 'Pull yourself together, Jake. Paul would be fucking ashamed of you,' he said before driving off and leaving Jake standing alone in the car park.

Chapter Sixteen

Michael was reviewing the CCTV from The Blue Rooms when his office door opened. Looking up from his laptop, he was surprised to see Lena standing in the open doorway.

'Lena? What are you doing here? I thought there was only me and Nick left,' he said as she walked into the room, closing the door behind her.

Lena continued towards him, crossing the room and walking around the desk. She stopped a few steps away from him. 'I wanted to make sure there was nothing else you needed, Boss,' she said softly.

Michael sat up straighter in his chair. 'I think I've got everything I need,' he replied as he watched her toying with the belt on her coat.

'Are you sure about that?' she said with a smile.

Michael's eyes narrowed. 'I'm pretty sure. What do you want, Lena?'

She took one step closer, so she was only a few feet from him. 'I wanted to let you know that I can give you *anything* you need,' she said as she began to undo the belt on her long coat. 'I've been flirting with you for weeks, but you don't seem to have taken the hint, so I thought I'd spell it out for you. Just to make sure you're absolutely clear.'

'Clear about what?'

'That you can have this,' she purred as she opened her coat fully, revealing that she was wearing only underwear beneath, 'anywhere, and anytime you want.'

Michael stared at her for a few seconds and waited for the punchline. Surely this was a set-up? But she continued to stand there, waiting for him to make his move. Waiting for him to claim her for his own.

He stood up. In one stride, he was standing before her, his face only inches from hers. She tilted her head to look at him and blinked, her long eyelashes fluttering across her cheeks.

Michael bent his head lower. He wanted to make sure she heard every word he said. 'I know you've been flirting with me,' he growled. 'I'm not fucking stupid. But I've been ignoring you and hoping that you'll get the message that I'm not interested.'

At this, she took a step back from him, her mouth open in surprise, and he realised she probably wasn't used to being turned down. There was no denying she was a beautiful young woman and she could have almost any man she set her sights on. Almost.

'In case you hadn't noticed, I'm married,' Michael went

on. 'And I happen to love my wife. You know her – Grace. She gave you this job. I suspect I'm not the first married man you've made a pass at, and I expect you've heard most of them say that they love their wives. But when I tell you that I love her, I mean, I fucking adore her. She is the only woman I have any interest in seeing, in or out of her underwear. So, as for how I want you, that would be fully clothed and out of my fucking restaurant.'

Lena pulled her coat protectively around her and, to Michael's relief, walked quickly out of his office.

Michael sat down with a sigh, and ran a hand through his thick dark hair. He should have put a stop to Lena's flirting weeks ago, but he'd hoped that just ignoring it would be enough to give her the message that he wasn't even remotely interested. He hoped that this was the end of it, and she didn't go trying to cause him any further trouble.

———————————

Michael slid into the driver's seat of his brand new Jaguar FX and took a deep breath, inhaling the car's still new smell. He loved cars. He always had done. He'd wanted to buy himself a Maserati, but Grace had talked him out of it, reminding him that they really shouldn't be drawing so much attention to themselves. Michael had reluctantly agreed and bought the Jag instead, but on the understanding that one day, before he was too old to enjoy it, he'd buy that Maserati. He had it all planned out. After he and Grace had got married, they'd sold her place in

Formby and moved back to Mossley Hill in the south of the city, to be closer to the rest of their family. But that was when everything had been okay, before Paul had been murdered. Now, Michael wanted out. He didn't want to have to bury another of his children – or his wife. As soon as they could, he wanted to move out of the city again. Not too far. They'd buy a big house in Southport or Lydiate. Then he'd get his Maserati and he wouldn't care who saw him driving it.

As he put the car into gear and pulled away from the kerb, Michael remembered his earlier encounter with Lena, and sighed when he thought about how he'd tell Grace that their newest waitress had ended up almost naked in his office. Grace trusted him, he knew that, but if it had been the other way around, he'd have been furious, his first instinct being to smash the cheeky bastard's head in. Although that wasn't Grace's style, it still wasn't a conversation he felt like having, especially after he'd have to tell her about what happened at The Blue Rooms too. There was no postponing it until morning either. He knew she'd be waiting up for him, even though he would be getting home later than he'd planned. The kids were with their grandparents for the night, so she'd wait up until any hour, knowing that she had the promise of an uninterrupted night's sleep and a lie in.

Belle and Oscar stayed at their grandparents' every Wednesday night, and sometimes on a Friday or Saturday too, if there was something going on that needed his and Grace's attention. It worked well. Michael's dad, Patrick, and his wife, Sue, adored all of their grandchildren, and played a big part in the kids' lives. Michael had already spoken to his dad about his plan to relocate to the suburbs, and he and Sue were keen to make the move with them. Michael loved Sue. She was a warm and good-natured woman, and, most importantly, she made his dad happy. Michael's mum had died when he was just eighteen years old. Marie O'Malley had been a force of nature. Everyone had been surprised when lung cancer had taken her at the age of thirty-eight. She'd gone from the most energetic woman he'd ever known to being bed-ridden within a matter of weeks, her body ravaged by the cruel disease. In those final days, it was Michael who barely left her side. Sean had been newly married with a new baby, and although he saw their mum every day, he had other priorities. Their dad had buried himself in his work, unable to comprehend that his vibrant young wife was slipping away before his eyes. He'd tried to pretend it wasn't happening. Every night he'd come home to her and would hold her in his arms until she fell asleep, but he just couldn't take the endless days sitting there with her. Michael's parents had adored each other. And not spending those final days with Marie was something Patrick Carter had regretted ever since, something for which he had never forgiven himself.

Michael had always loved to listen to his mum's stories about her childhood in Ireland and their large and eccentric family. He would listen to her talking for hours in her soft Irish lilt as she taught him all about his heritage. She knew all about the history of his dad's side of the family too, and the Carters' colourful past. One afternoon shortly before her death, they had been sitting in their lounge, which had become her bedroom, with the sun streaming through the windows, when she'd removed her engagement ring and pressed it into his hand.

'You've always been my favourite, you know?' she said with a wink.

Michael smiled and placed his other hand over hers. 'I know,' he replied even though he knew she was lying. She loved both of her boys equally and had never shown them anything other than that. He knew she would have told Sean the same thing at some point.

'I want you to have this ring,' she said softly. 'And give it to the woman you want to spend the rest of your life with.'

'Mum, I can't—' he'd started to protest, but she had cut him off with a wave of her hand.

'I want you to have it,' she insisted before breaking into a fit of coughing.

Michael had given her a drink of water, and then she'd recounted, for what he thought must have been the millionth time, the story behind her engagement ring and how it had belonged to his great-grandmother Elizabeth. It was a beautiful platinum band, set with three small but exquisitely cut diamonds. His great-grandfather, Albert Carter, had been a rag and bone man who had come from nothing. He had acquired the ring from a Romany woman whose life he had saved on one cold, rainy night in Liverpool. The circumstances of their encounter had become the stuff of Carter family legend, and there were numerous versions of the tale, but one thing that was universally agreed was that the ring was blessed – or cursed, depending on which way you looked at it.

The Romany woman had told Albert that the ring was so powerful, it would grant him any woman he wanted. All he had to do was give her the ring in a proposal of marriage, and she would be tied to him for ever, with only death able to part them. Albert had tested his good fortune on Elizabeth Campbell – the girl he'd adored since they'd become clandestine playmates at the age of eleven. Elizabeth was from a well-to-do family, the likes of whom would never allow their daughter to marry a humble rag and bone man. But the power of the ring had been proved when Elizabeth had immediately said yes to Albert's proposal, leaving her family's large detached house in Aigburth and moving to the tiny terraced house in Anfield that Albert shared with his mother. It had sent shockwaves around the local community. While Elizabeth wore her beautiful ring with pride, she dismissed any rumours about Romany magic, and swore that she'd been in love with Albert Carter since she'd first met him crawling through the hole in the fence of her family's back garden to steal apples.

Elizabeth had passed the ring on to her grandson, Patrick, before she died, and despite her insistence that she didn't believe in such folly as curses, she told him to be careful who he chose to give it to, as he would be tied to that person for life – and so it had been since he'd first set eyes on Marie O'Malley.

Michael had taken the ring with a smile, paying no heed

to his mother's talk of Romany curses either. He'd been seeing Cheryl, the woman who became his first wife, at the time, and while he'd loved her, he knew that the understated beauty of his mother's ring would be lost on her. Cheryl would need a diamond as big as a pebble, set in 24-carat gold, to agree to marry him – a fact which was borne out when he allowed her to choose her own engagement ring six months later. When Michael had proposed to his second wife, Hannah, many years later, after a whirlwind romance, he hadn't even considered giving her his mother's engagement ring, and wondered in hindsight whether that should have been a warning that their marriage was doomed from the outset.

He'd been packing up some of his house, after agreeing to move in with Grace, when he'd come across it in his safe. He and Grace had only been seeing each other properly for a month. They had got together just after she'd been kidnapped and almost murdered, and had spent almost every moment together since. Although they'd only been officially a couple for a month, their long history together, including the fact that they had a one-year-old daughter, meant that proposing marriage seemed like the most natural next step. Michael knew that after Nathan Conlon, Grace had sworn off ever marrying again, and he couldn't blame her, but he wondered whether there was any truth to the legend of the ring. If there was anyone it was worth testing on, it was Grace. That same evening, he'd cooked Grace her favourite meal, plied her with a few glasses of rosé and then asked her to marry him. He'd been as shocked as she was when she'd said yes. They'd married in their local church three months later. Maybe the ring was magical after all?

———————

Grace was making herself a cup of herbal tea when she heard Michael closing the front door behind him.

'In here,' she shouted to him.

He walked into the kitchen and made his way towards her before wrapping his arms around her waist and giving her a long, deep kiss.

'Is that an apology for being late?' she said with a grin when they came up for air.

'Nope. Just because I love you.' He returned her smile. 'But about me being late? Something happened tonight.'

'What? Is everyone okay?' she replied, wondering what fresh hell might be in store for them now.

Michael nodded. 'Everyone is fine. There was some trouble at The Blue Rooms. A couple of lads turned up there, all tooled up, and started causing bother. Murf and the lads sent them on their way, and no one was badly injured, but the doors and some of the mirrors were smashed up.'

'Do we know who these lads were?' Grace asked.

'No. Murf said he'd never seen any of them before. But they weren't from round here. He thinks they were from down south by the sound of them.'

'Down south?'

Michael nodded. 'Yeah.'

'What the hell's that about then?'

'No idea. But we'll find out,' he assured her.

'I know. But it's a worry we could do without.'

'Tell me about it,' he replied with a sigh.

Grace took his face in her hands. He'd been working so hard lately and he looked tired. 'I was going to suggest a nice herbal tea, but why don't we head straight to bed instead,' she said as she pressed her body into his.

Michael smiled at her. 'That's the best idea I've heard all day,' he said as he pulled her tighter to him. 'But there's something else I need to tell you.'

Grace frowned at him, fearful of what else he was about to say. 'What?'

He shook his head. 'I don't even know how to tell you this.'

'Tell me what?' she insisted. 'You're scaring me, Michael. What?'

He tucked her hair behind her ear. 'It's nothing like that,' he said. 'You know that new waitress, Lena?'

'Yes?'

'Well, she came on to me tonight.'

Grace laughed, mostly out of relief. 'I bet she's not the first woman to come on to you?'

'Of course not. I'm a catch, aren't I?' he replied with a grin.

'You certainly are,' she said as she pulled him towards her again for a kiss. The truth was, Grace had seen many women taking more than a second glance at her handsome, powerful husband, and she could hardly blame them. Michael, however, usually seemed oblivious to their attention.

'But this was different. She basically stripped to her underwear in our office and told me I could have her any time I wanted.'

'What?' Grace shouted in surprise and shock at the barefaced cheek of the woman. 'She stripped in our office?'

'Well, she was about to take her coat off, and she was only wearing her knickers and bra underneath.'

'Really?'

Michael nodded.

'Jesus Christ! What a fucking cliché. Don't tell me she was wearing a mac? Stockings and suspenders?'

Michael shook his head. 'I don't know, love. I didn't pay that much attention. I was too busy telling to her to get the fuck out of our restaurant.'

Grace frowned at him. 'Oh, you didn't fire her, did you?'

Michael stared at her. 'I didn't not fire her. Don't you think we should?'

Grace considered his question. 'I suppose so.'

'You suppose?'

'It's just that she's a great waitress. And the customers adore her,' she said with a laugh. 'But what a cheeky mare!'

'I can't believe you think this is funny,' Michael said incredulously. 'I've been worrying about how to tell you all the way home, and you don't seem to care that another woman offered herself to me on a plate.'

'Oh, behave yourself.' Grace wrapped her arms around his neck. 'Of course I care. But I trust you,' she said before kissing him on the lips.

'Glad to hear it,' he responded. 'But you could at least pretend to be a bit jealous.'

'Would it make you feel better if I threatened to scratch her eyes out?' Grace asked.

'Much,' he said with a laugh. 'Now, what were you saying about going straight to bed?' he asked with a glint in his eye as he took her hand and led her out of the kitchen and up the stairs.

Chapter Seventeen

Grace walked down the carpeted hallway of the upstairs landing towards the spare room she and Michael used as an office sometimes. She heard him on the phone.

'I want to know who they were, Murf. I watched the CCTV. They were too good to be just a pair of drunks looking for a scrap. And why come all tooled up? It was obviously planned. Get me the names by the end of the day.'

Michael was ending the call as Grace walked into the room. 'Everything okay?' she asked.

He shook his head. 'I've been thinking about last night. The hit on The Blue Rooms. It had to have been planned. Why else would they have had machetes and baseball bats with them?'

Grace nodded in agreement. She'd thought the same thing but hadn't voiced her concerns last night.

'They were good too,' he added. 'You should have seen the way they took out the bouncers. And Murf.'

'They hurt Murf? Is he okay?' Grace asked. Jack Murphy had worked for them for years and as well as a good employee, they considered him a friend.

'He's fine. They surprised him when he was coming out of the gents. Punch to the gut and he dropped like a sack of spuds.'

'I thought you said the bouncers got the better of them?' she asked, recalling their conversation the previous night.

'I said they saw them off. Eventually. But it was probably the thought of the bizzies turning up that did it, now that I think about it.'

'Is Murf going to find out who they were?'

Michael nodded. 'He'd better. I've told him I want the names by the end of the day. Or at least who they're working for.'

'Good. Then we can decide what our next move will be. Do Jake and Connor know about this yet?'

'No. I'll give them a call in a bit and let them know.'

'Tell them to stay out of it though. They can't afford to be getting caught up in anything right now.'

'I know. I will,' he replied as he ran a hand through his thick hair.

Grace perched herself on the edge of the desk next to his chair. 'Are you okay?' she asked.

He smiled at her. 'I'm fine,' he said and she knew he was lying. He was worried and he wasn't talking to her about it. No doubt trying to protect her. She was worried too, but she had faith that they could fix it all, as long as they were a team.

'You know we'll get through this, don't you?' she said as she placed a hand on his cheek.

Taking hold of her hand, he kissed her fingertips. 'I know,' he said quietly. Then he sat back in the chair and closed his eyes. 'I know.'

Grace had a feeling he was trying to convince himself as well as her. She wasn't going to sit about all day waiting for Murf to identify the culprits. Murf was a good soldier, but that wasn't exactly his field of expertise.

'Do you have the CCTV?' she asked.

Michael opened his eyes. 'Yeah. It's on my email.'

'Good. I'm going to send it over to Nudge. He has plenty of contacts down south and beyond. He might recognise some faces, or at least tell us someone else who might. I know Murf is your right-hand man, but he's not exactly Sherlock Holmes, is he?'

'And Nudge is?' Michael replied with a laugh.

Grace laughed too as she thought of her friend Nudge, who was a giant hairy man with a distinctive scar across his left eye – he was about as inconspicuous as a pink elephant. 'No, but he is well connected.'

Michael nodded and wheeled the chair back from the desk. 'It's all yours,' he said, indicating the laptop. With no other chair available, Grace perched on his lap and opened up his email inbox. She forwarded the email to Nudge with a request to identify the two intruders who had smashed up The Blue Rooms. Closing the computer again, she turned her body to face Michael. 'I bet my man comes up with the goods before yours,' she smiled.

'You think so?' he responded with a grin.

'I know so.'

'You're very sure of yourself, Mrs Carter,' he said with a twinkle in his eye before kissing her.

A few moments later, Grace was undoing the buttons on Michael's shirt when her mobile phone started to ring on the desk beside them. Glancing at the screen, she saw that it was Nudge calling and she held her phone up in triumph. 'Told you,' she said, grinning, although even she hadn't expected Nudge to be quite so efficient.

'Hi, Nudge,' she said as she answered the phone, putting it on speaker so Michael could hear too.

'Hiya, Grace, love,' he answered.

'Michael's here too. Do you have anything for us?' she asked.

'I know who one of those men is,' he replied, his tone flat. 'At least I know who he works for.'

'Who?' Grace asked, wondering what Nudge's reluctance was about.

'The one I've met before works for Alastair McGrath.'

Grace had never heard of him. 'Who?'

It was a few seconds before Nudge spoke. 'He is basically the Essex version of you.'

Grace felt Michael's grip on her tighten. 'What the hell is he doing sending his lads up here then?' she asked.

'That I can't help you with. I don't know Alastair myself, but I did some work years ago for his right-hand man, Jock Stewart. He owes me a favour or two actually,' Nudge added. 'I have no idea why his boss would send some lads to smash up The Blue Rooms though. Maybe it was a mistake?'

'If Alastair McGrath is who you say he is, I don't think he'd make those sort of mistakes, do you?' Michael said.

'I suppose not,' Nudge agreed. 'Want me to have a word with Jock and see what's going on?'

Grace looked at Michael and he nodded. 'Okay,' she agreed. 'I suppose it couldn't hurt. But be discreet, please, Nudge.'

'Of course, Grace. I always am,' he reminded her.

'Thanks, Let me know if you get any more information.'

'I will. Bye, love.'

'Bye, Nudge,' she said as she hung up the phone.

'Essex?' Michael said with a shake of his head. 'What the fuck is that about?'

'No idea. We've never had any dealings with Essex, have we?'

'No. But Connor might have. Him and Paul used to do work for all kinds of people before...' He trailed off.

'Let's see what Nudge comes back with before we decide what to do next then,' she suggested.

Michael nodded. 'I'll give Connor a ring and tell him about last night. I'll ask him if he ever did any work for Alastair while I'm at it.'

'I'll phone Jake,' Grace answered as she glanced at her watch and noticed it was only just after ten in the morning. 'Although I doubt he'll be up. I'll go and pick the kids up from your dad's first.'

'I'll come with you,' Michael said as she stood up. 'We can phone Connor from the car.'

Grace nodded. Maybe they should ask Michael's father Pat if he knew Alastair. Back in the day, it had been Patrick Carter who had first seen the potential in Grace. It was with his encouragement and backing that she had started her rise to the top. He had been her right-hand man and most trusted confidante for a very long time. He had known her father many years earlier and had always treated Grace like a daughter. He'd been over the moon when she and Michael had finally got together. He didn't get involved in business much any more and proudly declared his status as a happily retired man to anyone who cared to ask. He had married Sue, a former nurse and generally lovely woman, and now preferred to spend his days with his grandchildren.

Grace knew that Patrick's assault at the hands of her ex-husband, which had almost cost him his life and had left him with a permanent limp and two missing fingers on his left hand, had been a big contributory factor in his decision, and she always felt a pang of guilt about it. Nathan had targeted Patrick because he worked for her and because he was her friend. She was able to exact revenge for both of them a few months later when she put a bullet in Nathan's chest.

Chapter Eighteen

Jock Stewart was taking his wife Celia a cup of coffee in bed when he saw the unknown number flashing on his mobile. He debated whether to answer it, knowing that it was very likely going to be something that would stop him from climbing back into his warm bed with his even warmer wife. Cursing under his breath, he picked up the phone and answered it.

'Hello?' he snapped.

'Jock. It's Nudge.'

'Nudge? Fucking hell, mate. I haven't heard from you for years. What's going on?'

'I'll get straight to the point, Jock. Two of your lads smashed up Jake Conlon's club last night. They gave some of the bouncers a good kicking too.'

Jock sucked the air through his teeth. Hadn't he told those stupid bastards to keep their heads down and get the job done with minimum fuss? 'Fuck!'

'Can I take it from your reaction that they weren't acting on your orders then? Were they Alastair's?' Nudge asked.

Jock didn't answer. Nudge was a decent bloke, and they had always got on well, but Jock would never betray his boss. He wondered what Alastair had said to the boys before they left for Liverpool. Despite what orders Jock had given them, any from Alastair would override them. The problem was that Alastair didn't understand the hierarchy in Liverpool. Everyone who was anyone was loyal to Grace Carter and her family. You made an enemy of her and you made an enemy of them all.

'How do you know it was our lads?' Jock asked.

'One of them was that kid I helped out for you a few years back. I recognised the tattoo on his neck.'

Jock muttered under his breath as he realised that was true. Finn had stolen some antique jewellery from an East End gangster's wife. The shit was so hot that it could have melted lead. Finn had been a stupid kid who'd seen an opportunity to make some easy money, not realising who he'd been stealing from. Nudge was the best fence Jock had ever met and he knew he'd be able to get rid of the stuff before anyone found out. Taking pity on Finn, whom he'd always had a bit of a soft spot for, Jock had passed them on to Nudge, who had sold them to a wealthy American collector. They'd all earned a decent wedge and no one had ever found out who stole the gems. The gangster had wrongly accused the Russians and had started a war that had wiped out half of their respective firms, so it had worked out well for everyone concerned.

'I suppose you told Grace Carter who he was then?' Jock said with a sigh.

'Of course I did, Jock. She would have found out anyway. I like you, Jock, but she's Grace fucking Carter, and she's always had my back. I'm giving you the heads up in case you can do something about it and prevent your lads from being thrown into the Mersey with a pair of concrete wellies.'

'Look, Finn and Nev are good lads. They weren't sent there to cause any beef with Grace or her boys. They were there to collect some money someone owes us, and that was all.'

'Who owes you money?'

'Nobody important. Some fuckwit brothers. Anyway, is that really any of your fucking business, Nudge? Just try and hold off on World War Three until I have a chance to speak to the boss, eh? I'll come up to Liverpool myself if I have to. Maybe we can nip this thing in the bud before it gets out of hand?'

'I'll see what I can do,' Nudge replied. 'But I'm not promising anything.'

'Thanks, Nudge,' Jock said as he ended the call. He put his phone into the pocket of his bathrobe and slammed his fist onto the kitchen counter. This was exactly what he'd been afraid would happen. The last thing they needed was a war with Liverpool.

For fuck's sake! He was in his late fifties now and it was time to start winding down. He'd worked for Alastair McGrath for over thirty years, since they'd both been thrown out of a nightclub in Glasgow for selling ecstasy.

They'd decided to pool their resources and soon became the biggest suppliers to every nightclub in the city. When Alastair had moved to Essex after meeting his wife, Shannon, Jock had made the move too, and had remained loyal to his best mate throughout the years, through every takeover and turf war, but now was surely the time to start slowing down and enjoying the fruits of their labour, not making more enemies at every turn.

Alastair was keen to get a foothold in Merseyside. He had Essex in the palm of his hand, and they had a good supply chain in Scotland thanks to their former connections, but he saw Liverpool as a vital link in the supply chain and he wanted a piece of it. For some reason, he had trusted the fuckwit Johnson brothers to do that for him. If Jock was in charge he'd have tried to make an ally of Grace Carter. From what he'd heard about her, she was a shrewd businesswoman, although she was ruthless when crossed. She'd even murdered her own ex-husband. He shuddered to think what might be waiting for him when he arrived in Liverpool. Whatever happened, he needed to speak to Alastair before he made any moves. But before all that he'd be calling Jerry and asking him what the fuck he was doing letting Finn and Nev out of his sight.

Chapter Nineteen

Grace and Michael had just finished talking to Connor about the incident at The Blue Rooms the previous night when Grace's phone rang again. She answered it and the sound of Nudge's voice filled the car.

'I spoke to Jock. As I suspected, he didn't say much, but he did say that those two lads weren't working on his orders. They were here to collect a debt and that was all apparently.'

'A debt from who?' Grace asked, wondering if it was something to do with one of their bouncers – although surely she and Michael would know about it if it was the case.

'Well, I asked that, and he got a bit cagey – understandably, I suppose. He said it was nobody important. Some fuckwit brothers apparently.'

'Do you believe him?'

It was a few seconds before Nudge spoke, as though he was giving his response some serious thought. 'Jock is a ruthless bastard. He'd carve you into pieces if you crossed him, but I've always found him to be a straight talker. And I think if him and his boss wanted to get your attention, they'd have been a little more direct.'

'Did he say anything else?'

'Yeah. He said he'd come up to Liverpool and sort the mess out himself if he needed to.'

Grace watched as Michael's knuckles turned white as his grip on the steering wheel tightened.

'What the hell did he mean by that?' Grace asked.

'I got the impression he meant to deal with his lads, not cause any more aggro. He said he wanted to nip this all in the bud before it got out of hand. I think he has a bit of a soft spot for one of the lads involved, otherwise he'd probably leave them to be dealt with, if you know what I mean?'

Michael turned in his seat and frowned at her. 'So we've now got a gangster from Essex on his way up here to make sure nothing happens to his boys?' he snapped.

'Probably. But I honestly don't think he wants any trouble with you two,' Nudge offered.

'A bit fucking late for that now, isn't it?' Michael said.

'Did he say who these brothers were?' Grace interrupted.

'No, sorry.'

'It's okay. I've got a pretty good idea anyway. Thanks for the info, Nudge. Let us know if you hear anything else from your mate Jock.'

'Will do, Grace. Bye now.'

Grace ended the call and turned to Michael. 'I would bet our house on those brothers being the Johnsons.'

'I agree they're fuckwits. But why are you so sure they're involved with this Essex lot?'

'Think about it. A few months ago they tried to make a move on the lads' business. They were gobbing off about being responsible for Paul's murder. It was like they'd suddenly grown some balls. I bet that McGrath was backing them. Then Bradley Johnson suddenly disappears and McGrath's sending his henchmen up here to try and collect a debt. Bradley has obviously done a runner with the money and left the rest of them in this shit.'

Michael shook his head. 'Fucking hell, imagine doing that to your own brothers. Not to mention his wife and kids.'

'I know. But there's always been something dodgy about him.'

'So, what do we do now then? We've got enough on our plate without a war with some Essex gangsters.'

'Well, let's hope what Jock told Nudge was right and they want to nip this in the bud. We'll have to deal with them if and when they arrive. But I think the key to this whole thing is finding Bradley Johnson.'

Michael concentrated on the road ahead with his jaw clenched, so she went on. 'Bradley has the money, or at least he had it – he's probably gambled it away by now. So McGrath wants him, and no doubt his brothers want him too.'

'Maybe his brothers are in on it together? Maybe they

already know where he is and just nicked the money? They are fucking idiots after all.'

Grace shook her head. 'Most of them. But not that Craig lad. He's got some nous about him. I don't think the rest of them are involved, and I think they'd kill to have Bradley back. If the Johnson brothers were indebted to us – well, just think about it.'

'I'm not sure they'd agree with your way of thinking though, love. They believe our sons murdered their brother.'

'I know they do. But there are other things at play here. If they really owe this McGrath a substantial amount of money, then they are all in fear of their lives.'

'How are we going to find him then?' Michael asked.

Grace laid her head against the head rest and smiled. 'Leave it with me,' she said. Although she already had a plan, and it was going to fix everything.

Chapter Twenty

Jerry Smith was sitting on the small sofa in his hotel room, reading the newspaper and smoking a joint, when his mobile phone started to ring. Seeing Jock Stewart's name flashing on the screen, he answered it quickly.

'Everything okay, Boss?' Jerry asked.

'No, it's fucking not okay, Jerry,' Jock barked down the phone. 'In fact, it's as far from fucking okay as we can get. I thought I told you to keep an eye on that pair of meatheads last night?'

Jerry's heart sank. Finn and Nev had rolled back to their hotel room at seven that morning, looking worse for wear and stinking of booze and cheap perfume. They'd gone straight to bed and were still sleeping it off. He'd assumed they'd behaved themselves though, given that they didn't look hurt and after he'd warned them to.

'What have they done?' Jerry asked with a sigh.

'They've only gone and trashed the nightclub of one of

the biggest faces up there, that's all. And given some of his bouncers a good walloping in the process. This could start a fucking war, Jerry.'

'Shit!'

'What was the point of sending you up there with them if you were going to let them run amok?' Jock snapped.

'I told them to behave, Jock. But I can't babysit them twenty-four fucking seven. They're grown men.'

Jock sighed and was silent for a few seconds. 'I have a feeling Alastair told them to shake things up a bit when they got there. But believe me when I tell you that they have picked the wrong target.'

'I'm going to bollock the pair of them in a minute,' Jerry said. 'Then what do you need me to do?'

'Keep your heads down, and get all of your arses back here as soon as you've got that money back from Craig Johnson. Once Jake Conlon or the Carters identify Finn and Nev, they'll be dead men walking. Although they might wish they were dead when I get my fucking hands on them.'

'Will do,' Jerry said. 'Later, Jock.'

'Yeah, later.'

Jerry put his phone in his pocket and walked through to the bedroom where Finn and Nev were sleeping.

'You pair of fucking cretins,' he shouted as he pulled the covers off them both. Then he launched into a tirade while they held their pillows over their heads to try and drown him out. When he had no more breath left to shout, Jerry walked out of the room and out of the hotel suite. He needed some fresh air.

Chapter Twenty-One

After parking his Jag on the expansive drive, Jock Stewart walked up to the front door of Alastair McGrath's house. His wife Shannon opened the door before he'd had a chance to knock. She smiled at him – all boobs, white teeth and bee-stung lips. She'd had more work done than the Forth Bridge, but she was a good-natured woman with a heart of gold.

'Jock, I've just put the kettle on, love,' she said as he gave her a brief hug. 'Alastair is waiting in the lounge for you.'

Jock walked through their thickly carpeted hallway and into the lounge where he found Alastair sitting in his favourite leather wingback chair. His boxer dog, Beryl, was sitting beside him, enjoying the remainder of last night's leg of lamb.

'Everything okay?' Alastair asked as Jock gave Beryl a quick scratch on the head before taking a seat.

'Not really,' Jock replied.

'What's going on?' Alastair asked with a frown.

'Nev and Finn have smashed up a club in Liverpool.'

'So? I told them to have some fun,' he said with a shrug.

'But they didn't just target anyone's club, Al. They smashed up the club of Grace Carter's son, Jake Conlon.'

'Means nothing to me, Jock. Who the fuck are they?'

'Grace Carter, along with her husband and their sons, run Liverpool, Al. They have the whole place sewn up. If they're not involved in it, then they get a backhander for it. Everyone who is anyone operates under their orders, or at their discretion. I'm not talking about some cowboy outfit like those Johnson clowns. These are proper business people. Ruthless fucking business people.'

'Then why the fuck didn't you tell me about them when I was trying to make a move in Merseyside?'

'I tried to, Boss. But you weren't interested. That prick Craig Johnson had you convinced that he was the key to you getting a piece of the action. To be fair, the kid talked a good talk, but he hasn't delivered the goods, has he? Finn and Nev have gone and picked a fight with the biggest firm in the North West, and to be fucking frank, we could do without it.'

Alastair stared at Jock and chewed his bottom lip, a habit he had when he was deep in thought.

'I'm going up to Liverpool in a few days to try and straighten this mess out. I've got a meeting with the Russians tomorrow that I can't put off,' Jock said.

Alastair nodded sagely. 'I'd meet Alexei myself, but…'

'Yeah, I know,' Jock answered. Last time Alastair and Alexei had come face to face, Alastair had tried to chop

Alexei's fingers off with a machete over a woman. They had since come to an amicable business arrangement, but it rested on a delicate knife edge.

'I'll come to Liverpool with you, though,' Alastair declared as he stood up.

'You sure, Boss?' Jock asked.

'I've never been to Liverpool. If this Grace Carter is as big as you say she is, I think it's about time I met her, don't you?'

Jock nodded. Despite being prone to occasional bouts of psychopathic behaviour, for the most part Alastair was good at making money. Perhaps they could make some kind of deal with Grace Carter that wouldn't end in an all-out war.

'I'll get one of the lads to drive us up there,' Jock said.

'Yeah. Ask Colin. He can drive the Bentley. We might as well arrive in style, eh?' he said with a laugh.

They were interrupted by Shannon walking into the room carrying a tray of tea and biscuits. 'Here you go, boys. I even got the Hobnobs out especially for you, Jock,' she said with a giggle as she placed the tray on the coffee table.

'So, what are you boys up to?' she asked as she sat on the arm of the chair beside her husband.

'Just planning a little trip to Liverpool in a couple of days,' Alastair replied.

'Ooh, I've always fancied going there,' she squealed in delight.

Alastair patted her leg gently. 'Not this time, darling. But I'll take you next time. I promise.'

Shannon picked up her cup of tea and stood up, moving

to take a seat on the sofa. Jock could see she was disappointed, but she at least tried to hide it well. She was the perfect hostess and would never embarrass Alastair in front of guests by sulking. She had learned that from her own mother, the indomitable Ruby Shaw. Shannon's father, Harry Shaw, had been the biggest gangster Essex had ever seen. When Alastair had met Shannon and moved to Essex, Harry had recognised Alastair's talent and had eventually handed over the firm to him shortly before he died. Ruby had been the woman behind the great man in more ways than one and her parties had been legendary. As a result, Harry and Ruby had been a hit with socialites and gangsters alike and they had moved in the most influential of circles.

Shannon was a lot like her mother, but, unfortunately for her, Alastair wasn't much like her father. Whereas Harry had adored Ruby and had treated her as his equal, Alastair failed to see Shannon as anything more than something to look good on his arm. As she'd got older, despite her desperately trying to maintain her appearance to keep him happy, Alastair had replaced her with a string of younger models, but he would never divorce Shannon because she was the key to Harry Shaw's empire. All of Harry's properties and businesses were in Shannon's name and it had been written into his will that they'd stay that way. When Shannon died, they would pass to their only child, their nineteen-year-old daughter Evie. Evie hated her father and the way he treated her mother, and had moved out as soon as she'd been able to. She had a modest trust fund, set up for her by her adoring grandfather, and other than that she didn't take a penny from her mother and father.

Alastair had all but disowned his daughter and branded her a disgrace to the family name. He had banned Shannon from seeing her, although Jock knew that the two women met up in secret whenever Alastair was out of town. He was happy to keep their secret for them. As far as he was concerned it was unnatural to ban a mother from having contact with her child.

Jock felt sorry for Shannon. She was only fifty-two. If Alastair would just let her go, she could find herself someone who would love and appreciate her, and she could enjoy the rest of her life, instead of spending it waiting at home for Alastair to finally pay her a bit of attention.

Jock smiled at Shannon. 'I'll make sure he picks you up a nice present, Shan.'

She smiled back, although it was one that didn't quite reach her eyes. 'Thanks, Jock.'

Chapter Twenty-Two

After picking up the kids from Pat and Sue's, Grace had told Michael she needed to go out for an hour. She had a plan forming and she needed to test it out. After dropping them at home, she had driven to John Brennan's house. She was sitting on his sofa admiring the photographs of his sisters, nieces and nephews when he walked into the room, pulling a T-shirt over his large muscular chest.

'Sorry I disturbed your shower,' she said.

'No worries. I didn't expect you so soon,' he replied with a smile. 'What can I do for you, Boss?'

'I've been thinking about how to fix this mess with Jake and Connor. The thought that they might go down for life, John…' She shook her head.

'They won't,' he said quietly.

'Well, I hope not. But anyway, I have an idea.'

'Don't you always,' John said with a grin.

'And as they often do, this one involves you.'

John nodded 'Whatever you need, Boss.'

'I need you to speak to Craig Johnson for me,' she replied.

'Okay.'

Grace smiled. One of the things she admired so much about John was that he never asked too many questions, always trusting that she knew what she was doing. He was loyal to a fault and to someone like Grace, loyalty was everything.

———

Grace left John's house half an hour later. She climbed into her car and dialled Faye Donovan's number. Faye answered straightaway.

'Hi, Grace. Everything okay?'

'Yes, fine. Well, as fine as can be expected. I was wondering if you could look into something for me though, or at least have that new PI you use do it? I need to find someone, and quickly.'

'Wouldn't it be quicker to have one of your people do this?' Faye asked.

'Possibly, but the guy who I'd trust with this is on something else for me. I'd ask Webster but I don't want the police anywhere near it. I know he's discreet but I can't chance it.'

'Okay. Let me grab a pen and give me the name. I'll get him to put a rush job on it.'

'Thanks, Faye. I'll pay him whatever he needs.'

A few seconds later, Faye returned to the phone. 'Go on,' she said.

Grace gave Faye Bradley's name and address before hanging up the phone. Faye's new PI was an ex-NCA officer. She'd only had him working for her for the past few months, but Faye had told Grace that he'd already proved himself to be very skilled at tracking down people who didn't want to be found. John Brennan would usually handle that sort of work for Grace, but he was going to be tied up with other things.

Grace had a suspicion that finding Bradley Johnson could be the answer to all of their problems.

Chapter Twenty-Three

Michael was busy making a late lunch when Grace walked into the kitchen. Their youngest, Oscar, was drawing pictures at the kitchen table. She kissed him on his cheek before making her way over to Michael.

'Did you do what you needed?' he asked.

She leaned over him and took the lid off the saucepan, inhaling the scent of the pasta sauce and smiling her approval. 'Yes. And I spoke to Faye. She's going to have her PI find Bradley Johnson for us.'

'And what are we going to do when we find him?'

'Hand him over to McGrath or his brothers. I haven't quite decided yet. It depends on a few things.'

'Do you think getting involved with the McGrath fella is wise?' he asked as he picked up the packet of fresh pasta and began opening it.

'I don't know until we meet him. Maybe it would be good to have a connection in Essex. I think he's trying to get a foot in the door up here. Why else would he be working with the Johnsons? And if he does, it's better that we manage him than someone else, don't you think?'

'I don't know, Grace,' he replied. 'I thought we were trying to take a step back from all this, not get sucked further in.'

'Well, it's kind of been taken out of our hands now, hasn't it? I don't particularly want to work with Alastair McGrath, and we might not, but his right-hand man is on his way here and I intend to meet with him to see what the hell he wants and why he allowed his employees to smash up Jake's club.'

'Have you spoken to Jake yet?' Michael asked, changing the subject as he poured the pasta into the saucepan of boiling water.

'Not yet,' she replied with a sigh. 'Every time I phone him it rings and goes to voicemail. I think he's avoiding me.'

'I think he's avoiding everyone. Connor couldn't get hold of him either.'

Suddenly, Grace's stomach dropped through to her knees. 'Oh God, Michael. What if something's happened to him?'

He put his arms around her waist. 'He'll be fine. Connor said he was wasted last night. He's probably still in bed sleeping it off.'

'I need to go over there and see him.'

'Can it at least wait until after dinner?' he said.

She nodded. 'Okay.'

Grace barely touched the food as she watched her husband and Oscar tucking into theirs. She was so worried about Jake she couldn't face eating. The likelihood was that he was fine and would be sleeping off a hangover in bed, but even that was a worry to her. Until recently, Jake had never been much of a drinker, and he'd never done drugs much, despite selling them. But lately he seemed to be permanently drunk or off his face on drugs. She saw so much of his father in him sometimes that it terrified her. She could see her beautiful boy slipping away from her and it felt like there was nothing at all she could do about it. It broke Grace's heart and she knew that the longer he stayed on this road to self-destruction, the harder it would be to get the old Jake back.

Chapter Twenty-Four

G race walked along the corridor of the apartment building on Liverpool's waterfront. Since his split from Siobhan, Jake had moved back into his old place. He'd put their beautiful four-bedroomed house in Woolton on the market because he said it was too big for him, but Grace suspected it held too many painful memories. The flat had two bedrooms so he could have his daughter Isla staying over, although, from Grace's conversation with Siobhan earlier in the week, who knew when that was likely to happen again.

Grace knocked on the door and waited for an answer. When none came, she knocked louder, using the side of her fist.

Eventually, and much to her relief, Jake answered the door. She could smell the whisky on him as soon as he did, the stench seeming like it was seeping out of his pores.

'Mum!' he snapped, bleary-eyed and only half awake. 'What are you doing here?'

'Well, what do you expect when you haven't been answering your phone?' she answered. 'Can I come in?'

'Now's not a good time,' he said sheepishly.

'I don't care who you've got in there with you, Jake. I need to talk to you.'

'Oh, all right,' he said with a sigh as he held his door open wider.

Grace walked into the room and noted the stale smell of alcohol, weed and unwashed bodies. 'Jesus Christ, can you crack a window in here?' she said as she walked towards one of the large windows overlooking the river and opened it.

'Well, I was asleep,' Jake complained. 'If I'd known you were coming over to do an inspection, I'd have tidied up a bit,' he added sarcastically.

'Who was it?' Grace heard a voice coming from the bedroom and looked up to see a naked man walking out.

'Oh, God, sorry, Mrs Carter,' he said as he bowed his head and ducked back inside. She recognised him as one of their bouncers, although his name escaped her.

Jake looked at her, waiting for a reaction, but she didn't have one – not to that at least. She was glad he had some companionship after losing Paul.

'Did he tell you what happened at the club last night?' Grace asked.

Jake frowned. 'No, he wasn't on last night. Why, what happened?'

'Two fellas turned up with machetes and baseball bats and smashed a couple of mirrors and the doors. One of the bouncers had to go to hospital with a concussion, but other than that everyone is okay.'

'Do we know who they were?'

'Two lads from down south. They work for someone called Alastair McGrath. Ever heard of him?'

Jake shook his head. 'Should I have?'

'I suppose not. But, he's a big gangster from Essex, apparently.'

'So what were his lads doing in my club?' Jake asked.

'We've spoken to Alastair's right-hand man, at least Nudge has, and he swears the incident was nothing to do with them. He says they were just here to collect on a debt.'

Jake nodded and sat back in his chair, the glazed look returning to his face. Grace frowned. A few months ago she'd have been hit with a barrage of questions from him, about who these men were and what the hell they were doing in Liverpool, as well as his plan to deal with them. Now, Jake just sat there, looking detached and vacant.

'Jake,' Grace said.

He blinked rapidly. 'What?' he said with a scowl.

'I'm worried about you,' she said softly.

'There's nothing to worry about, Mum, I'm fine.'

'You don't look fine,' she replied.

He looked down at himself and Grace noticed that he'd lost some weight. Then he looked back up at her but he stared right through her, and he looked so much like his father that she felt winded. How many times had she watched Nathan after a heavy night, sitting looking like a dribbling mess. Well, it wasn't going to happen to her son too.

'Jake,' she shouted. 'You look like shit. You spend your days and nights drinking and taking God knows what, and it's affecting everything. Do you know Siobhan doesn't feel safe leaving Isla with you any more? You think you're invincible, Jake, but you're not. You've lost your edge and sooner or later someone is going to take advantage of that fact.'

He glared at her and she wondered if he was about to give her a tirade of abuse. She wouldn't mind if he did – it would be better than the pathetic figure she was looking at right now. At least it would prove that he still had some fight in him. But he didn't. Instead he put his head in his hands. It was only when she saw his shoulders moving up and down that Grace realised he was crying.

'Jake,' she said as she rushed to his side.

'I don't care any more, Mum,' he sobbed. 'I don't care if I lose it all. It means nothing without him.'

Grace sat on the arm of the chair and put an arm around him, hugging him to her. She had to fight back the tears herself. 'I know, son. We all miss Paul. But he would hate to see you like this. You know that.'

Jake sniffed and wiped his face with the back of his hand. 'I just miss him so much. It fucking hurts, and the only way to stop it is to shut it out.'

Grace kissed the top of his head. 'But you can't shut it out. It will still be there when you eventually sober up. And you owe it to Paul to grieve for him. It hurts like hell because you loved each other so much. That is the price we pay for love, son.'

Jake nodded and put his hand on her arm. 'Thanks, Mum.'

Aware that one of their bouncers was still in the flat, and that Jake would hate anyone to see him so vulnerable, Grace stood up. 'Come on,' she said. 'Let me make you a nice strong cup of coffee and something to eat. You can ask your mate to join us too if you like. What was his name again?'

Jake gave a half laugh. 'I can't remember. I'll go and tell him to go home anyway. If I let him stay for breakfast he might get ideas.'

Grace watched her son walk down the hall to his bedroom before walking into the kitchen. The sink was piled with dirty dishes and there was hardly any food in the fridge, but there were eggs and coffee, left over from the shopping she had brought him the week before. She'd wash the dishes and then make him a nice omelette. He'd always enjoyed those when he was a kid. God, how much easier things had been when he was little and she was his whole world. She'd been able to protect him from heartache and pain. That was the hardest thing about having kids: they remained your world long after they had grown up and left home. It broke her heart that she couldn't protect him from those things any more.

Chapter Twenty-Five

Craig Johnson stepped out of the café onto Breck Road and looked around to see if there was anyone resembling Jerry or his goons around. The street was busy with mid-afternoon shoppers and he hoped it would provide him enough cover should he be spotted. He knew the streets of Anfield better than anyone and was confident he could make a hasty getaway on foot if he needed to. He'd packed Gemma and the kids off to her auntie's house in Wigan after his visit from Jerry and Co. last night and he and Ged had driven to Formby beach and slept in Craig's car. They hadn't been able to get hold of Scott as his phone was going straight to voicemail. Craig knew he'd gone into hiding with an old girlfriend he'd had in college, after he'd stupidly become the key witness in their brother Billy's murder. Craig could hardly believe that Scott could be so bloody naïve. He allowed himself a moment to consider how fucking incredible it would be if Jake Conlon and

Connor Carter did go down for life – although he knew in reality it would never happen.

Out of the corner of his eye Craig saw the black BMW X5 pull up beside him as he continued walking along Breck Road. He readied himself to make a run for it, until he heard someone with a thick Scouse accent shout his name. He turned his head to see that it was John Brennan driving the car.

'Fancy a lift?' John asked with a grin. *The Smiling Assassin*. Craig shook his head. *Fuck!* John Brennan was Grace Carter's right-hand man. Damn Scott and his fucking blabbing to the filth.

'Come on. I saw a couple of heavies up the road there. Looking for you, aren't they?'

Craig turned around, scanning the street for any sign of Jerry and his two very large friends.

'I can help you, Craig.'

Craig stared at him. 'Yeah, right. Your boss sent you, has she?'

John shrugged. 'She wanted me to speak to you actually, but that's not why I'm here. I don't always do what she tells me to, you know.'

The car had stopped completely now, causing a build-up of traffic. Other drivers were beeping in annoyance, or shouting obscenities as they were forced to drive around John's car. Passers-by were starting to stare and the whole situation was becoming too much of a scene for Craig's liking. If Jerry and his goons were in the vicinity, it wouldn't be long before they spotted him.

'Look, Craig. If I wanted to hurt you, I'd just get out of

this car and do it. Or I'd have come into the café before when you were enjoying your bacon and eggs. But I don't. In fact, I have a business proposition for you.

Craig looked at the car. He'd barely slept. The constant beeping of the car horns was making his head feel like it was about to explode, and the thought that Jerry might pounce on him at any moment and relieve him of an eyeball was making his sphincter clench. He opened the passenger door of John's car and jumped in.

'Good. Now let's go somewhere we can talk,' John said with a grin as he sped off down Breck Road.

———

Thirty minutes later, Craig was sitting opposite John Brennan in a pub on Lark Lane. The place was closed, but they had opened the door especially for John, and Craig wondered what is was like to have the kind of power that someone like John Brennan wielded. It was a power he wanted for himself, and it had almost been within his grasp, if it hadn't been for his backstabbing cunt of a brother, Bradley. John ordered two Cokes from the woman who had opened the door and they waited for her to bring them over.

'I hear you and your brothers have got yourselves into a spot of bother with Alastair McGrath?' John asked.

Craig frowned. 'How do you know about that?'

'You'd be surprised, Craig. There's not much that happens in this city that I don't know about, mate,' John said with a smile as the woman approached with their drinks. 'Thanks, Bethan,' he said as he handed her a note.

'On the house, John,' she replied as she placed a hand on his shoulder.

When Bethan was out of earshot, John went on. 'So, how much do you owe him then?'

'Two hundred and fifty grand,' Craig answered. There wasn't much point in evading John's questions now.

'Were you working for him?'

'Yeah. We couldn't get a decent supplier from round here, thanks to your boss blacklisting us, and he wanted a foot in the door up here, so he gave us the gear and we sold it for him. It was good stuff. We shifted it easily enough once we found some buyers.'

'But Bradley fucked off with all the money?'

'Yeah,' Craig snapped. 'Look, are you just pumping me for info for your boss then? Or what?'

'Calm down,' John said as he picked up his glass. 'I told you, this is nothing to do with her. This is between me and you.' He took a swig of his drink.

'She wanted you to speak to me though?'

John nodded. 'She thinks you or your brothers had something to do with her and Michael's kids getting arrested. She wanted me to warn you off.'

'I had nothing to do with that,' Craig replied.

John shrugged. 'Not really that arsed, to be honest, mate. Doesn't bother me one bit if those arrogant pricks go down for murder. But just so I'm doing my job, consider this a warning,' he finished his drink and placed the glass on the table.

'Okay,' Craig answered.

'I can help you with your other problem though,' John added.

'You just have that kind of money lying around?' Craig snorted.

'For the right investment, I do.'

Craig remembered that John had been at the top of his game for decades – why wouldn't he have that kind of cash? 'Why would you help me?'

'Because I'm looking to branch out myself. I'm fed up of being Grace Carter's dogsbody and I want to be my own boss again. I figure if this Alastair fella wants to start operating in Merseyside, then I'm happy to help him. I can get you the money today. You can pay him back, and then you can tell him you're back open for business.'

'So you'll be running the show?' Craig asked. 'And I'm supposed to work for you?'

'You can work for me until you pay off your debt, and then you're a free man, Craig. This isn't one of those deals where you'll have to work for me for life. I'm not interested in having people around me who don't want to be there. I need people I can trust, and if you don't want to be one of those then that's fine by me. But I can't think of an easier way for you to make a quarter of a million quid, can you?'

Craig nodded. He had always heard good things about John Brennan. 'What if I did want to stick around?'

'Well, then you'd need to prove you could be trusted. But if you do that … well, you could have a lucrative career ahead of you.'

'And what about Grace? She just gonna let you branch out on your own and be in direct competition with her?'

John grinned. 'You just leave Grace to me. It's all about the spin, Craig. Besides, she believes everything I tell her. I'll get you the money later on tonight.'

Craig smiled and lifted his glass up in a toast. 'To the future then,' he said.

John nodded, and lifted his own glass, despite it being empty. 'To the future.'

Chapter Twenty-Six

Driving home from Jake's flat, Grace noticed she had a voicemail from Nudge. She pressed play and his voice filled the car. 'Grace, love. Just wanted to let you know that Jock is coming to Liverpool with his boss Alastair McGrath the day after tomorrow. He said they'd like to meet with you. Give me a bell when you can.'

Glancing at the clock on the dashboard, she saw it was almost 2pm and Belle would need picking up from school in just over an hour. She'd have to pass near Nudge's scrapyard on her way to Mossley Hill, so she decided to pay him a quick visit instead.

Walking up the rickety wooden steps to his portakabin, Grace called out his name as she knocked on the door. She had once walked in on him in a very uncompromising position with a lady friend of his and was determined never to repeat the experience. A few seconds later, Nudge's large frame filled the doorway and his face broke into a smile.

'Grace, love,' he said. 'Come on in.'

He stepped aside and Grace walked into his office and took a seat.

'Brew?' he asked.

'No thanks. I'll have to pick up Belle soon.'

'Did you get my message?'

'Yep. Did they say where and when they wanted to meet?'

'Jock said he would leave that up to you and that I should let him know what you decide. They should be here by lunchtime on Thursday.'

'Okay. I'll ask Pat and Sue to watch Oscar. I want to catch them as soon as they get here, so let's say 1pm at Grazia's. It's not as busy as the other restaurants and they have that room as the back we can use,' Grace replied. She had two days to prepare for a meeting with the supposed biggest gangster in Essex.

'Okay. I'll let them know,' Nudge replied.

'Have you ever met Alastair?' Grace asked.

Nudge shook his head. 'Only Jock. Jock's a good man though. Reminds me a bit of Michael's dad Pat. Wouldn't want to get on his bad side, but he's a gentleman too – you know what I mean?'

'Yes. Well, let me know if there's any problem with the meeting, Nudge. I'd better be going or I'll be late.'

'If there's anything else I can do, Grace, just let me know. Okay?' He stood up and Grace noted how old he was starting to look. His walk had a shuffling quality to it now that she'd never noticed before. She wondered how much longer he would be able to stay in this game and it saddened her. He was one of her oldest and most reliable allies. They had become good friends over the years too. Perhaps Michael was right and they were all getting too old for this game? She had to admit that his ideas about semi-retirement in the suburbs sounded like heaven sometimes.

'I will do, Nudge, and thanks for your help.'

'Anything for you. You know that, love,' he said and she knew he meant it. He was a truly good friend. She pulled him into an impromptu hug. 'Thank you,' she whispered, thankful for the few people in her life she could truly trust, and he hugged her back in response.

Chapter Twenty-Seven

It was a little after midnight and Craig Johnson shifted from one foot to the other as he stood in the deserted car park of Crosby swimming baths waiting for John Brennan to arrive. From his vantage point he could see his own car, an old Ford Fiesta, where his brother Ged was waiting armed with a shotgun should anything go wrong.

A few moments later, Craig saw the headlights of a car approaching in the distance and watched as it rolled into the car park and came to a stop beside him. As he peered inside the BMW X5, Craig was relieved to see that John had come alone.

'Sorry I'm late,' John said as he climbed out of the car. 'Grace had me running errands for her all night. I swear sometimes she thinks I have nothing better to do with my time than be her fucking gofer.'

'Women, eh?' Craig replied with a laugh.

'Tell me about it, mate,' John said as he opened the boot of his car and pulled out a large black holdall. In a few long strides, John had rounded the car and was standing a few inches from Craig. 'Two hundred and fifty grand,' he said with a smile as he held out the bag.

Craig took it from him and noticing the zip was open, he looked inside to see the bundles of fifty-pound notes. Until he'd seen the money there, he hadn't quite believed that John was going to deliver on his promise. He had half suspected that he was walking into some kind of trap, but he was backed into a corner and his options were limited. If he didn't get Alastair's men the money, he'd be a dead man anyway.

'I appreciate this, John. Thank you,' Craig said as he held out a hand to shake.

John reciprocated the gesture, his large hand dwarfing Craig's. 'I'm looking forward to us doing business together.'

'Be a nice change to be the boss, eh?' Craig said with a grin. 'Get away from Grace Carter?'

'And not before time, mate,' John agreed.

'If you don't mind me asking though – she might be a stuck-up bitch, but she's no fool. How are you going to pull this off?'

'I already told you, Grace Carter believes everything I tell her. She thinks I'm a loyal soldier, like a dog that doesn't mind living on scraps but stays loyal anyway. She doesn't suspect a thing and by the time she does, it will be too late. Just trust me.'

Craig nodded and smiled. This couldn't be working out any better for him and his brothers. Not only had John dug them out of a huge hole, but he was doing it by getting one over on Grace Carter at the same time. It was a win-win.

'Well, I for one can't wait to see that bitch taken down a peg or two. The sooner she realises she doesn't own this city, the fucking better.'

'Well soon enough, Grace will get what's coming to her. Don't you worry about it,' John said with a smile.

Then he walked away and climbed back into his car, driving away and leaving Craig standing alone in the dark.

———————

The following morning, Craig took the holdall full of cash out of the boot of his car. John Brennan had been true to his word and had given him two hundred and fifty grand in cash, as promised. Now all Craig had to do was wait at home for Jerry and his goons to arrive and hand it over. He and Ged spent a second night in Craig's car and were both looking forward to being able to get back to their own houses. He'd thought about having Ged there with him at the drop, but decided against it. Ged was a bad-tempered bastard at the best of times, prone to running his mouth off when he should be keeping it shut. Craig had weighed up the odds. Ged was a good scrapper, they both were, but even together they were no match for Jerry and his boys. Whatever happened, if shit went down, Craig was getting a kicking whether Ged was there or not. But there was no doubt that having Ged there significantly increased the chances that there would be a kick-off, so he'd decided to go it alone, and hope that repaying the money with added interest was enough.

Craig had been home for less than five minutes when

the front door was kicked open. As he suspected, Jerry and Co. must have been waiting for him. He'd left the door unlocked to avoid causing too much damage and was sitting in the kitchen waiting for them. He had a knife tucked into the waistband of his trousers – just in case. It made him feel slightly less anxious anyway.

'You were supposed to be here yesterday,' Jerry's voice boomed around the kitchen.

'I know. And I'm really sorry. I had Mr McGrath's money, but I had to get the other fifty as well. It took me a bit of time.'

Jerry frowned at him. 'So you've got the money then?'

'Yeah. Of course,' Craig said as he picked up the holdall and handed it over.

Jerry took it from him and passed it to the one with the shaved head. 'Make sure it's all there,' he ordered.

Craig sat under the scrutiny of Jerry and the other man while the third counted the money.

'It's all there, Boss,' he said after a few moments.

'Well, I don't know where the fuck you got that from, but that's not my concern. I have to say, I'm impressed,' Jerry said with a nod of his head.

'I know there's been some bumps in the road, but that was all down to my brother Bradley, and he's not on the scene now, so tell Mr McGrath it will be all plain sailing from now on. There will be no more delays with his money. I swear.'

'You still think he'd work with you after this?' Jerry asked with a flash of his grey eyebrows.

'It's all there, isn't it? And I paid the interest too.'

Jerry nodded. 'Well, Mr McGrath is on his way to Liverpool as we speak, so maybe you can tell him yourself?'

'He's coming here?' Craig asked. It wasn't like Alastair to get his hands dirty. He had plenty of people to do that for him.

'Yep, and he's not very happy,' Jerry replied as he glared at his two companions, making Craig wonder what else was going on.

'Well, if he has the time, I'd be happy to meet with him and apologise in person,' Craig offered. In prison he'd got on well with Alastair, who had seen the potential in him. Craig hoped that his offer to meet face to face would go some way to redeeming himself.

'We'll see. He's going to be busy, I expect,' Jerry replied, absent-mindedly rubbing his beard.

Craig's curiosity was piqued even further now.

'Well, we haven't got all day, lads,' Jerry said. 'Make it quick.'

Craig looked up as the two goons approached him. 'What the fuck? I gave you your money,' he shouted.

'But only after we had to come up here and get it,' Jerry reminded him. 'You're lucky I'm not taking your eyeball as a souvenir for my trouble.' Then he turned to his associates. 'Leave him walking and talking, lads. Mr McGrath may have use for him yet, and you don't want to end up in any more trouble, do you?' he said. Then with a final nod, he left the kitchen leaving his two heavies to it.

Craig reeled backwards off the chair, landing on the floor with a thud as the first punch connected with his jaw. Instinctively he pulled his arms and legs into his body, closing his eyes and bracing himself for the onslaught. But none came. He listened as the two men smashed up his kitchen. Then with a few final kicks to his arms and legs, they left.

Sitting up, dazed from the blow, and with his head spinning, Craig surveyed the damage to the kitchen. Gemma was going to have a fit. But he was alive. And he was relatively unscathed. He'd taken a worse beating than that from his own dad back in the day. To top it off, he was going into business with John Brennan. Craig smiled. His life was finally back on track.

Chapter Twenty-Eight

Grace checked in on Belle and Oscar before going downstairs. As she walked into the hallway, Michael was coming through the front door. He walked towards her, his damp hair stuck to his forehead and his T-shirt clinging to his skin with sweat. If that wasn't enough to set her pulse racing, he was also wearing shorts that showed off his muscular, toned legs. Grace grinned at him.

'And I thought you looked good in a suit!'

'Are you perving at me?' he asked with a twinkle in his eye as he dropped his gym bag onto the floor.

'I didn't know you were going boxing. You haven't done that for ages.'

'Connor asked me. He's been missing sparring with Paul – and Jake.'

'Oh yes, he must be,' Grace said as she approached him. 'Well, tell him you'll spar with him any time as long as you come home looking like this,' she laughed as she wrapped her arms around his neck, inhaling the smell of his Tom Ford aftershave mixed with fresh sweat.

'Are you kidding? He kicked my arse,' Michael replied as he put his arms around her waist and pulled her closer to him.

'Aw. Poor you. Would you like to me kiss anything better?' Grace asked.

'Well, actually…' he began, then his mobile phone started ringing. 'For fuck's sake,' he muttered.

'Ignore it,' Grace whispered, but then hers started ringing too.

Stepping apart, they each checked their phones.

'It's Jazz,' Michael said with a worried look on his face.

'Webster,' Grace added as her heart started to pound in her chest.

Grace answered the call, aware of Michael speaking to Jazz in the background. She stepped into the kitchen so she could focus on the one conversation.

'Grace,' Webster said when she answered and there was something about the tone of his voice that made Grace take a seat. 'Jake and Connor have been arrested.'

'Again?' Grace said with a sigh.

'Yes, but this time they're going to be charged.'

Grace's heart started beating violently. She could hear the blood thundering in her ears. 'With murder?'

'Yeah.'

'What's changed? Is there new evidence?'

'Something about a partial fingerprint was all I heard,' Webster replied.

'Christ! So, they'll be remanded straightaway then?'

'Yep. I'm sorry, Grace. There was nothing I could do…'

'I know. Thanks for letting me know,' she replied with as much composure as she could muster.

After Grace ended the call, she could still hear Michael talking in the hallway. His voice was calm and soothing and she realised that he would be trying to calm Jazz down. She was almost eight and a half months pregnant and Connor was about to go to prison. Grace closed her eyes and swallowed the bile as it rose in her throat. The reality of the situation was sinking in. There was a strong possibility that Jake and Connor could go down for life. Even if Faye Donovan could come up with some mitigation they'd both be looking at about fifteen years each before they'd be eligible for parole. It was incomprehensible. There had to be something they could do.

Grace was still sitting with her eyes closed when Michael fell silent. She heard his footsteps entering the kitchen. Opening her eyes, she looked up at him.

'Jazz is distraught,' he said with a sigh. 'I said she could stay with us for a while. I'll phone our Sean and ask him to pick her up.'

Grace nodded. 'Of course. She needs to be around family.'

Michael walked over to her and put his arms around her. Grace clung onto him.

'God, Michael, they'll be on their way to prison in the morning.'

'I know,' he said quietly.

'I can't believe this has happened. I knew they were

under investigation, but I thought we'd be able to fix it somehow.'

'There's still time. We'll get them out. It will be okay,' he said as he pulled her tighter to him and stroked her hair. Grace nodded, her cheek brushing against his T-shirt. It was nice to have someone else say that for a change. Usually it was she who had to be strong and tell everyone things would work out. She supposed that was why she and Michael made such a good team. He knew exactly when she needed him to pick up the slack, if only for a short while.

After a few moments, Grace disentangled herself from Michael's embrace. 'Do you want to phone Sean to pick up Jazz? I'll go and make sure one of the spare rooms is set up for her.'

'Yeah, I'll give him a ring now. Are you okay?'

'No, and I won't be until our boys are back home here they belong. But we've come through worse than this, haven't we? Let's get Jazz here and settled, get a good night's sleep and then we can plan our next move tomorrow.'

'Sounds like a plan,' Michael replied.

———————

One hour later and Michael's brother Sean was carrying in the many bags and giant maternity pillow that Jazz had brought with her, while Grace comforted her future daughter-in-law in the living room.

'Will you get them out, Grace?' Jazz asked through floods of tears.

Grace put an arm around Jazz's shoulder. 'I'll certainly do my best. If there is a way to get them home, then I'll find it.'

'But not before the baby's born?' Jazz sniffed. 'Connor will miss our baby being born.'

'We'll see. Who knows how long it will be before that little fella makes an appearance. It could be another four weeks yet if you go over.'

Jazz nodded and wiped her eyes with the tissue Grace had given her. 'Maybe. My mum was late with me.'

Grace couldn't help but smile as she remembered the birth of her three children. 'Jake and Oscar were both overdue by a couple of weeks. Belle was early though. I like to think it was because she couldn't wait to arrive. My waters broke while I was driving home from the supermarket. I detoured to the hospital and she was born just over two hours later. The quickest labour of the three of them.'

Michael and Sean walked into the living room as Grace was finishing her sentence. Talking about the babies seemed to have perked Jazz up a little at least.

'Were you there for all of your kids' births, Michael?' she asked.

Sean almost choked on fresh air and started to cough awkwardly before sitting down.

'For the twins, and for Oscar's, yes,' Michael answered as he sat on one of the armchairs.

'But not Belle's?' Jazz asked. A perfectly innocent question in her eyes, no doubt.

'No,' he replied sharply.

After an awkward silence, Sean spoke up. 'Anyone fancy a drink?'

'What is it? I feel like I'm missing something,' Jazz asked as she looked around at them all.

'Do you want to tell this story, or shall I?' Michael asked Grace.

Grace took a deep breath. 'Michael wasn't there when Belle was born because he didn't know I was pregnant. At least not with his baby, anyway.'

'What?' Jazz said, her eyebrows raised in surprise. 'I thought you two had been together since before Belle. I mean, you know, properly together?'

'Nope,' Michael said.

'After Jake's dad died, I moved away to Harewood. I didn't even know I was pregnant until after I'd gone.'

'But you still didn't tell Michael?' Jazz asked in surprise.

'Well, it wasn't quite that simple,' Grace explained. From the corner of her eye she saw Michael shake his head. She went on. 'Michael was married to Hannah then.'

'Oh?' Jazz said with a smile. 'How didn't I know this about you two? You pair of dark horses. So, you had a passionate affair.'

'Not quite,' Grace interrupted her. 'It was one time. We promised it would never happen again, and then I moved away.'

'So, how did you find out Belle was yours?' Jazz asked animatedly as she looked at Michael.

'I came back to Liverpool when she was almost nine months old, and well, it was pretty hard to keep it a secret then.'

'Did you freak out that Grace had had your baby and not told you?' Jazz asked Michael.

'I think I handled it pretty well,' he replied and both Sean and Grace laughed out loud, Grace recalling how understandably livid he'd been when he'd discovered that she'd kept Belle a secret from him. He'd vowed that he would never speak to her again.

'Was Hannah furious?' Jazz asked.

'We'd separated by the time I found out about Belle. But I'm sure she was, yes,' Michael replied.

'God. I can't believe Connor never told me this.'

'Well, it wasn't exactly our finest hour, was it, love?' Michael said as he winked at Grace.

'Nope. We mostly try and pretend it never happened now,' Grace said with a grin.

'And here's me asking all of these questions. I'm sorry,' Jazz said.

'Oh, don't worry about it. Each time we tell this story, Michael gets a little less annoyed with me,' Grace said. 'One day he might even laugh about it.'

'Don't push your luck, Mrs Carter,' he said with a smile.

'And at least it's given us something else to talk about,' Grace added.

'I need to get back,' Sean said as he stood up. 'But can I have a quick word?' He looked at Michael and Grace, who both nodded and followed him out of the living room.

'I've got some of that peppermint tea you like, Jazz, do you fancy a cup?' Grace asked on her way out.

'That would be lovely. Thanks, Grace,' she said with a faint smile as she sat on the sofa, rubbing her large bump.

As soon as they were in the hallway and out of Jazz's earshot, Sean turned to Grace and Michael. 'So, what happens now?' he asked quietly.

'The boys will be held in a police cell overnight to appear at the Magistrates tomorrow morning. Then they'll be remanded into custody. Faye will do her job and argue for bail, but they'll never get it on a murder charge. Especially not with our family's reputation,' Grace answered.

'And what can we do about it?' Sean asked.

'The investigation seems to rest on a key witness, who I suspect is Scott Johnson, the youngest brother.'

'Do you need us to take care of him?' Sean asked.

'Not like that,' Grace answered. 'Although I thought you were a respectable businessman now?'

'I'll be anything you two need me to be to get the lads out,' he said solemnly.

'Well, let's hope it won't ever come to that. I'm not sure offing the investigation's key witness does a lot to help Jake and Connor's cause, Sean,' Grace replied.

'I beg to differ,' Sean said.

Michael put a hand on his brother's shoulder. 'Look, Grace had a plan to get Scott to change his statement some other way. Let's try that first, and if it doesn't work…'

'We'll bury the bastard so deep he won't be found until the next ice age?' Sean offered.

'Something like that,' Grace replied with a smile.

Later in bed, Grace was lying with her head on Michael's shoulder. 'I wish you had been there when Belle was born,' she said.

'So do I.'

'She didn't cry, you know? She was born smiling, that kid. They laid her on my chest and I couldn't believe how beautiful she was.'

'Well, she would be, with you for a mum.' He pulled her closer to him.

'Actually, she looked just like you.'

He laughed. 'Poor kid. At least she's gorgeous now though.'

Grace gave him a playful shove. 'She always has been. I am sorry you weren't there though, you know?'

'I know you are,' he said quietly.

'So, have you finally forgiven me?' she asked, aware that they'd never really spoken about it since they'd started seeing each other again.

'I forgave you a long time ago,' he replied as he planted a kiss on the top of her head. 'You know that.'

Grace smiled and closed her eyes. 'I do now,' she whispered.

Chapter Twenty-Nine

G race noticed that Michael was quiet as they sat in the back room of Grazia's restaurant in Crosby village, waiting for the infamous Alastair McGrath to make an appearance. It had been the first restaurant that Grace and Sean had opened together, many years before. At the time, it had been their pride and joy and a huge success. It was still busy and gave them a decent return, but it paled in comparison to their bigger and more successful restaurants. However, it still had a special place in Grace's heart and always would. It had been the first legitimate business venture that she'd nurtured from the outset, and it had given her the bug. It was opening Grazia's that had made her realise she had a good head for business.

Grace had been made aware that the two idiots responsible for smashing up Jake's club had buggered off back to Essex with their tails between their legs, but that wasn't enough as far as she and her family were concerned. They had taken a massive liberty, and if they got away scot free then it would send a message that anyone could just walk into The Blue Rooms and do whatever the hell they wanted. With Jake and Connor locked up, it was more important than ever that nobody was seen to be taking the piss.

'You okay?' Grace asked her husband.

He looked at her and shrugged. 'We know nothing about this fella. He could turn up here with a firm and a semi-automatic for all we know.'

'I don't think he's going to pull anything in a crowded restaurant in the middle of the afternoon, Michael.'

'Well, let's hope so, eh?' he replied.

Before she could answer there was a knock at the door and the waitress opened it. 'Your guests are here, Mrs Carter,' she said, smiling at them.

Grace and Michael stood as two men walked into the room. Both of them were in their mid-fifties and dressed in suits. One of them was tall and well built. He had a scar running across the left side of his face. The other was smaller in stature but no less imposing. He had an air of arrogance about him that Grace recognised well and she suspected that he was Alastair McGrath.

'Mr and Mrs Carter,' he said as he extended his hand to shake.

Grace shook his hand first, noting how firmly he gripped hers. She was used to it – a reminder that she was a feeble woman and he could crush her if he chose to do so. She ignored it and smiled politely. 'Mr McGrath?' she asked.

He smiled back, a perfect row of white teeth which she

suspected were false. 'Please, call me Alastair,' he said as he released his grip and offered his hand to Michael instead. 'And this is my business associate, Jock Stewart.'

Grace nodded at Jock in acknowledgement and indicated the seats across the table. 'Shall we have a seat?'

After the formalities were over and Alastair and Jock had ordered some food from the menu, Grace was ready to discuss business.

'So, can you tell us why two of your employees smashed up my son's club and assaulted four of our bouncers?'

'They took out four of your bouncers?' Alastair said with a low whistle and Grace recognised it as another display of his power. If he wasn't careful, he would see a display of her own.

'I wouldn't call it taking out, but they put them on their arses, yes. They turned up all tooled up and took them by surprise. So, I want to know why?'

Grace was aware of Jock shifting uncomfortably in his seat, but her gaze remained fixed on Alastair.

'Well, what can I say, hen, but they're young and stupid and sometimes things happen,' he replied.

Grace could feel the anger radiating from Michael as he sat beside her.

'Although I want you to know that it wasn't on my orders, and I will pay for any damage that they caused.' He put his hand on his heart as though to emphasise his sincerity.

'It's not really about the money, though, is it?' Grace challenged him. 'Your lads come here, to our city, and start causing trouble for no apparent reason, and you expect us just to roll over and take it?'

'We'll deal with them. They won't be causing any more trouble,' Jock interrupted, earning himself a withering look from his boss. 'We'll make sure that word gets out that they were dealt with too.'

Grace turned her attention to Jock, whom she'd already decided she preferred of the two men. 'I heard the Johnson brothers were working for you?' she asked. 'Selling your product? In Liverpool?'

'In the Wirral, I believe,' Alastair replied with a smirk and Grace had to fight the urge to slap him herself.

'I think you'll find the Wirral comes under our jurisdiction too,' she said.

'Well, I wasn't aware of that at the time. But I've heard you're a good businesswoman, Grace, so now that I am aware, then I'm prepared to let you sell our product instead.'

Grace smiled. Now that she'd met him, she had no intention of working with Alastair McGrath. Jock was a different story, but unfortunately he wasn't the one who made the decisions. 'We have our own product, thanks. So I'm not sure we'll be needing yours.'

Alastair shrugged. 'That's fine. I have other connections in Liverpool.'

'You mean Craig Johnson?' Grace asked with a laugh. 'And how did that work out for you last time?'

'You just let me worry about that,' Alastair replied with a scowl.

It was then that Michael spoke for the first time. 'I think you'll find that anyone worth knowing in Liverpool is loyal to us. So why don't you think yourselves lucky that we allowed your two lads to leave Liverpool while they were still able to walk and talk, and fuck off back to Essex?'

Alastair stood up quickly, leaning forward as he did, another obvious intimidation tactic, but neither Michael or Grace flinched.

'I don't think you two have any idea who you're dealing with,' he said, signalling to Jock that they were leaving.

'Oh, we do, Mr McGrath, but do you?' Grace replied.

'We'll see,' he said with a grin before he and Jock left the room.

———

Jock climbed into the waiting car beside his boss. His jaw was aching and he realised he'd been grinding his teeth throughout the entire meeting. It was the best way to stop himself from interrupting Alastair when he was being deliberately confrontational – which he seemed to be doing more and more lately.

'You should have kept your mouth shut in there,' Alastair growled as the car pulled away from the kerb. 'I had it handled.'

Jock turned in his seat and glared at his boss. He could keep silent no more. 'Are you fucking serious?' he asked.

Alastair stared at him, open-mouthed. No one ever spoke to him like that. Jock went on before his boss could answer. 'I don't think *you* have any idea who *you're* dealing with—'

'Some tart, and her lapdog husband,' Alastair snorted.

'Don't underestimate her because she's a woman. And he ain't no lapdog, he's a fucking animal. Don't be fooled by him sitting there all nice and pleasant and well-behaved today. He would slit your throat while you slept and take a bath in your blood.'

'So they're a pair of nutters then?' Alastair said dismissively. 'Nothing we haven't dealt with before.'

'No! Not nutters. They are business people. Cold, calculated and ruthless when they need to be, but they are fucking smart. They employ more people than John Sainsbury. And from what I've heard, there isn't anyone who's anyone around here who doesn't owe that woman a favour.'

'Oh, calm down,' Alastair said. 'I'll sort it out.'

'Like you sorted the Russians?' Jock snapped.

'Oh, for fuck's sake, you're not dragging that up again. Look, Jock, I pay you to do as you're told. You don't need to think, or speak, unless I tell you to. Okay?' he snarled.

Jock sat back in his seat and remained silent as their driver drove them to their hotel in the city centre. Alastair McGrath thought he was fucking untouchable, and one day he was going to get the two of them killed.

'What an arrogant prick!' Grace said to Michael as they drove home from the restaurant.

'Fucking tosser,' he agreed. 'We're not going to work with him, are we?'

'God, no!'

'Good. So, what next?'

'Let's hope they take your advice and fuck off back to Essex,' she said with a smile, despite knowing that was very unlikely. 'But it wouldn't hurt to have someone keep an eye on Alastair for us in the meantime, would it?'

Michael nodded. 'Sounds like a good idea. Want me to ask Murf?'

'Actually, I was thinking of asking John,' she said. 'We could do with Murf focusing on the security in case Alastair and his lads target any more of our clubs. What do you think?'

'Hmm, makes sense,' he agreed.

'I'll go and speak to John now then, before I pick up the kids.'

'I was going to go into the office and catch up with Murf, but I can come with you if you want.'

'No, there's no need. I won't be long. Can you drop me off there? Then John can give me a lift home when we're done.'

Grace sat back in her seat. She considered herself a good judge of character and she could tell even from their brief meeting that Alastair McGrath wasn't going to slope off back to Essex quietly. She had a feeling he was going to cause them some problems, and the sooner she dealt with him, the better.

Chapter Thirty

Grace had sent John a text to say she was on her way and he was waiting at the front door for her as she and Michael pulled up.

Leaning over in her seat, she gave Michael a kiss. 'I'll see you later,' she said.

'Yeah, see you later, love,' he replied, although she noted the flicker of a scowl flash across his face when he looked at John.

Ten minutes later Grace was sitting in John's kitchen drinking a hot mug of tea. He sat at the table opposite her.

'Two home visits in the same week. I'm honoured,' John said with a grin. 'So, to what do I owe today's pleasure?'

'Can't I just visit my good friend?'

John laughed out loud.

'What's so funny?' Grace said.

'How long have I worked for you now, Grace? I know you better than that,' he said.

Grace smiled back at him. 'Okay. Why do I ever visit you at home, John?'

He nodded and took a sip of his tea. 'So, what do you need me to do, Boss?' he asked.

'You know me and Michael were meeting with that guy from Essex today?'

'Yeah?'

'Well, I think he's going to cause us some trouble, and I want to be prepared.'

'What makes you think that? Did he say something?'

'Nothing specific. But there was just something about him. And if what I've heard about him is true, we'll need to have our wits about us. He's big enough to cause us some serious problems, John. He could give us a real run for our money if he so chooses.'

'Okay. What do I need to know about the way this fella operates then, and what you need me to do?'

John listened intently as Grace told him all that she'd learned about Alastair McGrath in the last few days, including her own assessment of the kind of man he was. Then she told him all about the next stage of her plan.

Chapter Thirty-One

D I Leigh Moss frowned at the pile of paperwork on her desk. Sometimes she wondered if she'd made the right move, going for promotion. It seemed the higher you climbed up the ladder, the further you moved away from the action and the closer to a desk and a computer. Her thoughts were interrupted by the ringing of her office phone.

'DI Moss,' she answered.

'DI Moss, my name is DI Gavin Starkey, I'm calling from Essex police.'

'Hi, Gavin, what can I do for you?' Leigh asked.

'I'm calling to let you know that someone who is a significant person of interest to us has just landed in Liverpool. We don't know what he's up to yet, but if past history is anything to go by, he'll be involved in something dodgy and I wanted to give you the heads up that he was on your turf. Please don't attempt to intercept him though.

He's very dangerous and if he thinks you're onto him he'll go underground and we'll never find out what he's up to up there. But if you happen to hear anything could you pass on any relevant intel to me?'

Leigh's interest was piqued and she took a notepad and pencil from her desk drawer. 'Who is this guy, and what's he into?' she asked.

'His name is Alastair McGrath and he's into everything. If it's illegal and there's a profit to be made, he's involved. I've been after this prick for years, but he's as slippery as an eel. Like I said, if he gets a whiff of any police activity, he'll be in the wind.'

'Do you have any idea at all what he's doing in Liverpool? Who he's meeting with?'

'Not yet,' Gavin said with a sigh. 'We do know he's staying at the Radisson Blu hotel but little else. Actually, I was hoping that you might have some idea who he's working with or what he might be doing up there.'

'I have some ideas who he might be meeting with if he's as big as you say he is.'

'He is. He's the kingpin around here, but we can never get anything to stick to the jammy little bastard.'

'I know that feeling,' Leigh said with a laugh.

'So, who do you think he's working with then?' Gavin asked.

'My money would be on Grace Carter and her firm. But I'll look into it.'

'That would be good, but please don't make any waves. Just intel gathering. I want to play the long game on this one. All of his info is on his VISOR record anyway. Check him out and let me know if you hear anything. I'd do anything to bring this fucker down.'

'I'll check out his record, and I'll make some enquiries.'

'Brilliant. Thanks, Leigh.'

'No problems, thanks for the heads up, Gavin. I'll be in touch if I hear anything.'

Leigh hung up the phone and popped her head out of her office. 'Nick,' she shouted across the office. 'Have you got a minute?'

'Of course, Boss,' he said with a smile as he made his way over.

Nick closed the door behind him and sat down. 'What's up?' he asked.

'I just had a very interesting call from my oppo in Essex who wanted to let me know that one of their major players is here in Liverpool. Alastair McGrath. Have you ever heard of him?'

Nick shook his head. 'Can't say I have, but I've never worked outside of the North West before. Any idea why he's here?'

'This DI didn't know, but I'll bet my life on it being something to do with the Carters, wouldn't you?'

'Probably.'

'I wonder if it's anything to do with Billy Johnson's murder?' Leigh asked with a frown.

'What? You mean like they're bringing in reinforcements or something?'

Leigh shrugged. 'Maybe? But it's funny that he turns up shortly after Jake and Connor have been arrested.'

'It could be nothing to do with it though. And nothing to

do with the Carters at all. Let's not lose focus when we're so close to finally nailing two of them.'

'I know. But it wouldn't hurt to keep our eyes open and do a bit of digging, would it?'

Nick rolled his eyes. 'What did you have in mind?'

'McGrath is staying at the Radisson Blu. Doesn't your cousin work behind the bar in there?'

Nick nodded. 'Our Ben, yeah.'

'Why don't you pop by and see him when he's next on shift then? You might see Mr McGrath yourself, or Ben might be able to keep an eye on him for us? I'm sure he must be working with the Carters, because I doubt they'd allow him to stroll into Liverpool and start touting for business if he wasn't.'

Nick shrugged. 'I suppose it couldn't hurt. I do owe our Ben a visit. I haven't seen him for a few weeks. I'll see when he's next working. Maybe you could come for a drink with me?' he said with a wink. 'Meet some of the family?'

'I can't. Grace and Michael Carter might recognise me. I've met them before when Paul was killed, remember?

'All right. A boys' night it is then. Anything else I can do for you, Ma'am?'

'Yes. You can pick us up something nice for tea on your way home. I'll be stuck here until eight sorting this lot out.' She indicated the pile of papers on her desk.

'Will do,' Nick said before leaving her office.

Leigh sat back in her chair and rubbed her temples, trying to stave off the headache she already knew was on its way. She was sure that Alastair's sudden arrival in their city had something to do with Grace Carter, if only because Grace would have it no other way.

Leigh was ploughing through her paperwork when she saw the Chief Super, Henry James, making his way to her office. It was unusual for him to be on her floor of the building.

'Evening, Sir,' she said as he walked in.

'Evening, Leigh. Hard at it as usual, I see?' he said with a smile.

'Well, this paperwork doesn't file itself,' she said with a laugh.

'I heard our colleagues from Essex have been in touch?'

'Yeah.'

'Their Chief Super gave me a quick call too. She'd heard about your task force being quite new, and well…'

'Well, what?'

'I think she's worried that you're going to go after McGrath to try and make a name for yourself to promote the team.'

Leigh opened her mouth in surprise but didn't say what she was thinking, which was that Henry's opposite number was a cheeky, presumptuous bitch. 'Seriously?' she asked instead.

Henry nodded. 'There are other factors at play here. Factors that I'm not at liberty to disclose. Anyway, I assured her that while we would arrest Mr McGrath if he gives us any cause to, we would not be actively seeking him out – or stepping on their toes.'

'With respect, Sir, what exactly does that mean?' she asked.

'With respect, Leigh, it means stay the hell away from him,' he said before he bade her good evening and left her office.

Chapter Thirty-Two

'Thanks, Jock. We'll see you at four o'clock,' Craig Johnson said before ending the call and placing his phone in his coat pocket. He was contemplating the implications of a meeting with Alastair McGrath and Jock Stewart as he stepped out of his front door and saw John Brennan pulling up in his distinctive BMW X5.

'You got five minutes?' John asked through the open passenger window.

Craig checked his watch. He had over an hour to go before his meeting with Alastair.

'Yeah. I'm just off to The Grapes if you fancy a pint?' Craig suggested.

'Nah. Haven't really got time for one. But I can drop you off?'

'Sound,' Craig replied as he jumped into the passenger seat of John's car. 'What did you want to see me about?'

'This Alastair McGrath, do you still have any sway with him?'

Craig nodded, a surge of pride swelling in his chest. 'Yeah. I'm on my way to meet him now, in fact.'

'Good. Can you arrange a meeting with him for me? Tell him I'm looking to branch out on my own and could do with a supplier.'

'I suppose you can't use any local ones, seeing as you're about to screw over Grace Carter?' Craig said with a chuckle.

'Yeah, well, you just keep that to yourself for now, eh?' John snapped and Craig saw a glimpse of the John that could instil fear into the hardest of men.

'Of course I will. You can trust me, John.'

'I'd better be able to,' he replied as they pulled up outside The Grapes. 'Let me know what Alastair says about a meeting.'

'Will do,' Craig said as he jumped out of the car with a smile. 'But I'll square it with him, don't worry.'

'I'll look forward to hearing from you later then,' John replied before he drove off.

Craig strode through the doors of The Grapes as though he owned the place. Things were finally starting to look up. Not only had he found himself a new business associate in John Brennan, but he was about to impress his new boss by setting up a meeting with one of the biggest gangsters in the country. Alastair would be happy to learn that Craig had a new backer with some money and some credibility behind him. It was the perfect arrangement. And the icing on the cake was that it was all being done under the nose of Grace and Michael Carter. Craig was looking forward to the day

Grace found out that her right-hand man – her most trusted soldier – was actually conspiring against her, and he hoped he was there to see the look on her face when she did.

Chapter Thirty-Three

C raig and Ged Johnson were sitting at their usual table in The Grapes waiting for Alastair and Jock to arrive. When he'd received the telephone call an hour earlier from Jock to let him know that Mr McGrath would like a meeting, Craig had been relieved at first that he hadn't burned all of his bridges with the Essex gangster. However, as he sat in the pub waiting, his relief was starting to wane and was slowly being replaced with a with a sense of dread as he remembered who he was dealing with. He'd practically promised John Brennan he could arrange a meeting, but what if Alastair wanted nothing to do with him? What if he still intended to make an example out of him? Craig was slightly reassured that Jock had told him to pick the venue. Surely Alastair or Jock wouldn't blow his brains out in the middle of their local boozer?

It was nice to be able to sit in The Grapes again. He and Ged had only been in hiding for a few days, and it had been the most stressful thing ever. He'd rather do another year inside than have to go through that again.

'So, you think we can trust John Brennan then?' Ged asked.

'Well, he came through with the money for us, didn't he?' Craig replied as he took a swig of his pint.

'Suppose so.'

Their conversation was interrupted by two men approaching the table. Craig stood up, recognising Alastair immediately. He hadn't seen him for two years, since Alastair had left prison, and Craig noticed that he looked much better out of his prison issue tracksuit. 'Alastair, it's great to see you,' he said with a smile.

'Craig,' Alastair replied with a nod, not returning the smile. 'And you know Jock.'

'This is my brother Ged,' Craig added.

Alastair and Jock sat down at the table. 'I'm not fucking happy about having to come up here and sort this mess out,' he snapped.

'I know. And I'm sorry about that, Mr McGrath. It won't happen again. I swear.'

'Oh, I know it fucking won't. Because if you ever try and mug me off again, son, you and your brother here will be floating face down in the Mersey.'

Craig nodded. 'It won't. If you let us work for you again, we'll make sure you get your money on time every month.'

'Why should I trust you? What makes things different this time?'

'We have a new business partner for a start. John

Brennan. He's legit, and he's prepared to bankroll us too, so there'll never be a problem paying on time.'

'John Brennan works for Grace Carter,' Jock interrupted.

'Not for much longer,' Craig said with a grin. 'He's branching out on his own, and I won't lie, being able to stick it to that stuck-up cow is an added bonus.'

'Well, I wouldn't mind sticking it to her myself. In more ways than one.' Alastair laughed at his own joke.

'You think he's just going to turn his back on her though?' Jock asked.

'He's probably fed up of working for a woman,' Alastair said.

Jock shook his head but he didn't say anything else and Craig got the feeling he wasn't convinced.

'He's serious. He wants to set up on his own, and with that in mind, he'd like to meet with you, Alastair,' Craig insisted.

Alastair considered the request for a moment before turning to Jock. 'You said this bloke works for Carter?'

'He's her right arm.'

'So, he's legit then?'

'The best,' Jock replied. 'I always thought he was loyal to her though.'

'Seems not as loyal as she'd hoped,' Alastair started to laugh again. 'What does she expect though? Most men I know wouldn't take their orders from a woman. Why on earth would a woman like that even get mixed up in our business? She's a right looker, she should be at home with her kiddies and trying to hang on to that husband of hers. Don't you think?'

Craig nodded. 'It's what my bird does,' he replied.

Jock didn't answer and looked around the room instead.

'I'll never understand women,' Alastair said with a shake of his head.

'I couldn't agree more,' Jock replied and Alastair smiled at him. Craig grinned as he realised the dig Jock had made at his boss's expense, although Alastair hadn't cottoned on and assumed Jock was being his usual obedient self.

'Anyway, back to this meeting. Tell your mate John I'll meet him tonight at our hotel at eight. We're staying in the Radisson.'

'Will do,' Craig answered, with a sense of pride that he'd managed to deliver on John's request.

'Well, we might as well have a drink while we're here, eh Jock?' Alastair said. 'Your round, Craig?'

'Yeah, course, what you both having?' he replied with a grin.

Chapter Thirty-Four

G race took a seat on the bright orange plastic chair, fidgeting with the buttons on the cuffs of her shirt as she waited for the prison officers to bring their charge to meet her. She had only been to prison a few times before, when her ex-husband had been sent down for ABH shortly after they'd got married. He'd beaten some poor bloke to a pulp after he'd accused him of flirting with Grace – his wife and his property as far as he was concerned. At the time, Grace had been relieved to have a few months free of him – just her and Jake. Life had been so much simpler and happier without Nathan around, but she had still visited him every week, like the dutiful wife.

Scanning the brightly lit room, she noted the row upon row of wooden tables and plastic chairs fixed to the floor. Amateur artwork adorned the walls, no doubt an attempt to make the sterile environment look a little more welcoming.

Grace suppressed a shudder and forced her face into a smile as she saw Jake walking towards her in his prison-issue grey tracksuit, and a fluorescent orange vest to make the prisoners easily distinguishable from the visitors. Despite his attire, he stood out from the rest of the prisoners. It was something about the way he carried himself – the swagger, always full of confidence, just like his father.

Grace stood up and gave Jake a brief kiss on the cheek as he reached her table. One of the prisoner officers stopped his pacing and looked over at the two of them and Grace glared back at him until he shuffled past. They had enough prison officers from Walton nick on their payroll to ensure that Jake and Connor were ensured as comfortable a time as possible inside.

'How are you, son? You look well,' Grace said truthfully. Despite being on remand, he looked a hell of a lot better than when she'd last seen him. He was sober for a start.

'I'm all right, Mum,' he replied with a grin. 'It's not that bad in here,' he said as he scanned the room.

'Are you being looked after?' Grace said quietly.

He nodded. 'Of course.'

'We'll get you out of here, son. I promise,' she said as she placed a hand over his.

'I know, Mum,' he replied. 'Can you make it sooner rather than later though, eh? Sharing a pad with Connor is a fucking nightmare. He talks in his sleep, you know?' Jake said with a laugh but Grace knew the truth in his words. Michael had visited Connor the day before and despite both of the boys' bravado, Grace and Michael knew that they couldn't wait to get out of the place. No matter how comfortable they tried to make it for their sons, prison was prison and it was shit. And looking at a potential life sentence was enough to send anyone off the edge of a cliff.

'I'm doing everything I can. You and Connor are my number one priority right now,' she assured him as she gave his hand a gentle squeeze.

Jake looked into her eyes and she saw the little boy she had carried and raised and her heart almost broke in two. 'I know,' he said softly. 'We always are.' He said it so sincerely that Grace had to choke back a sob. She wanted nothing more than to walk around the table and wrap her arms around him and then walk him out of that place. She did neither, knowing that a lingering hug from his mother was not only prohibited but also would do little for his reputation inside Walton prison.

Instead she smiled at him, relieved to see glimpses of the boy she'd once known and the man she had hoped he would become, rather than the selfish drunk whom she'd feared her beloved boy was turning into. 'I have a few irons in the fire on that score anyway. If one plan doesn't work out, then another one will. Maybe they all will? But I want you to know that we have options, and all of them are very likely to lead to you and Connor walking out of here very soon.'

Jake didn't respond but simply nodded before falling silent for a few moments. Grace got the impression that he was trying to keep his emotions in check.

'Siobhan said I can bring Isla in to see you next week,' Grace said, trying to give him something tangible and positive to focus on.

It had the desired effect and Jake looked up. 'Really? I wasn't sure she would.'

Grace nodded. 'I know, and nor was I, but Isla really misses you, and while this place isn't the ideal place for little ones, Michael and I will make it a day out for her. We'll take her to McDonalds over the road afterwards and then she can stay at our house overnight.'

Jake smiled. 'How are Belle and Oscar?' he asked and Grace was happy to be able to talk about her youngest children with her firstborn. He adored his younger siblings and soon they had filled half an hour talking about Belle and Oscar and the rest of the family.

When it was time to go, Grace pulled Jake into a brief hug. 'I'll see you next week, son,' she whispered before he was led away by one of the prison officers. She swallowed the lump in her throat and looked around the room at all of the other relatives standing as she was – adrift, bobbing amongst the sea of people like a boat with no anchor. Mothers, fathers, wives, sisters and girlfriends – for it was predominantly women, all watching their loved ones being led away while being unable to do a single thing about it. Not at that exact moment, at least. Grace made her way through the crowd of people and consoled herself with the fact that before too long Jake and Connor would be walking out of this place too.

Chapter Thirty-Five

Grace sat in her car and watched the shoppers as they walked out of Sainsbury's with their trolleys laden before packing their cars. She was waiting for one particular shopper. Thanks to DI Tony Webster, she knew that Leigh Moss popped into Sainsbury's every Friday after her shift.

Fifteen minutes later, Leigh walked across the car park to her red BMW. Grace stepped out of her own car and walked over to Leigh, who turned in shock as Grace walked up behind her.

'Are you following me?' Leigh snapped.

'I don't need to follow you to know where you are. You're a creature of habit, DI Moss,' Grace replied.

'What do you want?' Leigh asked as she looked around the crowded car park.

'You charged them with murder?'

'It's my job.'

Grace shook her head. 'Your fucking job! Is that all you

215

can say? You arrested my son and my stepson for murder,' Grace hissed through clenched teeth.

'What else is there to say, Grace? It's the truth. They don't get special treatment just because…'

'Because I saved your life?' Grace snapped as she felt her heart hammering in her chest.

'That doesn't mean you and your family get a free pass to do whatever you want in this city.'

'I should have let Nathan strangle you and leave you for dead in that alleyway.'

'If it wasn't me, it would be someone else going after them. You know that. They are out of control.'

'I can get them back under control. I promise. If you'll just give me a chance.'

Leigh shook her head. 'You had your chance, Grace,' she said as she turned away.

'I haven't finished,' Grace barked and Leigh turned back towards her.

'Then I'll ask you again, what the hell do you want?'

Grace took a step closer. 'I wanted to look you in the eye and tell you that you will regret making an enemy of me, Leigh. One day you'll need me and you'll come running back, begging me to save you again. Perhaps, next time, I won't.'

'Is that a threat?' Leigh asked, her eyes narrowed and her face pulled into a frown.

'It's a promise,' Grace snapped before turning on her heel and walking away.

Chapter Thirty-Six

J ock Stewart stood beside the bar in their hotel and watched as his boss Alastair chatted up the blonde barmaid, who was young enough to be his daughter. He resisted the urge to remind him that he had a wife waiting for him at home. He was used to Alastair's philandering ways. *A girl in every port* as his old mum would have said.

Jock kept his eye on the door waiting for John Brennan. He'd met John once many years earlier when Jock had visited The Blue Rooms, although he doubted that John remembered their encounter, as he and his then boss, Nathan Conlon, had been wasted. A few moments later, Jock saw the unmistakeable figure of John Brennan walking through the door.

Jock gave a wave and signalled him over. He nudged Alastair in the ribs. 'Our meeting is about to start.'

'I'll get your number later, sweetheart,' he said to the barmaid and she giggled in response.

'Mr Brennan,' Jock said as John reached them. 'I'm Jock, and this is Alastair McGrath.'

John shook each of their hands in turn. 'Nice to meet you both. Shall we go somewhere a little quieter?' he asked.

'Of course,' Jock replied and ushered them all to a quiet table in the corner that he'd reserved earlier.

'So, why did you want to meet with me, lad?' Alastair asked when they were seated.

'I'm not sure how much Craig has told you, but I'm interested in setting up on my own and I need some people with some good quality merchandise to help me do it.'

Alastair sat back and nodded as though he was deep in thought. 'I understand why you want to work with me. But tell me why I should work with you? I don't know you from Adam, and Craig hasn't exactly proven himself to be a reliable judge of character.'

'I have the money and the connections in Liverpool to make this work. I'd say ask around, but I'd rather you didn't.'

'And why's that?' Alastair asked, despite knowing the answer.

'Because I currently work for Grace Carter, and she wouldn't be very happy if she knew that I was meeting with you, and certainly not if she knew I was setting up in direct competition with her.'

'Why are you?' Jock interrupted. 'I always heard you worked well together. You also have a reputation as being loyal, John.'

John frowned at him.

'I like to do my homework,' Jock said.

John nodded appreciatively before he answered. 'Don't get me wrong, I've enjoyed working for Grace. But it feels like I've worked for someone else for most of my life, and I'm fed up of being someone else's lackey to be honest. I think now is the time to strike out on my own before I get too old to deal with the fallout.'

'Fed up working for a woman, eh? Let's face it, women like that are only good for one thing, aren't they?' Alastair laughed to himself.

'How do you intend to do that though? Just walk away?' Jock asked, ignoring Alastair's crude comment and seeing him scowl at him from the corner of his eye. He knew his boss hated it when he asked too many questions.

'Like I told Craig, Grace believes everything I tell her. I could have her eating out of the palm of my hand if I want to. She trusts me completely.'

'More fool her,' Alastair said and started to laugh again.

'I'm not sure it's going to be quite as easy as you think to walk away from someone like her,' Jock added. 'You must know where all of the bodies are buried?'

'I know enough,' John said pointedly.

'Well, it's nice to have you on board,' Alastair said as he sat forward and patted John on the shoulder.

'So, what's the next move then? Are you staying in Liverpool for long?' John asked.

'A few—' Alastair started.

'What the fuck has that got to do with anything?' Jock interrupted.

'Just asking,' John said. 'No need to take offence. I just

wondered if you were planning on hanging around for a bit, that's all.'

'We'll be here for a few days,' Alastair snapped, glaring at Jock before turning his attention back to John. 'It would be good to do a bit of business before we head back, John. And I'd be very interested to know more about Grace's operations up here.'

'Oh? What exactly do you want to know?' John asked.

'As much as you can tell me.' He cackled. 'Then it will be much easier to take it all from her.'

DS Nick Bryce was sitting at a small table in the bar of the Radisson hotel. He'd spoken to his cousin Ben the previous day and they'd arranged to meet after his shift ended at ten o'clock that evening. As Leigh was busy with paperwork again, Nick had left her a lasagne in the oven and decided to head to the bar early, looking forward to a long overdue catch-up with his favourite cousin and one of his closest mates. He doubted that he'd see anything of Alastair McGrath while he was there, but nevertheless he had studied the man's photograph from his VISOR record just in case. It was an old image taken from a time he'd been arrested for drink driving twelve years earlier, but Nick hoped he'd still recognise him. And even if he didn't, even if he didn't learn anything, he would score some brownie points with Leigh, and have a laugh with Ben while doing it.

Nick was sipping his second pint when he saw John Brennan walking through the glass doors of the hotel. From his vantage point, Nick could see the foyer and bar area clearly and he watched as John approached two men near the bar. Now that he looked closely, Nick could see that one of those men was indeed Alastair McGrath, thought he hadn't aged well at all. The man on the photograph had thick black hair, whereas now he was almost bald. He'd put on quite a bit of weight too and jowls had replaced his once square jawline. But it was definitely him, Nick was sure.

He watched John shake the hands of the two men. So Leigh was right all along. Alastair was working with the Carters. Why else would their number one solider, John Brennan, be here meeting with them?

Nick pulled out his phone and dialled Leigh's number.

'You're going to bloody love me,' he said when Leigh answered.

'You're not drunk already, are you?' She laughed.

'Nope,' he whispered. 'But our friend Mr McGrath is here in the bar with his associate, and you will never guess who he's meeting with.'

'Who?'

'John Brennan.'

'What?' Leigh almost squealed with delight and Nick could imagine her smiling as he told her the news. 'I told you, didn't I?'

'Yes. Seems you were right after all.'

'I knew it, Nick. I knew they were up to something. John doesn't know you, does he?'

'I don't see how he could.'

'Brilliant. Can you stay on them? See where they go next?'

'What? You want me to follow them around all night? I'm not trained in surveillance, Leigh. What if they see me or something?'

'Not all night. Just see where they go next if you can. Tell me if they leave together, and then you can go back to your night out with Ben.'

'Okay,' he replied with a sigh. 'But only because I love you.'

'I love you too,' she whispered. 'Be careful.'

'I will,' Nick said with a smile as he hung up the phone. He had waited a long time to hear that from Leigh Moss. As he put his phone back in his pocket, Nick thought he saw John Brennan staring at him from the corner of his eye. But when he turned his head, John was talking to Alastair McGrath again. Nick shook his head. He was being paranoid. There was no way John Brennan knew who he was.

Chapter Thirty-Eight

G race was finishing up some paperwork in her office at Sophia's Kitchen and had nipped out to the bar to get a drink when she spotted Alastair McGrath and Jock Stewart sitting at one of their tables. She frowned, wondering how on earth they'd managed to bag themselves a table on a Friday night. Carlos, the maitre d', was passing by and she took hold of his arm.

'Do you know those two men in suits in Lena's section?' she asked him.

'No. But John Brennan asked us to squeeze them in. I assumed it had come from you?'

'Thanks, Carlos,' Grace said with a smile, assuming John had used the table as a way to ingratiate himself and get to know a little more about their competition. She took a seat at the bar and watched the two men. Alastair – loud and obnoxious. His thick Scottish accent could be heard across the restaurant. Jock, on the other hand, appeared to be the complete opposite. Quiet, understated and considered.

Together they made quite the pair, and she supposed that in business they probably complemented each other well.

Lena was making her way over with their food and she gave them one of her brightest smiles as she reached their table. Grace knew that Carlos always gave Lena the best customers – and Alastair, with his expensive suit and gold jewellery, looked like a big tipper. Grace noticed how he made a grab at Lena as she stood beside him, which she expertly dodged. Undeterred, he put an arm around her waist and pulled her towards him. Grace could see Lena laughing it off as she took a step back and placed his plate of food in front of him. Taking a step towards Jock, Lena bent forward slightly and placed the second plate of food down. Alastair took the opportunity to slide his hand up Lena's skirt, and whatever he did next made the young woman jump in pain, shock or both. The bouncers generally just covered the door and therefore didn't witness the assault. But Grace had.

Putting her drink on the bar, she marched over to Alastair's table, by which time he had pulled Lena onto his lap and was holding onto her with both arms. He was laughing, as though it was all some big joke, and Lena was doing her best to extricate herself from the situation while not causing a scene.

'Alastair,' Grace said as she reached the table. 'Let her go, now!'

Alastair scowled at her. 'We're only having a bit of fun, aren't we, lass?' he said to Lena.

'I said let her go, you disgusting old perv,' she snapped. 'She's a waitress, not your fucking toy.'

Alastair released his grip and Lena took the opportunity to jump up from his lap, pulling her skirt down as she did so.

'Now get out of this restaurant and don't ever let me see you in here again,' Grace snapped.

'Who the fuck do you think you're talking to?' Alastair snarled, his teeth bared like a rabid dog. 'John Brennan got us this table. He understands what it means to work in this business. You don't piss off your paying customers, least of all customers like me.'

'Well, in case you'd forgotten this is my restaurant and John Brennan works for me. Now get out!'

Noticing Grace had confronted one of the customers, two of the bouncers came walking over. 'Everything okay, Boss?' they asked.

'Please escort this piece of shit out of here,' she snapped.

'You'll fucking regret this,' Alastair shouted. 'You've picked a fight with the wrong man this time. And all for some little whore who wears skirts short enough to show her minge and then complains when people come on to her.'

'Come on, Boss, let's go,' Jock said as he pushed back his chair.

'You heard the lady,' one of the bouncers added.

'You'll pay for this, Grace. No one makes a cunt of me,' Alastair said, almost foaming at the mouth now with rage.

'No, you do a good enough job of that yourself,' Grace added. 'Now get out of my restaurant and out of my city.'

With that, the two bouncers approached him and Jock held up a hand. 'It's fine,' he snapped. 'We're going.'

The two men walked out of the restaurant, with Alastair still ranting as he left.

'Thank you, Grace,' a tearful Lena said as she continued to fiddle with her skirt.

'Come into my office,' Grace said. 'Carlos, can you bring us a brandy each? The good stuff?'

'Of course,' Carlos said as he dashed off to the bar.

Grace sat down at her desk and Lena sat opposite her, her hands still trembling. 'Are you okay?' Grace asked.

Lena nodded. 'Yes. I think so. I didn't know what to do. He grabbed me. He put his hand…'

'I know. I saw him. Dirty old pig,' Grace added.

Lena blushed and looked down at her hands, not daring to maintain eye contact. Grace had never had a chance to speak to her about the night she had propositioned her husband and wondered if Lena was thinking the same thing.

'I heard you stepped in and did the rotas and drinks order for Jamie last week?' Grace asked.

'Yeah. He was off with food poisoning for two days, and Kerry was on leave, so I had a go.'

'And there were no complaints? No issues?'

'None that I'm aware of,' Lena answered.

'It's not easy doing the rotas for this lot. Someone's always complaining that someone else got the best shift, but from what I could see you were fair.'

'I tried to be,' Lena replied with a shrug.

'You've got a nice way with the customers, Lena. You've obviously got some brains too. You could be an asset. You're aware that we own quite a few restaurants and bars, and you could go far if you wanted to? Do you want to?'

Lena looked up and smiled, nodding her head furiously. 'Yes I'd love to. I really enjoy working here, and I'd absolutely love to manage a place like this one day. You really think I could?'

Grace nodded back. 'If you work hard enough, I think you've got what it takes, yes.'

'Thank you, Grace,' she said as her cheeks turned pink.

'You're welcome, Lena. I don't give compliments when they're not deserved. But if you *ever* come on to my husband again, I will make sure that you never work in another decent bar or restaurant for the rest of your days.'

Lena blinked rapidly and was about to reply when Carlos entered the room carrying two glasses of brandy. 'Here you go, ladies,' he said with a smile as he handed them over.

'Thanks, Carlos,' Grace said. 'You are a truly gracious host.'

'Why, thank you,' he said as he gave a mock bow.

'Yes, thank you. You are very gracious indeed,' Lena added although she looked at Grace when she spoke.

Chapter Thirty-Nine

Alastair McGrath was almost foaming at the mouth as he walked along Liverpool's waterfront back to their hotel. 'Who the fuck does she think she is talking to me like that?' he shouted as he stomped along. 'Cheeky, arrogant little slag. She will rue the fucking day she ever met me, Jock. She will rue the fucking day.

Jock resisted the urge to tell Alastair that he had brought that whole scene on himself and watched instead as his boss, who was half drunk, fished around in his pocket for his mobile phone. He pulled it out and started flicking through his phone contacts, mumbling and grumbling to himself.

'Who are you looking for?' Jock asked.

'John fucking Brennan,' he snapped.

Jock took the phone from him and scrolled through his list of contacts until he found John's name. He pressed dial and handed the phone back to his boss and went on to listen to the one-sided conversation.

'John. I think it's about time we stepped up our plan to work together. In fact, I think it's time we showed that nasty little bitch just exactly what happens to little girls when they try and mess with the big boys, don't you?

'Well, if you want to work for me, this is how it's got to be. It's about time someone took her down a peg or two, and I'm the fucking man to do it. So, you're either with me, or you're against me. Which is it?

'Good. Meet me and Jock tomorrow at our hotel. Ten o'clock. Don't be fucking late.'

Alastair ended the call and turned to face Jock, his face an angry shade of purple now. 'Phone the boys, Jock, and tell them all to get down here. I want a fucking small army here by tomorrow night. We are going to prove to that cunt and her husband that *no one* makes a fool of me.'

'Why don't we—'

'Just fucking do it!' Jock shouted.

'Okay.' Jock took his own phone out of his pocket and phoned Jerry Smith, who had only a few days earlier headed back to Essex with a flea in his ear after what had happened at The Blue Rooms. He told him to assemble as many men as he could and be prepared to head back to Liverpool when they were told to. Jerry was as dumbfounded as Jock was, but they both knew better than to question Alastair when his mind was made up.

Jock listened to his boss ranting all the way back to the hotel and prayed for them to get there as quickly as possible to he could go to his own room, phone Celia and go to bed. He'd need his beauty sleep if they were about to take on the biggest firm in Merseyside. He and Jerry would stand by him as they always did, and the lads were always up for a scrap regardless of who they were fighting with. Alastair had an ego big enough for the lot of them, and one day it was going to get them all killed.

Chapter Forty

L eigh was asleep when Nick came home from his night out. She'd tried to stay awake but had fallen asleep reading the latest Kimberley Chambers novel.

'Leigh,' she heard him whisper as he picked up her book and put it on the bedside table. She blinked and was about to reprimand him for waking her up, when she remembered who he'd seen earlier. 'Did you follow them? Where did they go?' she asked anxiously.

Nick nodded and smiled, like a little kid on Christmas morning. 'The three of them left together. I followed them for a bit like you asked, and they all went into Sophia's Kitchen together.'

'The Carters' restaurant?'

Nick nodded. 'Exactly.'

'I fucking knew it, Nick. I knew we were onto something. What happened after that?'

'I tried to get a table. I figured I could wait there for our Ben to finish his shift, but they were fully booked. I had a quick drink at their bar, but you can't see much from there, and I couldn't see their table at all. So I only had one drink and then I left. John had gone too by the time I did and Alastair and his mate were sitting on their own.'

'Oh, I bet they were waiting for Grace or Michael,' she said. 'If only you could have waited a bit longer?'

'I sat there drinking my pint for half an hour, Leigh, and I couldn't see a thing. Maybe she met them while I was there, I wouldn't have known. I'm not MI6, you know!'

'I know,' she said with a smile, realising she'd offended him. 'And you've confirmed our suspicions at least. So, thank you,' she said as she pulled him to her for a kiss.

'Any time, Ma'am,' he replied with a grin.

Leigh slipped out of bed and left Nick snoring as she sat by her dresser and switched on her laptop. Although she'd been exhausted earlier, now her head was buzzing. She was desperate to find out what was going on with Alastair McGrath and the Carters. If she could, then she'd let the DI in Essex know and maybe they could bring the whole lot of them down? God, what a sting that would be. It would cement her career in the police force. She's probably make DCI in a year or two and would have her pick of any job she wanted. It was all she'd ever wanted. At least it had been at one time. She looked back at Nick and wondered if it still was. Nick was happy being a sergeant and would never go for promotion again. He said that he'd never be able to hack the longer hours, and Leigh knew that the higher you climbed the longer the hours were. As a previous boss of hers had once told her when she'd gone for her first promotion – *your salary goes up, but your hourly rate goes down.* And it was true. Suddenly, it seemed like her job wasn't the most important thing in her life any more.

Chapter Forty-One

Jock Stewart and Alastair McGrath were sitting at a table in the hotel restaurant eating their breakfast when Jock saw John Brennan walking into the room. The waiter approached him and asked for his room number but John quickly dismissed him with a wave of his hand and headed over to their table.

'Morning, gents,' John said as he sat down.

'Morning,' Alastair responded gruffly. He was suffering from a hangover, something of which Jock had extensive experience.

John ordered a coffee from the waitress and helped himself to a piece of toast from the rack on the table. 'So, you have a plan?' he asked before taking a bite.

Alastair nodded. 'I want to know who your boss's suppliers are. I want to know when her next shipment is coming in, and then I'm going to take it from right under her nose. Then when she comes after me, I will wipe out as many of that fucking family as I possibly can.'

239

John didn't flinch. If the thought of taking out his boss was in any way unpleasant to him, he didn't show it. 'Your plans have certainly escalated since we last spoke, Alastair,' he said with a smile. 'But, I do enjoy a challenge.'

'So you're in then?' Alastair grinned.

John nodded. 'All the way.'

Alastair started to laugh. 'See, I told you, Jock. I said he couldn't wait to get shot of her, didn't I?'

Jock nodded but he didn't share Alastair's enthusiasm and he didn't trust John Brennan at all. He was about to stab the woman for whom he'd worked for years in the back and was smiling about it. From what Jock had heard, Grace had always treated John well, and she counted him as one of her friends. No, a man like that was not to be trusted, but who was Jock to question the plans of the great Alastair McGrath?

'As luck would have it, Grace has a massive shipment coming in in two weeks. The biggest we've ever handled, in my time with her anyway. I think she's trying to prove something to everyone after her kid got nicked.'

Alastair's eyes lit up. 'Two weeks?'

'Yep. Well, two weeks on Monday. Coke and shooters. If we can nick that, then not only would we be quids in, but it would leave Grace in a very vulnerable position.'

'How so?' Jock asked.

'Like I said, this shipment is huge and I know for a fact we are running low on supplies – of everything. Losing this would disrupt the Carters' supply chains massively. Plus, we take the guns and we leave them without an arsenal.

Grace will only let us use clean weapons – and like I said, we're running low.'

Alastair nodded as he stuffed a piece of black pudding into his mouth. 'Perfect. You give me the details of where and when and we'll take it right from under her nose.'

'If this shipment is so big, and so important, it's not going to be as easy as that, is it?' Jock said as he looked between the two men.

'I never said it would be easy,' John snapped. 'But Jake and Connor are out of the picture, so this may be your best shot. Michael will be there but if you ask me, he's lost his edge lately and I don't think he'll give us too much trouble. He won't even carry a gun any more, he's turned into such a shithouse. Then there's usually up to eight men on the pick-up. I don't expect there'll be any more than that. Half of them will have guns, and one of those men will be me.'

'Sitting ducks?' Alastair said.

'The Carters aren't used to being challenged. They won't have a clue what's hit them.'

'Sounds perfect,' Alastair said.

'Too perfect,' Jock interrupted.

'Well, not quite,' John went on. 'We have two potential problems. The first being that Grace is going to be on this one too.'

'Grace?' Jock asked while Alastair nodded enthusiastically.

'Yep. She sometimes oversees them, so it's not that unusual, and with the lads inside, she wants to make sure it runs smoothly.'

'Oh, this gets better,' Alastair said.

John shook his head. 'Not for me. I might be happy to take her business from her, but I don't want to see her hurt. I'll go in on this with you, and I'll give you all the details you need, if you promise she doesn't get hurt.'

Alastair glared at him. 'I thought you were as hard as nails, lad?' he said.

Jock looked at John and saw the turmoil on his face. So, it wasn't so easy to stab your boss in the back then? For some reason, that made him like and trust John just that little bit more.

'They're my terms, Alastair. I don't care what happens to anyone else, but Grace walks out of there intact. She'll be no threat to us after this.'

'Sounds fair to me,' Jock said.

'If you insist,' Alastair added.

'What's the second?' Jock asked.

John rubbed a hand across his face. 'It could be nothing, but…'

'What?' Alastair demanded.

'I recognised a copper in here last night watching us,' John said. 'It could have been a coincidence. Maybe he was just having a pint, but…'

'I don't believe in coincidences,' Jock said.

'Me neither,' John agreed. 'Grace has quite a few of them in her pockets and I think he's one of them. If he's seen me talking to you, then our cover could be blown.'

'Fuck!' Alastair snapped.

'Nothing to worry about just yet. I could explain one meeting away easily enough. A chance encounter. Grace wouldn't even think not to trust me. But I think we need to meet somewhere a bit more discreet in future.'

Alastair nodded. 'Fine.'

'Great. So, two weeks then? The details could change up to a day or two before so we could talk a few days before to finalise plans?' John offered.

'Jock and I will head back here the day before. Another chance to stay in this fine establishment,' Alastair replied with a grin and Jock knew that he was really thinking about another chance to bang the blonde behind the bar, who had finally succumbed to his charms.

'We'll wait to hear from you,' Alastair added.

'Great doing business with you both,' John said as he glanced at his watch. 'I'd better get going. I've got to drive to Wales now. Another fucking errand to run. But not for much longer, eh?' He smiled as he picked up another piece of toast.

Chapter Forty-Two

John walked down Old Hall Street to the waiting car and climbed inside.

'All right, Murf,' he said as he closed the passenger door. 'You haven't been waiting long, have you?'

'Only five minutes. What were you doing in there anyway?' Murf asked.

'If I told you, I'd have to kill you,' John replied with a grin.

'Oh, top secret mission, was it?'

'Something like that. Now come on, let's get going. I want to be back handy, I've got shit to sort out today.'

'Do you know where this place is?' Murf asked.

'I've got an idea. Head for Bangor and I'll direct you from there.'

'Will do,' Murf said as he pulled the car away from the kerb.

An hour later, Murf pulled his old Land Rover into Perryman's caravan park near Bangor in Wales. He parked outside the club house and he and John got out of the car.

'Any idea where his van is?' Murf said as he looked around the site.

'Nope, but I know a man who will,' John said as he pushed open the door to the small sales office next to the club house.

Five minutes later and John was down fifty quid, but he had the location of Bradley's caravan. He and Murf jumped back into the car and drove to the remote spot on the site where the Johnson family caravan had sat for over thirty years.

'Jesus, what a dump,' Murf said, his nose wrinkling in disgust as he and John exited the car and walked up the door.

'What do you expect, it's almost as old as I am,' he said with a laugh.

'Shall we knock?' Murf asked.

'Okay,' John replied as he raised his foot and kicked the door with all of his considerable strength. It caved in easily and they both went inside to see Bradley Johnson's fat arse trying to squeeze out of the kitchen window.

John grabbed him and pulled him back inside. 'Hello, Bradley,' he said with a grin. 'There's a few people who'd like a word with you.'

Bradley's face turned the colour of boiled shite. Beads of perspiration started to appear on his forehead.

'Please,' he started to say as he held his hands up in defence. 'I can get the money back—'

Before he could say any more, John punched him in the face, causing him to stumble backwards and onto the sticky caravan floor.

'We'll need to knock him out if we're going to get him back to Liverpool without any hassle. Go and get the chloroform,' John said to Murf.

'What? I didn't bring it,' Murf said.

'For fuck's sake!' John snapped. 'I told you we needed to knock him out.'

'I know. But I didn't know you meant with that. I didn't want to drive all the way to Wales with it in case we got pulled. Can't one of us just knock him out?'

'Well, yeah. But it's not an exact science, is it? And he needs to be returned in one piece.'

'Sorry,' Murf said. 'I didn't think.'

John shook his head in annoyance and looked down at Bradley, who was watching the whole exchange in horror.

'You at least brought the gaffer tape and the cable ties?' John asked.

'Yeah, I'm not an amateur!'.

'Good. Go and get them then.'

Murf walked out of the caravan, leaving John and Bradley alone.

'What's this about? You don't work for Alastair McGrath?' Bradley asked as he shuffled away from John.

'I do now,' John replied with a grin. Bradley must have

realised who he was. Well, of course he would, everyone in Liverpool knew that he worked for Grace.

Murf returned, holding the tape and ties in his hands. 'Who wants the pleasure of chinning this piece of shit then?' he asked.

John shook his head. 'What did I just say about getting him back in one piece?' Ignoring Bradley's protestations, he bent down and grabbed him, easily manoeuvred him into positon so that he had him in a choke hold and applied the appropriate amount of pressure. A few seconds later Bradley was unconscious and slumped to the floor.

'Right, let's get him tied up and into the boot before anyone notices,' John ordered.

The two men worked quickly and expertly, neither of them strangers to such a task, and before long Bradley Johnson was safely bound and gagged and in the back of Murf's Land Rover.

'Is your place ready?' John asked as they drove back up the A51 towards Liverpool.

Murf nodded. 'Yeah. I'll park in the garage so no one will see us getting him out the car. Then the cellar is all geared up. Looks like something from a bad porno down there.' He laughed. 'Marie was not happy with me when I told her, but it's only a couple of weeks, right?'

John nodded. 'Yep. All you need to is keep him alive for a few weeks and then he'll be out of your hair.'

'Do you know what Grace has planned for him?'

John nodded.

'Anything I should know about?'

'If I told you, Murf—'

'You'd have to kill me.' Murf finished his sentence for him and started to laugh. 'Who am I to question the boss?'

'You'll find out all you need to know when you need to know it. It's always the way,' John reminded him.

Murf nodded. 'Fancy grabbing something to eat when we've dropped this fucker off? I'm starving.'

John looked at his watch. 'Yeah, all right. If you put your foot down we can get to Antonelli's before Steph clocks off.'

'You've got a bit of a soft spot for Steph, have you?' Murf grinned. 'You'd better hope Sean doesn't find out.

'Got a soft spot for her puttanesca, that's all,' John said.

Stephanie Carter was Sean Carter's daughter. At thirty years old, she was seventeen years younger than John, but he had a lot in common with her. Over the years, he'd watched her date a string of obnoxious and immature idiots whom she discarded after a few months, and wondered when she would wake up and realise that she needed someone with a bit more about them to keep her interest. Steph was intelligent, funny and beautiful. She had a fiery Italian temper like her mother, Sophia, but she also had a very sweet, soft side. John had known her for years and they got on well together. But he had never looked at her that way. Not until very recently anyway.

'Yeah, okay?' Murf laughed again. 'Is that what you call it?'

'Just get us to your house before this cretin wakes up, Murf.'

Murf nodded and obviously saw the good sense not to push any further.

Chapter Forty-Three

John and Murf had polished off their late lunch and Murf had left to check on his charge before his wife Marie got home. John was chatting to Steph at the bar when Grace walked into the restaurant.

'Afternoon, you two,' she said as she took a seat at the bar next to John.

'Hi, Grace,' Steph said as she leaned over the bar and gave her a kiss on the cheek.

'I didn't know you were coming in today, Boss?' John said.

'I wasn't planning to but Steph mentioned you were in and as I had to drop some invoices off to her, and I wanted to catch up with you about this morning, I thought I'd kill two birds with one stone.'

John nodded and smiled but there was something about his demeanour that was off. As though he wasn't entirely happy to see her.

'I'm not staying long. I've got another meeting shortly,' she said with a smile.

'Can I get you a bite to eat?' Steph asked.

'No thanks. I'll have a quick coffee though?' Grace replied.

'Coming right up,' Steph answered as she walked over to the espresso machine.

'So, how was this morning?' Grace asked.

'Perfect. Everything went according to plan,' he said with a smile, his manner returning to normal.

'Good. And Bradley is safely tucked away?'

'Yep. Murf is looking after him until you need him. I'm sure he won't be a problem.'

'Well, let's hope so,' Grace said as Steph returned with her coffee.

'Hot and steamy – just how you like it,' Steph said with a wink.

'Perfect,' she said as she pulled a folder out of her handbag. 'Here's those invoices you needed.'

Steph took the folder from her. 'Thanks. I'll sort them out later. What are you two conspiring about anyway?' she asked.

'Nothing important,' Grace replied before John had a chance to.

'Actually, I could do with a word, Boss,' John said. 'About Craig and Ged Johnson and what you want me to do next?'

Grace was aware that Steph was listening intently and while she trusted her niece implicitly, she didn't like to talk about certain aspects of their business in front of her.

'Leave them to me for now. I think I need to have a word with them myself, now that we have Bradley,' she said.

'But what about—'

'You know the game plan, John. How you execute it is up to you. I don't need to know the finer details. Unless there's anything in particular you wanted to talk about, I'll leave it in your very capable hands?'

John shook his head. 'Not really. I'll sort it.'

'Good,' Grace said with a smile as she picked up her cup of coffee. 'Now Steph, tell me about this new fella you've got your eye on.'

Steph blushed, which was unusual for her and Grace suddenly realised why John had seemed so awkward when she'd first come in. She had obviously interrupted something. Taking that as her cue to leave, she checked her watch. 'Do you know what? I should really run or I'll be late for the kids,' she said, taking a quick mouthful of the hot coffee. 'I'll leave you both to it.'

Steph and John hugged her goodbye and Grace walked out of the restaurant smiling to herself. John and Steph would make a great couple and it was about time they both met someone special.

Chapter Forty-Four

M ichael felt his phone vibrating in his pocket and cursed under his breath. He was struggling to put Oscar, who was teething and cranky, into his car seat. Picking his son back up with one arm, he took his phone out of his pocket and glanced at the screen to see it was Grace calling him.

'Hiya, babe. Is everything okay?' he answered.

'Yes, but I could do with your help. Is your dad still at our house?'

'Yeah, we were just going to take Oscar to the park for a bit. What do you need me for?'

'I need to pay a visit to Craig and Ged Johnson today. I think it's about time we test their loyalty and see if they're willing to convince Scott to withdraw his co-operation. It's been a week since we picked Bradley up and I think it's about time we let them know we have him. I'm not sure how they'll react to that news. I could really do with you with me.'

'Of course. I'll ask my dad to take Oscar and pick Belle up from school. Where are you?'

'I'm at Sophia's Kitchen. I've got my car, so, shall I pick you up in forty-five minutes?'

'Yeah. I'll be ready,' Michael answered.

Pat was walking out of their house as Michael ended the call. 'Change of plan, Dad. Grace needs me—'

Before he could finish his sentence, Pat interrupted. 'No problem. I'll take the little fella and me and Sue can pick Belle up from school.'

'Thanks, Dad.'

'Not a problem, son,' he said as he took Oscar from his arms. 'Be careful, won't you?'

'Always am,' Michael said with a smile. 'Bye, sunshine,' he said with a kiss on Oscar's head.

'Bye, Dada,' he said in response.

'You sure these two pricks are in here?' Michael asked as he and Grace walked into The Grapes. 'It's a shithole.'

'I know, but it's their local. And they came in here about an hour ago.'

Grace and Michael walked through the doors and saw Craig and Ged sitting at a table in the corner of the almost empty pub. The two of them were laughing and looked very happy with themselves. Their good humour probably wouldn't last once Grace had a word with them, but it was necessary. It would be like ripping off a plaster – painful, but needed to move forward. Despite all of the aggro he'd caused, Grace thought that there was a slim chance that they could work with Craig. It would all depend on how he conducted himself in the next seven days.

As Grace and Michael approached the table, both Craig and Ged looked up in surprise.

'Happy to see us?' Michael said as he took a seat.

'What do you two want?' Ged snapped.

'What I want is a word with you two,' Grace replied as she sat down next to her husband.

'About what?' Craig snapped.

'About you owing me,' Grace said with a smile.

'We owe you fuck all,' Craig spat.

Michael glared at him and Craig sat further back in his seat.

'I think you'll find you owe me more than you think, Craig. Shall I tell you why?'

The two brothers stared at her with their mouths hanging open, so she went on. 'For a start, I didn't bury the lot of you last year when you were stupid enough to try and muscle in on our family business. I let that slide because I thought you weren't worth the bother. Then, I gave you two and your idiot little brother another pass when he fingered my son and stepson for a murder that he couldn't possibly have witnessed. And finally, I had a word with Alastair McGrath and he hasn't put your head on his trophy wall yet, has he?'

Craig glared at her, but it was Ged who spoke. 'You might have met with Alastair McGrath, but stopping him from killing us is a bit of a stretch. That was nothing to do with you, you arrogant fucking bitch.'

Before he could finish talking Michael had jumped up and punched Ged in the face, causing blood to pour from his nose. Ged wiped it on the back of his sleeve as Michael sat back down.

'What my brother is trying to say,' Craig said as he shot Ged a sideways look, 'is that we dealt with the mix-up with Mr McGrath ourselves.'

'Oh, really? And how did you manage that?' Grace asked.

Craig shifted in his seat. 'We found a backer. Someone who wants to go into business with us.' He looked directly at her then and could hardly hide the smirk on his face.

Grace frowned at him. 'Oh? And who might that be?'

'None of your fucking business,' Ged snapped.

'Oh, come on. Who in their right mind would back you two idiots?' Grace said.

Grace had been aware of Ged's face getting redder and redder throughout the whole exchange, but she was still shocked when he launched himself across the table at her, screaming about what an evil bitch she was. Fortunately for her, he collided with Michael's fist instead and fell onto the floor.

Michael kindly picked him up by the neck of his T-shirt and sat him back down in his chair before delivering a swift kick to his groin for good measure. 'You ever try and touch my wife again, and I'll cut that off and shove it down your throat, you little cunt,' he spat before sitting back down.

'Are you going to tell us who this mysterious backer is then?' Grace asked with a smile.

Craig looked between the two of them. 'Not a chance. So, why don't you tell us why you're really here?'

'I want your little brother to retract his lies about Jake and Connor.'

Craig shook his head. 'Even if I wanted to do that, I don't know where he is.'

'He's in hiding, or so I'm told. We thought he was in witness protection but my sources tell me otherwise. I hear he's a bit of a delicate flower, and it won't be long before he contacts you or Ged here for some reassurance. When he does, you can bring him back into the fold.'

Craig laughed. 'You say that like it's easy. My little brother may be a bit of a quilt, but Billy was his favourite brother...'

'I get that. He wants revenge. You all do. But that's where I can help you out. I have a deal for you.'

Craig stared at her, while Ged sat back in his seat clutching his bleeding nose with one hand and his groin with the other. 'Go on,' Craig said.

'A few friends of ours have recently spent some time at a dodgy camp site called Perryman's. Ring any bells?'

Craig nodded. 'We used to go there when we were kids. My dad had an old van there.'

'Well, it seems that old van is still in the Johnson family.'

Craig's eyes widened and he sat forward in his seat. 'What?' he said quietly.

'Yep. Your beloved big brother Bradley was holed up there for the past few months. He's not there any longer, you understand? But don't worry, he's somewhere safe. Now, I can either hand him over to Alastair McGrath – or to you. You get your baby brother to fall into line, and Bradley is all yours.'

'And what then? Billy's murderers just walk free?'

'There's a difference between revenge and justice, Craig. I imagine there was a reason your brother Billy was murdered. We've all lost people we love – it's the nature of the world we live in. I know that doesn't make it hurt any less, but that's the way it is. Let's not pretend that we don't know who was ultimately responsible for Billy's death. Who was the one who went around taking credit for Paul's murder? Who was the one who disappeared and left you all to pick up the pieces of that fallout, not to mention nicking Alastair McGrath's money? He is the man responsible for Billy's death, and you both know it.'

Grace stood up and Michael followed suit. 'As soon as Scott retracts his statement and our sons are out of prison, Bradley is all yours and you can all get whatever justice you think you deserve for Billy's murder.'

Then, without a backwards glance, Grace and Michael walked out of The Grapes.

Chapter Forty-Five

Grace kicked off her heels and walked down the hallway towards the kitchen with Michael following close behind her.

'Do you fancy a drink?' she asked him when they reached the kitchen.

'Yeah. I could do with one,' he replied.

She poured them both a brandy and walked over to where he was standing near the breakfast bar, removing his shirt. She raised an eyebrow at him.

'It's got blood on,' he said as he held it up. 'I'll stick it in the wash.'

Grace watched him loading the machine while she sipped her brandy. He kept himself in good shape and she loved his body. He'd recently got himself a new tattoo on his side and she could just make it out as he bent over – *Cuimhnigh I Gconai* – 'Always Remember' in Gaelic. When he was finished, he walked back over to her and she handed him his drink.

'Today was just like old times,' she said to him.

He took a swig of the brandy and winced slightly as it went down. He didn't drink much as a rule and it was one of the many things Grace loved about him. Having once been married to a man who could down half a bottle of whisky and snort a bag of coke before lunch had left an indelible mark.

Michael placed his glass on the counter. 'No. It's different now,' he replied with a slight frown.

'How?'

'Because back then we were…'

'We were what?'

'You weren't my wife, for a start. Or the mother of my children.'

Grace scowled at him. 'So the fact that I'm now a wife and mum changes everything, does it?'

'The fact that you're *my* wife does, Grace. Yes.'

She wanted to interrupt him but she was lost for words. It was bad enough that almost every other man she dealt with held the fact that she was female against her, without her husband starting too.

He stared at her, his brown eyes almost black. She could feel the anger radiating from him like the heat from a furnace and wondered where the hell this was all coming from.

'I'd forgotten what it was like,' he finally said as he took a step towards her. 'To have to protect you from dickheads like Ged Johnson. I haven't had to do that for a long time.'

Suddenly, his anger made sense. It wasn't directed at her

at all. And there was more than anger in him now. He was scared too. Paul's death had changed him so much; sometimes he was unrecognisable from the man she had first met all of those years ago. But Paul's death had changed both of them. How could it not?

'Well, fortunately that's because it doesn't happen very often,' she said as she placed a hand on his cheek. 'And there is no one I would trust to have my back more than you.'

'But I can't be with you twenty-four hours a day.'

'And you don't need to be. I can look after myself too, you know.'

'I know you can. But—'

'But nothing. Today didn't go as smoothly as we'd have liked. Just as I expected it wouldn't. Why do you think I asked you to come with me in the first place?'

He pulled her closer to him and wrapped his arms around her waist. 'I worry about you. I can't help it. And this afternoon just reminded me of the arrogant gob-shites you have to deal with on a daily basis.'

'Yes and I deal with them just fine, don't I?'

He nodded. 'You certainly do. But if anything happened to you…'

'It won't. I'm titanium. Remember?'

Her comment had the desired effect and he laughed at the reference to the song they had danced to at their wedding – after the obligatory romantic first dance to Phyllis Nelson's 'Move Closer'. 'Titanium' had since become the unofficial Carter family anthem.

He pushed a strand of hair from her face. 'Do you have any idea how much I love you?'

'Why don't you remind me?' she said as she pulled his face towards hers and kissed him.

Chapter Forty-Six

C raig passed Ged the bag of frozen peas and he held it to his swollen face as they sat in Craig's kitchen.

'Do you really think they've found Brad?' Ged asked as he took a seat at the table, wincing as his groin area came into contact with the solid wood.

'How else would they know about our Da's old caravan?'

Ged nodded in agreement. 'I can't believe that sly little shit kept it and didn't let on, can you?'

'I think that's the least shitty thing he's done to us. He fucked off with all of Alastair's money. He gobbed off about killing Paul Carter and then left poor Billy to take the fall for it. As much as I hate to admit it, Grace Carter was right about one thing, and that is that Bradley is as responsible for Billy's death as anyone.'

'I always told you he was a wrong un, but none of you ever believed me,' Ged muttered.

'Oh, all right, what do you want, a fucking medal?'

'And I'll bet you he had something to do with us getting such long stretches for that job in Manchester. How else did he avoid getting sent down like the rest of us? Backstabbing cunt.'

'I hate to say this, Ged, but you're probably right. But it seems if we want our big brother back we need to get Scott to withdraw his statement.'

'We could just leave him for Grace Carter to deal with.'

'What? He's still our brother, Ged. Besides, she said she'd hand him over to Alastair and take all of the credit, and we don't want anything getting in the way of our business with him, do we? Once John cuts his ties with the Carters we'll need all the allies we can get. I wonder if any of John's lads will walk with him. They're pretty loyal to Grace.'

Ged shook his head in annoyance. 'And that's the problem, isn't it? Almost everyone who is anyone in this city is loyal to her.'

'Everyone except John Brennan,' Craig reminded him.

'So, what do we do about it?' Ged asked as he shifted in his seat, transferring the frozen peas to his groin for a moment.

'If we are ever going to make a name for ourselves around here then we need to take Grace Carter and her family out of the game.'

'Are you for real? And just exactly how are we supposed to do that?' Ged snapped.

'We're not. Alastair McGrath and John Brennan are.'

'And we'll be stuck in the middle of it all. It's suicide. I thought you were supposed to be the fucking smart one?'

'I am. You haven't heard the rest of my plan yet. We'll speak to Scott and get him back onside. Convince Grace that we're calling a truce, get Bradley back and deal with him in our own way. We can even blag Alastair McGrath that we've done it for him, as a gesture of goodwill.'

'So we help to set Billy's killers free? You and I both know that Jake Conlon and Connor Carter murdered our Billy. And now you're saying we're supposed to play nice with them and just take it on the chin? Billy would turn in his fucking grave.'

'We're only pretending to play nice, you daft fuck! Billy would be relieved that we were finally doing something that could make us some actual cash, Ged. Do you really want to stay in that grotty little flat in Everton for the rest of your life? Do you think I want to stay here? The girls are growing up and they can't go on sharing a bedroom for much longer – there's World War Three almost every fucking morning. And I'm tired of it, Ged. I'm tired of grafting my arse off and never getting anywhere. We hedge our bets. We make a truce with Grace Carter, but we hope that Alastair takes them out with John's inside information. Whoever comes out on top, we'll be okay.'

'What about John? You don't think Grace will mention that we're helping get Jake and Connor out of prison?'

'We'll tell John we're only trying to get Bradley back. I don't think he gives a shit one way or another about Jake and Connor, he thinks they're a pair of arrogant pricks. And with Grace and Michael out of the picture, those two won't last five minutes. Think about it, Ged. With Alastair's backing, John could become the top dog in Liverpool, and we could be his right-hand men.'

Ged stared at him, considering his proposal. 'Well, what the fuck else have we got to lose? What's a busted bollock or two between friends?' he said as he shifted uncomfortably in his seat.

'Sound. I'll call Grace first thing tomorrow and let her know we're on board.'

Grace and Michael were eating breakfast when Grace's phone started to ring. The caller was an unknown number.

Michael raised his eyebrows at her as she answered.

'Grace,' the caller said and she recognised Craig Johnson's voice.

'Morning, Craig. What can I do for you?'

'I've spoken to our Ged. We'll get Scott onside if you promise to hand Bradley over to us.'

'Smart move, Craig. I'll make sure your brother remains relatively unharmed, and as soon as Jake and Connor are in the clear, we'll hand him over.'

'Good,' he said and then he was silent.

'Great. Let me know when you speak to Scott.'

'Will do,' Craig replied.

Grace ended the call without any further exchange and relayed the conversation to Michael.

'You think they'll be able to persuade Scott to change his statement?'

'I think Bradley's return might be enough to sway him.'

'Let's hope so,' he said as he stood up to clear the table. 'Because if your plan doesn't work, Scott Johnson will be our only way out of this. Besides, Murf is getting twitchy having to keep that cunt Bradley chained up in his cellar for so long. I don't know about you, but I can't wait for this whole fucking shit-show to be over with.'

Chapter Forty-Seven

Craig and Ged Johnson walked up the short flight of steps to the first floor of the block of flats in Widnes.

'Number thirteen, I think,' Craig said as they walked along the corridor.

Ged stopped in front of a bright pink door. 'Thirteen,' he said before banging loudly on the glass.

A few seconds later, a young woman with shocking purple hair answered. 'Who are you?' she asked as she looked the brothers up and down.

'We're looking for our brother, Scott,' Craig answered.

'He's not here,' she said as she went to shut the door, but Ged put his foot in the doorway.

'Look again,' Craig snarled. 'Because we're not leaving here without speaking to him.'

She rolled her eyes and opened the door wider. 'Scott. Your brothers are here,' she said as she walked back into the flat.

A few seconds later a sheepish-looking Scott came to the

door. 'How did you know I was here?' he asked. 'I thought no one knew about me and Rosie.'

'You're not quite as clever as you think you are, Scottie. I followed you here one night when I wanted to know where you kept disappearing off to. You're not exactly inconspicuous about it, are you?'

Scott blinked at them both. 'Do you want to come in?' he finally offered.

Craig and Ged sat in the surprisingly well furnished living room of Rosie's flat while she made herself scarce, offering to go to the corner shop to get a jar of coffee.

'If you've come here to convince me to change my statement, then you've had a wasted journey,' Scott said defiantly.

'Stop playing the fucking hard case and listen up,' Craig snapped. 'We've come to tell you that we've been busy since you did your little disappearing act, and we can get justice for Billy another way.'

'A better way,' Ged added.

'Better than sending Jake Conlon and Connor Carter to prison for life?'

'For fuck's sake, Scott!' Craig shouted. 'How many times do I have to tell you that they will not go down for this? Do you honestly think you could hold up on a stand telling outright fucking lies?'

'I know they did it,' he snapped.

'Yes, but you didn't see them. Billy told you they were coming, but you didn't see them. I bet you never told the coppers that, did you? I bet you said you saw them coming in the house, didn't you?'

Scott shrugged. 'So what? They did come in the house, and they fucking killed Billy.'

'Fucking give him a slap before I knock him out, will you?' Craig said to Ged.

Ged was happy to oblige and stood up to give Scott a slap around the back of his head.

'Ow,' Scott yelped as he rubbed his head.

'Listen to me, you little knobhead. Grace Carter has found Bradley,' Craig said.

That seemed to get Scott's attention. 'What?' He sat forward in his chair.

'He was hiding out in our Da's old caravan in Wales. She has him and she's willing to hand him over to us if you'll drop this fucking nonsense with the police.'

Scott shook his head. 'I can't.'

'So, you're prepared to let Bradley be fucking tortured to death by Grace Carter and her firm? I know he's screwed us all over, but he's still our brother. Don't get me wrong, I'd happily kill the fucker myself, but I don't want that for him.'

'I'll tell that DI that Grace has him—'

At this Craig jumped up off his chair and pulled Scott up by the collar of his polo shirt. 'Are you fucking listening to me?' he snarled. 'These are not the type of people you grass up to the filth. If her son goes to prison because of you she will have Bradley tortured and flung in a fucking hole where no one will ever find him. Then she will hunt each and every one of us down and do the same to us, you stupid little prick!'

The colour drained from Scott's face and Craig pushed

him back into the chair. He let what he'd just said sink in for a few moments before he tried a different tactic. 'Look, Scott, we're all in this together. The three of us need to stick together, and we can't do that without you. We all know that Bradley was as responsible for Billy's death as much as anyone. We get him back and we'll make him pay in our own way, but it has to be us, not Grace Carter or Alastair McGrath.'

Scott stared at Craig, his eyes brimming with tears.

'Tell him what else we've been doing,' Ged said.

Craig nodded. 'You want to get back at the Carters so badly? Then the best way to hurt them is to help take what's theirs right from under their noses. Grace's right-hand man, John Brennan, has paid Alastair off for us and he wants to go into business with us. With him and Alastair backing us, we'll be able to pay Grace Carter and her whole fucking family back one day, one way or another, and we won't be the ones in the firing line.'

Scott looked at them both. 'I don't know. What am I supposed to say to this copper? Sorry, I've changed my mind?'

'You don't say nothing to her. You get your brief to tell them you're withdrawing your statement. You say you were mistaken. Job done.'

'And you're sure she'll hand Bradley over?'

'Why wouldn't she? He means nothing to her. What I do know is that she definitely won't hand him over if you don't drop this shit. And I am telling you she will kill us all if they go down for murder. All she's interested in is saving Jake and Connor.'

Scott sat back in his chair and appeared deep in thought.

'You can do what you want with your own life, Scott, but you're sentencing the rest of us along with you if you go ahead with this. And if you can't do it for me and Ged, think of my Gemma and the girls, and Bradley's kids an' all. Who knows how far Grace Carter will go to get her revenge?"

After what seemed like an eternity, Scott nodded. 'Okay. I'll speak to my solicitor later.'

Craig picked up Scott's mobile phone from the coffee table. 'Why wait when you can do it right now?'

Scott took the phone and Craig listened as he spoke to his brief and told him what a huge mistake he'd made.

Chapter Forty-Eight

J ock and Alastair were watching the Sunday afternoon football in Jock's hotel room when John Brennan phoned.

Alastair answered the phone and put it on loudspeaker. 'Where are you? I thought we were meeting for a pint during the match? I want to go over some final details for tomorrow,' he asked.

'I was just on my way into your hotel, but, well, let's just say there's been a last-minute change of plan.'

'Why? What's happened?' Jock asked.

'Remember that copper I told you about who I think works for Grace? Well, I've just seen him in the hotel bar. It all feels like too much of a coincidence to me, so I left—'

'Is the fucker still down there?' Alastair snapped.

'No, he left just after I did. He was looking around for a bit when he walked outside, but he didn't see me and now he's headed towards the car park. I'm going to follow him. We need to nab him before he has a chance to report to

Grace. That's twice now he's seen me at your hotel, and I'm not sure I can explain today's visit away so easily.'

'What are you suggesting?' Jock asked.

'That we grab him,' John replied.

'You want us to kidnap one of the Old Bill?' Jock asked. 'Are you serious?'

'I'm not asking you to do anything. I think it's about time we made Craig and Ged earn their keep, isn't it? You two don't need to be anywhere near this. And it will be a good test of their mettle. We'll nab him and I'll make sure Craig and Ged keep an eye on him until after tomorrow night's deal, and then Grace will know everything anyway. It's either that or we call off the whole thing now. It's your choice, Alastair.'

Jock watched as his boss sat back in his chair. He licked his lips, deep in thought. He was never one to back down from a challenge, or miss out on some money to be made, but John was talking about kidnapping a copper, and that wasn't something that should be done lightly. It wasn't the type of thing that could be easily explained away. The Old Bill were like a dog with a bone when one of their own was taken, and who knew if this copper would end up dead at the end of it all?

'Okay. Do it,' Alastair finally said. 'But let those two idiots take the fall if anything goes wrong. I want my name nowhere near this.'

'Of course,' John replied.

'Let me know when it's done,' Alastair said and then he ended the call.

'We're getting in deeper and deeper here, Boss,' Jock

said. 'We were only supposed to be coming up here to get your money back from the Johnson idiots, and now we're knee deep in a fucking takeover.'

'Relax, Jock. It's all sorted. This John fella is legit – you told me that yourself. He's obviously been thinking about this for a long time, and who are we to stand in the way of progress? I'm happy to help him out if it puts that stuck-up bitch in her place, and makes me a few quid in the process.'

'Whatever you say,' Jock replied, but he wondered if Alastair would be as keen to take over Grace's firm it if was a man at the helm. The level of anger he seemed to feel for a woman whom he'd met only twice was excessive to say the least. For some reason, Alastair could not bear a woman who stood up to him, and if one ever dared to challenge him in public, as Grace had a couple of weeks earlier, then he wouldn't rest until he had exacted his revenge and evened the score. It was this blind need for vengeance and score settling that was clouding his judgement, but what was Jock supposed to do about it? Alastair had always been this way and he wasn't about to change now.

Chapter Forty-Nine

C raig and Ged had been driving home from Widnes feeling very pleased with themselves when they'd received a phone call from John Brennan telling them he wanted to meet them in half an hour at Craig's house. They now sat patiently in Craig's kitchen waiting for him.

'What do you think this is about?' Ged asked.

Craig was about to answer when he heard the doorbell ringing. He answered it and John walked through to the kitchen.

'You both all right?' John asked.

'Yeah,' they said.

'Been up to much today?'

'Nothing interesting, why do you ask?' Craig said with a frown.

'Just making small talk,' John replied with a shrug as he sat down at the kitchen table. 'Any chance of a brew? I'm gasping.'

'Yeah,' Craig replied and he put the kettle on. 'What did you want to see us about?'

'I spoke with Alastair and Jock today and I think we're all going to work well together – all of us.'

'Great,' Ged said as he rubbed his hands together. 'Where do I sign?'

'I like your enthusiasm, Ged.' John laughed. 'And with that in mind, Alastair has a job for us.'

Craig leaned against the kitchen counter as he waited for the kettle to boil. 'Oh?'

'Yep. There's someone who needs dealing with. I suspect he's been spying on Alastair and Jock, and possibly me, for Grace, and he could cause some problems for all of us, if you know what I mean? But we need to act fast. Like in the next hour. I know what gym he goes to and he's there the same time every day. I'll drive the van and you two can grab him. I have a place we can take him to in Walton. Then you'll just need to watch him for a day or two until Alastair decides what to do with him. If we can sort this out for him, we'll prove that we're worth going into business with. That we can be trusted.'

'That we're indispensable?' Craig added.

John nodded. 'Exactly.'

An hour later John was parked in an old Transit van near to Cooper's gym in Crosby waiting for DS Nick Bryce to come out. He glanced at his watch and turned to Craig and Ged who were waiting anxiously in the back of the van, each armed with a baseball bat.

'Are you two ready?' he asked.

'Yeah,' they said.

'This is your big chance. Don't fuck this up, lads,' he warned them. 'Just grab him, get him in the van and tie him up. You might have to knock him out to get him in. He takes care of himself, this fella, he might give you a run for your money.'

'We can handle him,' Ged said, full of confidence.

John turned to face the gym again, just in time to see Nick walking out with a holdall slung over his shoulder. John knew Nick's car and it was parked about a hundred metres behind them so he would have to pass the van to get to it. 'Here he is,' John said. 'He'll be walking past us any second now. Go!'

Craig and Ged jumped out of the van and John was impressed with the speed and efficiency with which they overpowered Nick and had him bound and gagged. He wrestled and shouted a little before Craig and Ged shut him up with a quick blow to the head. John smiled to himself as he pulled the van away from the kerb. Job done, and, best of all, Nick hadn't had a chance to see his face.

'Good job, you two,' John said they drove towards Walton. 'I'm going to drop you off at the old taxi garage on County Road. There's plenty of food and water in there for you both. There's a couple of beers too, but don't get pissed! It will last you for a few days if needs be, but he should be out of there by tomorrow night. The place hasn't been open for a few years but there's a working toilet and electricity, and a couple of couches if you need to get your head down. I hope it goes without saying that only one of you should have a kip at any one time though?'

'Of course. We've told you before, we're not amateurs.'

'I know,' he replied. 'You've just proved that. But this is only the first step. Now you have to keep Sleeping Beauty here alive, quiet and restrained. That's the hardest part.'

'Are we allowed to mess with him?' Ged said.

'Mess with him? What the fuck do you mean?' John asked, wondering if Ged had some twisted tendencies that he wasn't aware of.

'You know, slap him about a bit? It will get boring in that garage with nothing to do.'

John shook his head and sighed. Ged really was a fucking plant-pot. 'By all means give him a dig or two if he gives you any bother, but don't be slapping him about just because you're bored. Alastair wants him intact. There's a portable DVD and a few pornos in there if you get that bored.'

'What the fuck do you usually use this place for, mate?' Craig asked with a laugh.

'Wouldn't you like to know?' John replied with a grin.

Chapter Fifty

Jock watched as Alastair McGrath paced up and down his hotel room.

'They should have picked him up by now,' Alastair said as he looked at his watch. 'So, why haven't we had the phone call yet?'

'I'm sure he'll phone as soon as it's done. Maybe they got caught up? Maybe kidnapping a copper isn't quite as easy as John made it out to be?' Jock replied. 'Anyway, do you honestly think those fuckwit brothers can be trusted with this?'

'Well, John seems to think so, and let's face it, if it all goes south it won't be our necks on the line, will it? We were nowhere near the job. It'll be him and those Johnson twerps who take the rap,' Alastair replied and took a seat in the armchair.

'I suppose so,' Jock agreed.

'Anyway, have you spoken to Jerry? Are the lads all okay for tomorrow?'

'Yeah. We've got nine men altogether and they'll be here tomorrow at four o'clock. I said we'd meet them at that service station on the M62 and then we can sort out who's going to do what.'

'Nine? I asked for twelve!' Alastair barked.

'Well, he struggled to get twelve.'

'He struggled to get twelve men together? Why? What the fuck were they all doing that was more important?' Alastair snarled.

Jock resisted telling Alastair that some of the hired muscle they usually worked with would no longer put their necks on the line for him, on account of the fact that he had screwed a fair number of them over in one way or another – it would only cause an argument that he didn't have the energy for. 'They've got other jobs on, Boss. Besides, he got nine and that includes four of our best. With me, you and Jerry on board, as well as John Brennan on the inside, that will more than suffice.'

Before Alastair could answer, Jock's mobile phone rang.

'Hello,' he answered.

'The job's done. The brothers are dealing with him,' John Brennan said.

Jock put the phone on speaker so Alastair could hear the call too. 'Good. But do you think he managed to speak to your boss first?' he asked.

'No. I followed him. He went straight to the gym after we spoke.'

'You're sure?'

'Do you think I'd be this calm if I wasn't?'

'Fair point. Are we all set for tomorrow then?' Alastair asked.

'Yeah. We'll be arriving at the warehouse at eight to make the exchange.'

'Will your suppliers get in the way? Are they likely to take Grace's side?' Jock asked.

'No. They're only interested in money. They won't come armed, Grace won't allow it, so they'll duck out as soon as anyone starts shooting. Trust me.'

'We're trusting you an awful lot,' Jock said.

'And I you,' John replied.

'We'll see you tomorrow at eight then, Johnny boy,' Alastair said.

'Tomorrow it is,' John replied before the line went dead.

Alastair looked at Jock as he placed his phone back in his pocket and grinned. 'Looks like we're all set then,' he said as he rubbed his hands together. 'Now let's go somewhere and get ourselves a nice glass of Scotch.'

'Okay, but you're paying,' Jock replied as the two men left the hotel room.

Chapter Fifty-One

G race walked through the restaurant area of Sophia's Kitchen towards the bar. She was supposed to be on her way home but Michael had asked her to pick up a takeaway on route, telling her he fancied some Italian. One of the perks of owning a string of Italian restaurants was being able to have a delicious meal boxed up and ready to take home whenever they fancied.

'It will just be a few minutes, Grace,' Lena told her as she reached the bar.

'No problem. I'll wait in my office, I need to send an email anyway.'

Grace walked towards her office and noticed the door was open. She wasn't expecting anyone to be using it at that time of night. As she got nearer she saw John Brennan in there, rummaging around her desk.

'Looking for something, John?'

He looked up at her. 'Sorry, Boss. Just looking for a pen,' he replied nervously.

'I didn't expect you here tonight,' she said to him as she handed him a pen from the holder.

'Thanks,' he replied as he took it from her and put it in his pocket. He was fidgeting. What was going on with him?

'I'm not here working. I'm waiting for Steph to finish her shift,' he replied.

'Oh, I see,' Grace replied with a smile. 'No wonder you're a bit twitchy.'

'I'm not twitchy,' he replied as he pulled at the collar of his shirt with his index finger. 'Is it hot in here?'

Grace laughed. 'I'm not surprised you're nervous. Does Sean know you're off out on a date with his daughter?'

'It's not a date,' John snapped. 'We're just mates going for a drink.'

'Oh?' Grace replied as she sat in her chair, not believing him for a second. 'I know what will distract you from your date that's not a date, anyway. Tell me, are we all set for tomorrow?'

'Yep. Everything is good to go. Eight o'clock!' He flashed his eyebrows at her.

'Good.'

'Are you sure you want to be there? It's not necessary. Me and Michael can handle it.'

'I know you can, and it's sweet of you to worry about me, but I want to be there.'

'Okay. Who am I to argue with the boss?' he replied with a smile.

'Do you think it will all go to plan?' Grace asked him.

John shrugged. 'Your plans usually do, but who can say? In the heat of the moment, anything can happen.'

'Well then, let's just hope that it doesn't,' Grace said.

John looked down at his feet.

'You sure you're okay?' Grace asked.

'Yeah. Just nervous, like you said.'

'Well, even though Sean and Michael might threaten to chop your bollocks off if they find out about you and Steph, I think you make a great couple.'

'Thanks, Grace.'

'You're welcome. You deserve to be happy. Both of you do.'

Just then Lena popped her head through the door. 'Your food's ready, Grace,' she said with a smile.

Grace stood up and gave John's arm a squeeze on her way past. 'I hope tonight goes well, and I'll see you tomorrow.'

'See you tomorrow,' he replied.

Chapter Fifty-Two

G race had just placed the hot food on the passenger seat of her car when she came face to face with Leigh Moss.

'Leigh? What the hell do you want?'

'Nick has disappeared,' Leigh snapped. 'Did you have anything to do with it?'

'Who the hell is Nick?' Grace frowned at her.

'He's my sergeant.'

'Your sergeant has disappeared? So you obviously assume I had something to do with it?' Grace laughed. 'Do me a favour, Leigh and piss off!' She walked round her car and was about to get in.

'Grace!' Leigh shouted, the desperation in her voice clearly audible.

Grace turned on her heel. 'What?'

'Nick is not just my sergeant,' Leigh said. 'He's much more than that.'

'Oh, like that, is it? Well, good for you, but I still had

nothing to do with him disappearing,' she snapped as she opened the car door.

'I think it was Alastair McGrath,' Leigh said.

Grace closed the door and stared at Leigh. 'What makes you think that? Are you sure he's even disappeared? Maybe he's at the pub or something? It's only nine o'clock.'

Leigh blinked back the tears. 'He was looking into Alastair for me, and then he didn't come home from the gym earlier this afternoon. I've phoned and phoned his mobile but he's not answering. It's not him at all. He's as reliable as clockwork. I just know something's happened to him.'

'Well, if you're right about it being anything to do with Alastair McGrath, then I suggest you call your boys in blue and get them to find him sharpish, while there still some of him left to find, because Alastair and his men do not mess around. He is an evil bastard.'

'I can't do that.'

'Why? Scared in case they find out you're screwing one of your subordinates?'

'No,' Leigh said and frowned. 'But I wasn't supposed to be looking into Alastair. I was specifically asked not to by my superiors.'

'So you had your boyfriend do it for you on the side instead?'

Leigh looked down at her shoes.

'Well, I see your dilemma, but I'm still not sure why you're telling me all of this.'

'Because you know Alastair. I thought you might know where he would take someone?'

Grace laughed out loud. 'You're asking me for help? Are you fucking serious?' She shook her head and opened her car door again to get in.

'Please, Grace? I don't know where else to turn. I know you have a connection with Alastair—'

'Oh, spying on me too, were you?' Grace snapped.

'No, but I know that he met with you.'

'Yes, we met, and he is a dodgy, nasty bastard. Even I draw the line at working with him. I suggest you make peace with the fact that you'll never see your boyfriend again.'

'Grace.' Leigh glared at her. 'You know I can't do that, and you know how hard it is for me to come to you for help. But I have nowhere else to turn.'

Grace stared at Leigh. She was feisty and passionate and was always willing to fight for what she believed in. She was prepared to do a deal with the devil in order to save the person she loved. They were so alike in many ways, but still so very different.

'Why would I risk a potential war with Alastair for you?' Grace asked.

'For the same reason you helped me all of those years ago – because it's the right thing to do. Nick is a good man, Grace. He does his job and he treats people with kindness and compassion. He doesn't deserve to die at the hands of someone like Alastair McGrath. I know deep down that you're a good woman, Grace, and you would never let an innocent man suffer if there was a chance you could help him.'

Grace shook her head. 'You're unbelievable, Leigh! I'll

help you, but if I find Nick…' She didn't finish her sentence. She didn't need to. Both of them understood the cost of what they were about to do.

———————

Grace walked into the kitchen and put the bag of food onto the kitchen counter. Michael walked in behind her. 'That smells gorgeous,' he said as he approached her and started unloading the bags.

'I just had a very interesting chat with DI Moss,' Grace said. 'Apparently, her boyfriend has been kidnapped and she'd like our help to find him?'

Michael raised an eyebrow at her. 'Well, who could have predicted that?' he said.

Grace was about to reply when Michael's phone started to ring.

'Jesus Christ. Do we ever get a minute's peace?' Michael snapped but then his face softened as he saw who was calling.

'All right, bro?' he said when he answered and Grace listened to Michael's half of the conversation.

'Seriously? Are you sure? We've got it covered, you know?

'Sound then. It will be nice to have you on board. Be just like old times.

'See you tomorrow.'

Michael ended the call and smiled at Grace. 'Sean wants to be in on the action tomorrow night.'

'Sean? Does Sophia know?'

'I didn't ask,' Michael replied with a shrug. 'I'm just glad he's on board. You can never be too prepared with things like these. No matter how straightforward it all seems, something can always go tits up.'

Grace nodded. 'Of course.'

'Are you okay?' Michael asked.

'Yes. It's not like I haven't done anything like this before, Michael.'

'I know that,' he said as he pulled her into a hug.

Grace leaned against him and enjoyed the feeling of his arms wrapped around her. The truth was, she *was* nervous about tomorrow night. As much as she had every detail worked out, she hadn't been involved in one of these things for a long time, and it made her feel queasy. She supposed that a small dose of nerves was healthy.

'Let's get this food while it's still hot,' Michael said as he released her from his embrace.

'Yes, come on. Then I'll phone Murf and speak to him about Nick.'

Grace followed Michael into the living room with a bottle of wine in her hand while he carried the food. She smiled. This time tomorrow it would all be over.

Chapter Fifty-Three

Alastair McGrath surveyed the group of men in front of him as they huddled in the far corner of the now empty carpark near to the warehouse where he was shortly about to ambush Grace Carter and her firm. Him and his boys were going to steal their entire shipment, while also taking out as many of those fuckers as they could. There were twelve of them in total, including him. They were all suitably armed. Eight of them, including him and Jock, had 9mm pistols and the rest had machetes and baseball bats. Grace Carter wasn't going to know what had bloody hit her. And he could not wait to see the look on her face when she realised that her own most trusted soldier was now working for him. God, it was going to be priceless.

'Right, lads,' he said, addressing his adoring audience. 'This ain't no Mickey Mouse outfit we're dealing with here. This is a firm of top-class nutters, so while we will most definitely have the element of surprise, do not underestimate what these people are capable of. Don't get cocky. Keep your wits about you, but shoot anything that moves,' he cackled. 'Except for the woman. Leave her to me.' Alastair had promised John that he wouldn't hurt Grace, but he wasn't intending to keep that promise. Nevertheless, he wanted the pleasure of that for himself.

The men all nodded their agreement.

'Right, into the vans then. It's nearly go time,' he said.

Grace Carter looked out of the window at the Liverpool skyline as Michael drove them to the old warehouse on Bridle Road in Bootle. She tried to focus on the song on the radio but the words were making no sense to her. Sean and John were silent in the back of the car.

'You okay, love?' Michael asked her, breaking the silence.

'Yeah. I always get a bit nervous before these things though. You can never fully predict how they're going to turn out.'

He placed his warm hand on her leg and gave a gentle squeeze. 'It will be fine,' he said with a reassuring smile. 'In a few hours we'll be back at home with our feet up watching telly.'

Grace nodded. 'Yeah,' she said with a sigh while the passengers in the back seat remained silent.

Jock Stewart looked at the assembled men, all in balaclavas and carrying weapons, outside the warehouse on Bridle

Road. His heart was hammering in his chest and his blood pounded in his ears as he signalled them to advance towards the door. They stopped just outside and he turned to them, their faces frozen in anticipation – or fear? Jock fingered the safety on his Glock, ensuring that it was off. Then he took a deep breath, preparing himself for what was about to go down. People were going to get killed tonight, quite possibly a few of them, and while that wasn't an entirely unusual event in his life, it was never one he'd got used to.

Alastair came up beside him. 'Remember, lads. Shoot anything that moves,' he whispered. The men nodded, like soldiers being given their orders.

Alastair raised one gloved hand and then gave the signal – the signal that they should storm through the large double doors that John had assured them would be open. The men charged on, with Jock and Alastair bringing up the rear. But there were no gunshots fired. In fact, the men in front of him stopped stock still, so much so that Alastair and Jock almost tripped over them as they rushed inside. Jock pushed his way to the front of the throng and the sight that greeted him almost stopped his heart.

Spread across the width of the warehouse were at least twenty men, including Michael and Sean Carter, as well as John Brennan, holding semi-automatic machine guns that were pointed directly at them. It seemed Michael Carter had got over his fear of carrying a gun then. Or John Brennan had been talking complete bollocks.

'What the fuck?' Alastair whispered as he came up beside him.

Jock blinked as his heart pounded so hard he thought it might burst out of his chest at any moment.

'Put all of the weapons on the floor, six feet in front of you, and then keep your hands up where we can see them,' Michael ordered.

When no one moved, he shouted. 'Now!'

'Do as he says,' Jock said to the men, knowing that they wouldn't get a single shot off before at least half of them were gunned down.

One by one, each of the men laid their weapons down on the ground, then stood with their hands in the air as instructed. Six of the armed men stepped forward and started to collect the weapons while the remaining ones kept their guns trained on Jock and his men.

'Take off your masks and get on your knees,' Michael ordered.

'Fuck you!' one of the men, whose name Jock couldn't recall, shouted, and without missing a beat, Sean Carter shot him in the knee, causing him to drop to the floor and howl in pain. One clean round straight through his kneecap. It had the desired effect and every other man dropped to their knees before removing their balaclavas.

'Easy, tiger,' Michael said to Sean but then he smiled and Jock saw a glimpse of the violence that these men were capable of. Sean and Michael Carter had a reputation that had followed them around like an urban legend all of their lives and Jock had always wondered whether it was true. Kneeling on the cold concrete floor of that warehouse, he knew the answer, although he wished he didn't.

Michael walked over to the line of men and crouched

down in front of one of them – Charlie Ross. 'Who's your boss?' he asked. 'Other than those two cunts, Alsatair and Jock. Who gives you your orders?

Charlie closed his eyes and shook his head. Michael stood up and pointed the gun at Charlie's head. 'I want to know who gives this man his orders. Who brought this shower of cunts to our city to try and take what was ours?'

'I do,' Jock answered.

'Nah, not you, Jock. You're his second.' He indicated Alastair. 'You two have been here since last night, so who bussed this gang of muppets here today? Who is your second, Jock?'

Nobody spoke and Michael pressed the barrel of the gun to Charlie's head, causing him to whimper.

'I do,' Jerry Smith answered. 'I give the lads their orders.'

Michael glared at Jerry and then looked up and down the line at the remaining men before speaking. 'Thank you. That wasn't so hard now, was it?'

Michael summoned a few of his men over to him. 'Round the rest of them up and put them on a bus back to Essex,' he growled as he looked at the men kneeling before him. 'But if I ever see any of your sorry faces again, I will personally put a bullet in each and every one of you,' he shouted.

Chapter Fifty-Four

Murf and two of his bouncers, Carl and Gary, forced a bound and gagged Bradley Johnson into the back of Murf's Land Rover. Murf and Gary climbed into the back seat so they were sitting either side of Bradley while Carl drove.

Bradley had spent the last two weeks chained up in Murf's cellar with limited food and water, wondering what the hell was going to happen to him. He'd asked Murf over and over but, as he'd been instructed to, Murf had not uttered a single word to his captive. Luckily for him and Marie, the cellar was soundproof so they were both spared the sound of Bradley's shouting and pleas for help, except for the few seconds when the cellar door opened. But now, Murf had a specific message to deliver.

'You are quite possibly about to take your last trip anywhere on this earth, Bradley,' Murf said quietly to him. 'Alastair McGrath wants you dead, mate. And he has had paid me very good money to make sure you disappear for ever,' he lied.

Bradley tried to talk but the gaffer tape over his mouth prevented him from doing anything but mumbling.

'But he doesn't just want me to kill you. No, he'd like you to suffer first. That's why I'm taking you to a nice little garage I know of. I don't want to be cleaning your blood up from my cellar for the next six weeks, do I?'

Bradley shook his head as tears started streaming down his face.

'Look, mate. If it were up to me, it would be quick and clean. I don't really go in much for this torture lark, I haven't really got the stomach for it. But well, I'm being paid to do a job and he's a crafty bastard, that Alastair, he wants me to keep certain parts of your body for him. I won't tell you which ones just yet, wouldn't want you to shit your pants in my car, but my own eyes watered when he told me.' Murf shook his head and winced.

'And did you know that you can tell whether parts of someone's body were removed while they were alive or after they were dead?' Murf asked.

Bradley started to scream.

'Well, I didn't either,' Murf went on, ignoring Bradley's muffled screams. 'But Alastair tells me it's true. He says he'll know and I can't take a chance, can I? Not when he's paying me so well.'

Murf sat back in his seat and listened to Bradley crying.

'You do have a choice though, Boss,' Gary said after a few minutes. 'Remember what Grace said?'

'Nah, there's no way Bradley will agree to that.' Murf

dismissed Gary with a wave of his hand while Bradley looked between the two men. Bradley started shouting.

'What's that you're saying?' Murf asked him with a grin. 'I can't hear you with that tape over your mouth.

'For fuck's sake, Boss,' Gary said with a sigh and tore the tape from Bradley's mouth.

'What did she say?' Bradley blurted out. 'What?'

Murf narrowed his eyes and looked at Bradley. 'Well, my boss, Grace Carter, she happens to hate Alastair McGrath as much as he hates you, so she did say she'd be willing to deal with him for you. She'd pay your debt and square it with him, but you'd have to do something for her in return, obviously.'

'What?' Bradley shouted. 'I'll do anything.'

Murf shrugged. 'You need to tell the police that you murdered Billy.'

'Billy? My brother? Why would I do that?'

'Because, Bradley, Grace's son and stepson are currently in prison awaiting trial for Billy's murder, when we all know that you were really the one responsible. You may not have actually done it, but it was your fault, wasn't it?'

'But, but, I'll go to prison for life,' he stuttered. 'And my brothers will never forgive me.'

'Ah well, your brothers already hate your guts. Craig and Ged are at the garage too. Because of your little stunt Alastair isn't happy with them either. So, it looks to me like you have two options. You can come with us now and know for certain that you and two of your brothers are going to die a slow and painful death, or you can go to prison for the next ten to fifteen years, safe in the knowledge that you have helped Grace Carter out of a hole and therefore she will make sure that no one tries to slit your throat or bum you in the showers while you're there. What do you think?'

Bradley hung his head and sobbed.

'Which is it to be?' Gary asked.

'I'll tell them I killed Billy.' Bradley sniffed as snot and tears ran down his face.

'Good choice,' Murf said as he patted Bradley's back and winked at Gary. 'We'll take you to your brothers and when the police arrive, you can confess all. But remember, should you change your mind later down the line, that Grace and Michael Carter have lots of very good friends in very high places. There is nowhere you can go that we won't find you,' Murf warned him.

Bradley sat back in his seat, thoroughly defeated. Murf sat back too and swallowed the bile that rose in his throat. Thank fuck for that!

Chapter Fifty-Five

Murf and Carl jumped out of Murf's Land Rover while Gary stayed behind to keep an eye on Bradley. They walked over to Mitch and Geoff, two more bouncers from Cartel Securities. Along with Mitch's huge Alsatian, Woody, they had been drafted in for the night and were standing in the cold outside the former taxi garage on County Road.

'They all in there?' Murf asked.

The two men nodded.

'And the copper is still tied up?'

'Yeah,' Geoff replied.

'Conscious?' Murf asked.

'Doesn't look like,' Mitch said.

'Right then, gents, let's get this over with.'

The four men pulled balaclavas over their heads and then along with Woody stormed into the garage catching Craig and Ged Johnson entirely unawares. Craig picked up a nearby metal pole to defend himself while Ged scrabbled around on the floor. Woody pounced on Ged and Mitch followed him, kicking Ged to the jaw as he struggled to shake off the dog and stand upright. Meanwhile Geoff and Gary easily overpowered Craig, who, to his credit, put up a good fight. It wasn't long though before the two Johnson brothers had their wrists and ankles bound. Ged continued to challenge them to a fight, despite being restrained, so Mitch punched him in the jaw and when that didn't work, he stuffed an old dirty rag into Ged's mouth.

Craig was slightly more reserved. 'What's this about? Do you know who we're working for?' Craig asked.

Murf nodded. 'I know who you *think* you're working for.'

'What?' Craig snapped.

'You do know he's a copper, don't you?' Murf asked as he walked over to Nick and checked him over. Nick groaned, his eyes flickered open for a few seconds and then he lost consciousness again.

'What? Fuck! He's not,' Craig said as he looked between Murf and Nick.

Murf nodded. 'Afraid so, mate.'

'But...' Craig said as he started to shake his head.

'Oh, I can't be arsed with all of this,' Murf snapped. 'Someone would like a word with you, Craig,' he said as he took his mobile phone from his pocket and dialled a number. As he waited for it to be answered, he turned to Mitch. 'Leave the dog in my car, would you, and bring that other soft prick in.'

Mitch nodded. 'Come on, Woody,' he called and his dog ran after him.

———————

Craig watched as Murf put the phone to his ear as it was picked up on the other end. 'Grace,' he said with a smile and Craig frowned. What the fuck was going on? He didn't have a clue. Why on earth had John not told him that they'd kidnapped a bizzie? He listened intently to Murf's half of the conversation in the hope he might learn some answers.

'Yes, he's here. He's been slipping in and out of consciousness while we've been here but I checked him and he seems okay.

'Yes, he's here too. I'll put you onto him.'

Murf moved closer and held the phone to Craig's ear.

'What the hell have you got yourself mixed up in, you stupid bastard?' Grace said.

'What do you know about it, and what the fuck is going on?' Craig barked.

'You tell me. Because there is all hell breaking loose. Something's not right and I can't quite put my finger on it,' she replied.

'It's because you're being betrayed, Grace,' Craig replied, no longer knowing who he could trust. John had lied to them, and now they were at the mercy of Grace Carter's men, not to mention that they had kidnapped a bloody police officer. Craig had to take a gamble and hope that it paid off. Grace had offered them a deal before and he hoped she might be amenable to another one.

'Really? By who?' Grace asked.

'John Brennan. He has tried to fuck you over big time. He's been working with Alastair McGrath all along. They're planning to take you down, Grace.'

'Really? You expect me to believe that? How would you even know something like that?'

'Because he asked us to help him. I was the one who arranged the meeting with Alastair for him. He's a two-faced backstabbing cunt. He's left us here to take the rap for kidnapping a fucking bizzie.'

'Well, whatever happens next, Craig, you just remember our agreement. You've kidnapped a copper and the police are going to be on their way to you at any minute. I'm about to deliver your brother, as I promised I would. Now, whatever happens next, I will look after you and your brothers, but only if you keep your end of the bargain. You know exactly what I want, so make sure I get it.'

'Okay,' Craig said. Then he looked up at Murf. 'She's gone,' he said.

'Good, now, as per my boss's instructions, we have one final surprise for you two,' Murf said as he straightened up. 'Bring him in, boys,' Murf shouted.

Mitch and Carl pushed Bradley through the door.

'Bradley, you lying two-faced piece of shit,' Craig shouted. 'Are you behind any of this?'

Bradley, who was still crying, started to shake his head. His hands and feet still bound, he shuffled forward as Mitch and Carl guided him further into the room. When he reached his brothers, Mitch pushed him down onto the floor beside them.

'I'm sorry,' Bradley mumbled.

'So you fucking should be,' Craig snarled while Ged, who was still gagged, glared at his eldest brother.

'I can make all of this right,' Bradley whimpered.

'Oh, fuck off!' Craig said and turned his head away.

Chapter Fifty-Six

J ock Stewart felt the cold steel of the gun barrel pressed against his temple as he had his hands tied behind his back by another one of Michael Carter's men. He glanced to the side to see Jerry and Alastair receiving the same treatment. Both he and Jerry were silent but Alastair had started mouthing off – he just couldn't seem to help himself. It was when he started getting personal about Grace Carter that he earned himself a swift kick to the solar plexus which make him vomit onto the cold concrete floor. It shut him up at least.

Once their hands were tied, the men stepped back and Jock was finally able to look forward again. Standing directly in front of him were Sean and Michael Carter and John Brennan. John was still holding a semi-automatic in his hands, but the Carter brothers had no such weapons now, and that made Jock feel slightly more at ease. He looked at John for some reassurance and was greeted by a wide smile. That made him feel better for a few seconds, until he realised that they were still surrounded by Michael and Grace Carter's men. John would have to shoot his way out if they were going to escape – but perhaps that was his plan?

Now that Alastair had stopped ranting, the place was quiet, and only the sound of cars in the distance could be heard in the deserted warehouse. But then Jock heard a sound that sent shivers down his spine. He saw Jerry's head snap up beside him too to see where the noise was coming from. The clicking of heels on the concrete floor echoed around the empty warehouse.

A few seconds later Grace Carter was before them, dressed in a skin-tight pencil skirt, white blouse and expensive shoes. She looked every inch the woman Jock had feared she was. She certainly knew how to make an entrance. She stood beside Michael, Sean and John and stared at the three bound men on the floor before surveying the entire room. She owned them all. Even John?

'Fucking bitch!' Alastair spat onto the floor in front of him.

'Watch your mouth,' Michael Carter growled.

Grace looked like she was about to speak when the sound of a mobile phone ringing stopped her in her tracks. It was Michael's. He took it out of his pocket, glanced at the screen and passed it to Grace. Jock listened to the one-sided conversation.

'Hello, Murf. Did you find Nick Bryce?'

Jock flinched at the sound of Nick's name. John's cover was about to be blown and they were going to lose any advantage they had.

'What the hell have you got yourself mixed up in, you stupid bastard?

'You tell me. Because there is all hell breaking loose. Something's not right and I can't quite put my finger on it.

'Really? By who?

'Really? You expect me to believe that? How would you even know something like that?

'Well, whatever happens next, Craig, you just remember our agreement. You've kidnapped a copper and the filth are going to be on their way to you at any minute. I'm about to deliver your brother, as I promised I would. Now, whatever happens next, I will look after you and your brothers, but only if you keep your end of the bargain. You know exactly what I want, so make sure I get it.'

Grace hung up the phone without any goodbyes and turned to John Brennan. Jock braced himself for what was about to happen next.

'Craig just grassed you up, John,' she said coolly – far too nonchalant for Jock's liking.

John shook his head. 'Bastard. I was hoping he might have a bit more about him than that. Looks like we won't be working with him after all, eh?'

'I told you both he was a Grade A wanker,' Michael added.

Grace shrugged. 'I like to try and see the best in people. I was wrong. No harm done. Now we know he's not to be trusted.'

'He's the one who can't be trusted.' Alastair nodded towards John. 'He's been undermining you every step of the way. Can't wait to be rid of you. He hates you. He said you're a fucking bitch. Go on, ask him!' he shouted.

Jock shook his head in disbelief at the stupidity of his boss. It was as though a lightbulb had just switched on in his head and he suddenly realised he'd spent the last thirty years working for an absolute buffoon. It was a pity that it had taken being tied up and held at gunpoint in a freezing cold warehouse on the outskirts of Liverpool to make him come to his senses. And now he was going to die because of him.

Grace turned to John again. 'Did you call me a bitch?' she said with mock horror.

John shook his head. 'I don't think so. Who knows though? I was in the moment, Boss. I had to make it all convincing, didn't I?'

'But…' Alastair started to stutter.

'Oh, for fuck's sake,' Jock snapped, unable to stand his boss's incompetence any longer. 'Isn't it obvious? This whole thing has been a set-up. He's been working for her the whole fucking time. I told you it was all a little too convenient but you never fucking listen.'

Grace looked at Jock for a few seconds and smiled at him. 'At least one of you has some brains.' Then she walked over and stood a few inches in front of him. She was so close he could smell her expensive perfume, could see that her shoes were the distinctive Louboutin brand that his own wife favoured. 'Jock, isn't it?' she asked.

'Yes.'

'John has actually told me good things about you, Jock.

He says you're a man who says what he thinks and also that you're very loyal. Some would say to a fault.'

Jock nodded. 'Well, you got that right,' he said through gritted teeth.

'Well, I already know your boss is a gob-shite with more brains in his knob than his head, but what about this fella here?' Grace asked as she pointed to Jerry.

'Jerry just does what he's told to do. He's only here because he was told to be. If you let him go, he won't give you any bother.'

Jerry didn't say a word and Jock's admiration for him only grew further. Some men would have started agreeing and pleading for their lives at that point.

Grace nodded and walked back to Michael, Sean and John. 'I suppose that settles it then.' Then she turned to her right-hand man, 'John?'

Jock watched as John raised his right arm, the gun pointed in the direction of the three men on the floor. Jock closed his eyes and prepared for the worst. Then one lone gunshot rang out through the air. Opening his eyes, Jock looked around him. Jerry remained beside him, looking just as puzzled as he was. Alastair, however, was face down on the concrete, a pool of blood already spilling out around his head.

'Clean that up, will you, Kev?' Grace said to one of the men standing behind him. Jock swallowed, wondering if this was a temporary or a permanent reprieve.

'What will happen now, Jock?' Grace said as Alastair's body was dragged away. 'Will you take over?'

Jock shrugged. 'I don't know.'

'He will,' Jerry answered. 'And I can't think of anyone who won't be relieved to be working for you instead of him.' He nodded towards Alastair's body before turning his attention back to Grace. 'And I'm pretty sure his wife would give you a medal if she ever found out about this, which of course she won't.'

Grace nodded. 'So where will Mrs McGrath, and the rest of Alastair's minions, think their beloved hero has disappeared to then?'

'He met up with one of his many mistresses here in Liverpool and decided he was jacking it all in to move to the Costa del Sol, where he plans to live out his days drinking cocktails and fishing,' Jerry answered without hesitation.

'I think I like you,' Grace said to Jerry with a smile. Then she turned her attention to her heavies behind them again. 'Let these two go,' she ordered and Jock almost passed out with relief as he felt the ties on his wrists being cut.

'Thank you, Mrs Carter,' he said to Grace as he stood up, rubbing his wrists.

'Please, call me Grace.' She smiled again and he was struck by how beautiful she was. Perhaps because she'd just saved his life? 'But Jock, in future, don't come to Liverpool unless we ask you to, okay?'

He nodded. 'Deal.'

'And who knows, maybe I will ask you to,' she said finally before she turned on her heel and walked away. Michael, Sean and John fell into step beside her as they started to make their way out of the warehouse while he and Jerry were ushered out of the back door. Jock took the opportunity to take one last look back before he left the building and watched Grace striding across the floor, flanked by the three men and with her head held high. She hadn't even broken a sweat throughout that whole exchange, while Jock had felt like he was going to have a stroke.

He smiled to himself. What a fucking woman!

Chapter Fifty-Seven

Michael opened the passenger door and Grace climbed into the warm car. She took her mobile phone from her handbag as Michael, Sean and John got into the car with her, and dialled Leigh Moss's number.

Leigh answered on the first ring and Grace could hear the desperation in her voice.

'We've found Nick,' Grace said, putting Leigh out of her misery.

Leigh let out a long breath. 'Is he okay?'

'He's got a few cuts and bruises. Maybe a concussion and a broken bone or two by the sounds of it, but otherwise he's fine. My men got to him just in time. Now this is how this is going to play out. I have two conditions. I will tell you where Nick is but some of my men are in there, and I want your assurances that if the boys in blue turn up they will walk out of there entirely unscathed – and not in handcuffs.'

'Okay.'

'The two men who took Nick are there. My men have detained them, and I think you might be surprised to learn that it was the Johnson brothers who were responsible.'

'What? But that makes no sense,' Leigh started.

'Look, Leigh, I don't know why they did what they did, and to be honest, I don't really care, but you came to me. You asked me to find your boyfriend before he ended up chopped up into pieces and buried in an unmarked grave, and I did. Why those knobheads took him is not my concern. That's for you and your colleagues to figure out.'

'Okay,' Leigh said. 'I didn't mean…'

'I'm sure you're not going to be surprised by my other condition, but I want the investigation into Connor and Jake dropped. I want them out of Walton by tomorrow.'

'But Grace, you know that's not within my gift. I'll do what I can, but these things take time. It will have to play out a while longer yet. I can't just drop the charges for no reason.'

'I beg to differ, Leigh. It is well within your gift, but what you mean is that your superiors will start asking you some difficult questions if you do. Well, fortunately for you, I'm not asking you to drop it with no reason. When you see the Johnson brothers shortly, I want you to ask them who really killed Billy. As luck would have it, the man actually responsible is there with them too. I am about to deliver Billy's murderer to you, Leigh, by hand. Not only is he going to confess to the murder, but there will be two witnesses who will swear that he is the killer you're looking for. I also have it on good authority that Scott Johnson has withdrawn his co-operation, so that will all tie up nicely, won't it?'

'I suppose so, if what you say is true.'

'It is. You make sure you ask Craig and Ged who killed Billy after you arrest them for Nick's kidnapping.'

'Okay,' Leigh said with a sigh.

'You'll find Nick at the old taxi garage on County Road. Let me know when it's done,' Grace said.

'Okay. And thank you, Grace,' Leigh said.

'You're welcome,' Grace said as she ended the call.

'Where to now?' Michael asked as he drove out of the warehouse carpark.

'Home,' Grace said with a smile. 'Let's go home and wait for the good news.'

'I can't believe you pulled this whole thing off,' Sean piped up from the back seat.

'Really?' Michael said as he looked at his brother in the rear-view mirror. 'I never had a doubt.'

'Me neither,' John added.

'Liars,' Grace said to the pair of them and they all started to laugh.

'Seriously though, Grace, you are a fucking genius,' Sean said.

'I agree,' Michael said as he lifted her hand to his lips and kissed her fingertips.

'That's why I'd never work for anyone else,' John said.

Grace reached back and gave his knee a squeeze. 'And you have no idea how much I appreciate that. It all comes down to one thing in the end, doesn't it? Those people you can trust, and those you can trust to screw you over.'

Michael nodded. 'You can't buy loyalty.'

Chapter Fifty-Eight

L eigh put her foot down on the accelerator and sped through the streets of Liverpool towards County Road. As she raced down Scotland Road she phoned the job in, knowing that she was only moments away and she would get there first. She wanted to make sure that she spoke to Grace's men first. If at all possible, she would rather the whole force didn't find out about her past, or her connection to Grace Carter. She'd rather Nick didn't find out either, but she knew now that was much less likely.

Leigh pulled up outside the taxi garage, which had been closed down years before, and parked on the double yellows outside. Grace's men were expecting her, but despite that her instincts kicked in and she crept around the side of the garage, being careful not to bring any attention to herself before she was ready to be seen.

Leigh stepped through the side door and saw four men bound and gagged. Three of them were sitting with their backs against the wall, looking up in horror at their captors

– five large men who paced the room in silence and who Leigh assumed must work for Grace. The fourth man on the floor was lying on his side in the recovery position, and Leigh immediately recognised him as Nick. It was the sight of him lying motionless on the floor that gave her the courage to walk into the room.

As she did, all of the men except Nick looked up at her.

'DI Moss?' one of Grace's men asked. He was the oldest of the bunch and something about the way he carried himself made Leigh think he was the one on charge.

'Yes, and you are?'

'Jack Murphy. But you can call me Murf,' he said. 'I work for Grace and Michael. Grace told me you'd be coming. She also said I could let my boys go home once you arrived. Is that right?'

Leigh nodded. 'Yes. The police are on their way, so you'd better leave now.'

'Go on, lads, get out of here,' Murf said to the other four men.

'Cheers, Boss,' one of them said before they made a swift exit.

As the men jogged out, Leigh rushed over to Nick and knelt beside him.

'He's okay,' Murf said. 'His mouth is bleeding so I put him on his side to stop him choking. He's in and out of consciousness but I don't think they've done any lasting damage.'

Leigh nodded and cradled Nick's head in her lap. 'I've phoned an ambulance too. They shouldn't be long.'

'Great. I'll hang around for your colleagues to show up.

It would be better if you let me do the talking when they arrive.'

Leigh blinked at him, wondering how he was going to explain how both of them came to be there. But she nodded, as she had no plausible explanation to offer other than truth, and no one wanted that coming out. 'Can you take the tape from their mouths?' she said as she indicated the men she now recognised as three of the Johnson brothers, Craig, Ged and the lesser spotted Bradley.

Murf ripped off the tape and they each winced in turn.

'My name is DI Leigh Moss, and I've been told to ask you two a question,' she said to Craig and Ged. 'Who killed Billy?'

Ged and Craig looked at each other. 'What if we can't trust her?' Ged whispered.

'I think we're all out of options at the minute, bro,' Craig replied before looking up at Leigh. 'It was him,' he said indicating his eldest brother, who was sitting next to them in silence.

Leigh stared at the three of them. 'Why?'

'Billy found out what a backstabbing piece of shit Bradley was, and he confronted him about it. Bradley here lost his temper and beat him to death. We saw it all, didn't we, Ged? Why else do you think Bradley disappeared for a few months? He was terrified that you lot were going to lift him.'

'So, you two actually saw him killing Billy?'

Craig and Ged nodded.

'So why did Scott swear it was Jake Conlon and Connor Carter?'

Craig laughed. 'Well, that was nothing to do with us, but can you think of a better way to get rid of those two? It was good business.'

'And what do you have to say for yourself?' Leigh asked Bradley.

He looked at the floor for a few seconds and then he looked up at Leigh. 'It's true,' he said, his voice shaking. 'It was me.' Craig and Ged looked at each other with their mouths open in shock and Leigh wasn't sure who was more surprised by Bradley's confession.

Before she could probe any further Leigh heard the sound of sirens approaching and a moment later the room was filled with armed response officers.

'It's okay,' Leigh said as some of her uniformed colleagues entered the room too. 'These are the men responsible.' She pointed towards the Johnson brothers. 'And this one has just confessed to the murder of Billy Johnson too,' she added, indicating Bradley.

Three uniformed officers grabbed hold of Craig, Ged and Bradley and frogmarched them out of the garage as they read them their rights.

'And what about him, Ma'am?' One of the uniformed officers, whom Leigh recognised as Sergeant Anthony Bird, looked at Murf.

'Mr Murphy was the one who found Nick,' she said. 'I'll let him explain.'

'Thank you,' Murf said with a smile as he took a step towards Bird. 'I work for Cartel Securities. We look after a few of the pubs along County Road and one of them is the one just at the back of here. I was just doing my rounds tonight, like I usually do, when I heard some weird noises coming from inside here. I knew the place hadn't been open for years, and, well, it sounded like someone was in trouble, so I crept in and I saw those three men you just took out beating the shit out of this guy here. I managed to overpower them—'

'You overpowered three men on your own?' Bird asked with a flash of his eyebrows.

'I've been in this game for almost thirty years, mate. I know every trick in the book when it comes to fighting. I've dealt with more mass brawls than you lot, I expect. Anyway, I had a little help – my Alsatian, Woody, was with me. He's outside in the car now though if you want me to get him?'

Bird shook his head. 'Go on.'

'Anyway, I sorted those three out, which believe me wasn't as difficult as you might expect, and then I checked the fella's pockets. His mobile phone was in there and I just dialled his last number, and it was this lady here. Couldn't believe my luck when she turned out to be a copper.' He laughed.

'How did you know his pass code to get into his phone?' Bird asked.

'Because he told me,' Murf replied. 'He's in and out. You could do with getting him to a hospital pretty sharpish.'

'Why didn't you phone 999?' Bird asked.

'Because I didn't know what kind of trouble this fella was in, did I? Seemed like he'd had enough of a bad day without you lot showing up and quizzing him.'

Bird nodded and Leigh smiled at him. 'It was lucky Mr Murphy was passing,' she said.

'Wasn't it just,' Bird replied and Leigh couldn't quite tell whether he had believed Murf's tale or not.

'We could check the CCTV, Ma'am,' Bird suggested.

'Ah, I don't think that will be much help to you. The CCTV round here hasn't been working for weeks. I reported it myself but you know how it is. Cuts and all that,' Murf said with a shake of his head.

Leigh had to admit that Murf was convincing, and she had no doubt that a trawl of CCTV cameras in the area would prove his last statement to be true. If Grace Carter wanted CCTV to stop working, then it usually did.

'We'll need you to come into the station tonight and make a statement,' Bird said to Murf.

'No problem. Can I just take Woody home first though? The wife will be missing him.'

'Of course, Mr Murphy,' Bird replied.

Suddenly, two paramedics came running into the room and made their way over to Nick.

'I'm going to go with him to the hospital, Sergeant,' Leigh said.

'Of course, Ma'am. I'll send a uniform over there to take your statement later.'

Leigh nodded. 'Okay.' Then she turned to Murf. 'I can't thank you enough for your help, Mr Murphy. If it wasn't for you, Nick would…'

'It's no bother at all,' Murf replied, saving Leigh from her emotion. 'Happy to do my bit for you fine officers.'

Leigh was sure she saw Bird roll his eyes, but she bade

both men goodbye and made her way over to Nick and the paramedics.

Leigh was in the ambulance with Nick, on their way to Royal Liverpool Hospital when her mobile phone rang. It was one of the constables in her team, who expressed her sympathies for what had happened to Nick, but also informed her that Scott Johnson's solicitor had been in touch to say that Scott was withdrawing his statement regarding Jake Conlon and Connor Carter's involvement in Billy's murder. He claimed that on reflection he had been entirely mistaken and said he was deeply sorry for any inconvenience he had caused.

Leigh put the phone down and shook her head. That tied everything up nicely, didn't it? Just as Grace had predicted.

Chapter Fifty-Nine

Grace, Michael, Sean and John were sitting in the kitchen of Grace and Michael's house. Sean had whipped up his famous spaghetti and pasta sauce – a recipe he'd stolen from his Italian wife Sophia and adapted to make his own, since cooking eased his nerves – and the three men were tucking into a large bowlful each. Although the smell was making Grace's stomach growl, she was too nervous to eat. Until she had the phone call from Leigh, she wouldn't be able to relax. Although she had planned the whole operation down to the last detail, there was always a chance something could go wrong.

'So, how did it feel conspiring with Alastair McGrath and the Johnson brothers?' Sean asked John.

'Well, to be honest, at first I thought it would be no problem, tell a few porkies and blow some smoke up some people's arses. But Alastair and those Johnson brothers were such pricks that it felt like I spent most of my time trying not to put a bullet in their heads. Shower of incompetent, arrogant fuckwits. There was only Jock with an ounce of sense between the lot of them, and he could hardly get a word in edgewise.'

'It must have been torture,' Sean said as he swallowed a mouthful. 'I'm not sure I could have kept my cool around them. But I suppose you knew it would all be worth it in the end. Only what if—'

Grace cut him off. 'No "what ifs",' Sean. Not yet. We don't know for certain that everything has worked out exactly as planned.'

'Fair enough,' he said with a nod as he turned his attention back to his food.

Grace listened to the three men making small talk as she stared at her mobile phone on the table, willing it to ring. A few moments later she saw Leigh's name flashing on the screen and grabbed it.

'Leigh?'

'Grace. It's done. We've arrested Bradley Johnson for Billy's murder. Bradley confessed and his brothers have both given statements that it was him, and, as you predicted, Scott Johnson has retracted his. Your solicitor has already been notified and Jake and Connor should be free men by the morning.'

'Good,' Grace said with a smile and noticed that Michael, Sean and John started smiling too. 'Thank you, Leigh.'

'Any time,' she said before hanging up.

Grace looked up at the three expectant faces. 'They're coming home,' she said, her face beginning to hurt from smiling so widely.

Michael rushed around the table and picked her up from her chair before planting a kiss on her lips. 'You are fucking incredible,' he said to her.

'Oh, leave it out. I'm trying to eat here,' Sean said with a laugh.

'Well, I couldn't have done it without the three of you,' Grace said. 'I mean that. I'd be lost without you all by my side.'

'No you wouldn't,' John said. 'But it's nice to be appreciated, Boss.' He raised his bottle of Bud in the air and everyone did the same.

'To loyalty,' John said.

'To Liverpool loyalty,' Grace added.

Leigh Moss looked at the clock and saw it was just past midnight. She had just left Nick in the hospital. He had a broken wrist and some cuts and bruises, but he was going to be fine. They'd kept him in for observation because he had received a nasty blow to the head that had rendered him unconscious for a time.

Nick hadn't seen who'd taken him. They'd worn balaclavas and had bundled him into the back of a van. Given that he'd been following Alastair McGrath around, both Nick and Leigh were convinced that he was the most likely culprit. It seemed like he had hired the Johnson brothers to do his dirty work for him, although they denied actually taking Nick, but his blood and prints were in Ged's van. The brothers had been arrested but there was not a scrap of evidence to tie Alastair McGrath or any of his men to the crime, so he was going to walk away from it all without so much as a blemish.

Fortunately, the whole thing had played out in such a way that Nick hadn't discovered Leigh's connection to Grace. She wasn't sure if he would forgive her if he ever found out who she'd sent to rescue him. He would probably understand about her past and although he'd be shocked, she doubted he'd hold it against her – he wasn't that sort of guy. But hiding her deep-rooted connection to Grace Carter was a different matter. He would never look at her the same way again. She could never be sure that he wouldn't go over every arrest they'd ever made and wonder if she'd held something back. Rethinking every time one of Grace Carter's many minions slipped through their hands, and wondering if there was any chance that she'd had a hand in it. She couldn't blame him. She'd do the same thing.

Leigh poured herself a glass of wine and sat on her sofa, her legs tucked beneath her. It had been a long day but she couldn't face going to bed alone, not when she usually had Nick's warm body to cuddle up to. Leigh blinked back the tears as she recalled walking into that garage earlier and seeing Nick bloodied and battered. She had run over to him and cradled him in her arms. He'd looked up at her as though she was his knight in shining armour and she had realised at that moment how much she had come to need him in her life. She had always been a loner, it was how she'd survived – never let anyone get too close. Well, like it or not now, Nick was as close as anyone could get to her.

Leigh downed her wine in one and placed the empty

glass on the table. She knew now what she had to do. It was too dangerous for her and Nick to maintain the current status quo. After the favour Grace Carter had done her today, Leigh knew that she was on Grace's hook for the rest of her life. Perhaps she always had been? Tomorrow morning she was going to hand in her resignation as the DI of the Organised Crime task force and ask for a transfer to a division where she would be less of an asset to the Carter family. She'd always disliked high-volume crime stuff like shoplifting and burglaries, but it seemed a place where she would be less valuable to Grace. It was either that or traffic – and she hated traffic.

Leigh knew that questions would be asked about her departure, especially after she'd fought so hard for the job in the first place, but she would use Nick's kidnap as the perfect excuse and claim that she just didn't feel safe in the OCG task force any longer. It would stick in her throat to say the words, when they were so far from the truth. It was also the kind of revelation that would make the likes of Tony Webster rub his hands with glee, but it was a damn sight better than admitting the truth, which was that she was now indebted to the biggest crime family that had ever set up shop in the North West.

Chapter Sixty

Grace walked into the kitchen after seeing Sean and John out. Michael was still sitting at their large kitchen table. He held a glass of brandy in one of his large hands and she noticed there was another on the table beside him which she assumed was for her.

He looked up at her as she walked in and leaned back in his chair. 'I think we need to talk,' he said before downing his drink in one.

We need to talk! Four of the most loaded words in the English language. Walking over, she sat beside him and picked up the second glass before taking a sip. The expensive cognac warmed her throat as it slid down. 'I know,' she replied.

'Where do we go from here, Grace? What's our next move?'

Grace stared at him. His dark hair was greying at the temples now. Flecks of grey peppered his beard too and there were lines on his face that she was sure hadn't been there just a few months earlier. The last few months had taken their toll on both of them. He looked into her eyes now and she couldn't help but smile at him. He still gave her butterflies.

'I know you want to leave this all behind—' she started.

'I want our family to be safe. I want you and the kids to be safe,' he interrupted her.

'I know that,' she said. Because she did, she knew that was all he wanted in life. It was what she wanted too, but lately they'd had different ideas about how to make that happen. Was it time to walk away and hand over the reins to Connor and Jake completely? Perhaps it was? Maybe she and Michael were too old for this game now?

'I know that we haven't been agreeing on the best way to do that,' he said as he moved his face closer to hers. 'But I hope after everything that's happened…'

Grace placed her free hand on his cheek. 'We are stronger now than we've ever been, Michael,' she said. 'You and me are a team. There is nothing we can't face together.'

He smiled and turned his face to kiss the palm of her hand. 'I know that. And I think we both know what we need to do.'

'Are you really sure this is what you want?'

Michael nodded. 'It's the best way to protect our family.'

Grace leaned back and took a sip of her drink.

'I love you,' Michael said to her.

She smiled at him. 'I know, and I love you too. But I don't want you to turn around in a year's time and regret this. I don't want *us* to regret it.'

He shook his head. 'We won't.'

Grace downed the rest of her brandy. 'I hope you're right, Carter,' she said as she stood up.

Michael stood up and pulled her to him, wrapping his arms around her waist and looking into her eyes. 'I am,' he said. 'Besides, I'd bet everything I have on you.'

Chapter Sixty-One

Michael leaned against his car, enjoying the morning sunshine as he waited outside Walton prison for Jake and Connor to be released. He spotted them coming out of the gate and his face broke into a smile. They jogged over the road to him and as soon as they reached him he pulled them both into a massive hug, kissing each of their heads in turn and not caring that passers-by were staring.

'God, it's so fucking good to see you two,' he said as he took a step back and looked them both up and down. He was pleased to see that that they both looked well, and Jake in particular looked like he'd gained the weight he'd lost in the few months preceding his short holiday at Her Majesty's pleasure.

'It's good to see you too, Dad,' Connor replied.

'Yeah,' Jake agreed.

'Your mum wanted to come, but I persuaded her not to. To be honest, lads, I know we've visited a few times, but I wasn't sure what state you'd both be in. I didn't want her to get upset, but the pair of you look like you've been on fucking holiday,' he said with a laugh.

'I'll still feel better after a hot shower and putting some decent clothes on,' Jake said.

'Get in then,' Michael said. 'I'll take you to our house so you can freshen up, and you can see Jazz, Con. She's been on fucking pins all morning. Then we can go and meet your mum at the club.'

'The club? Why there?' Jake asked as he climbed into the back seat next to Connor.

'We have some business to sort out there. Well, the four of us do, so she thought it would be better to do it there. There's quite a few people looking forward to seeing you both as well, so we figured it would be easier for you both to get it all over and done with this afternoon in one go. Then you can both have a few days off, Relax and take it easy for a bit before you have to get stuck back in.'

'We've done nothing but relax for the past three weeks, Dad,' Connor said.

'Oh come on, Con,' said Jake. 'It will be nice not to have to deal with everyone's shit straightaway though, won't it? A few days hiding out at my mum's sounds good to me.' He laughed. 'Besides, Jazz is about to drop that baby any minute, you need to do all your relaxing while you still can.'

'He's right, son,' Michael added. 'Once the baby comes, you'll wonder what the word relax even means.'

'So everyone keeps telling me,' Connor replied with a smile. 'Anyway, what's this business at the club then?'

'Me and Grace have decided to make a few changes.

We'll tell you all about them properly later, but the last few months have made us re-evaluate things. We've decided we need to focus our attention on the stuff that really matters, and part of that is selling off some of Cartel Securities. As you two own part of the business, it involves you too.'

'Fucking hell. Selling the security firm?' Connor asked.

'Just part of it. We want to take a step back from it. It's still going to be ours, but we're merging with Sable Securities, and Danny Alexander and Luke Sullivan will be the new managing directors.'

'Wow! I can't believe my mum is giving up control of something,' Jake said with a laugh. 'How'd you manage that, Michael?'

'It was her idea. Like I said, boys, we're making some changes. But we'll tell you more about it properly later. Right now, I want to know how you found your time in the nick.'

Soon Connor and Jake were in full flow, giving Michael a rundown of their three weeks inside. He smiled to himself as he listened. It was good to have his boys back where they belonged.

Chapter Sixty-Two

Grace sat in one of the meeting rooms in the Radisson hotel, with John Brennan by her side. A few moments later, Jock Stewart was escorted into the room by the head of hotel security.

'Thank you, Colin,' Grace said.

'No problem, Grace,' he replied with quick nod of his head before slipping out of the door and closing it behind him.

Jock stared at the two of them as he took a seat. 'You've got friends everywhere, haven't you? Being knocked up at ten o'clock by security isn't exactly the nicest way to wake up, especially considering the night I've had,' he said with a wry smile.

'What can I say, Jock? We manage the security contract for this hotel. Didn't you know?'

'Are you serious?' he said and started to laugh. 'We were fucked from the outset really, weren't we? And I thought I did my homework too.'

'Well, you wouldn't find this place under Cartel Securities, it's registered under one of our subsidiaries.'

'You really are quite the businesswoman, Grace Carter,' he said, then he turned his attention to John. 'That was quite a show you put on. Are you out of character now? Back where you belong?'

'That's right. No hard feelings though, eh?'

'So everything you did was on your boss's orders then?' Jock asked.

'Yeah. Everything. Took me all my strength not to knock Alastair out quite a few times.'

Jock laughed. 'I bet it did. He really didn't like you, Grace. He made that quite clear.'

Grace wasn't sure what the purpose of his comment was. Was he trying to cause some tension between her and John, or was he simply making an observation?

'Well, I've lost count of the number of people who didn't like me, Jock, or underestimated me because I'm a woman. And now that I think about it, things don't usually turn out well for those people.'

'I have no doubt about that. I consider myself very lucky to be breathing, but Jerry and I are heading back to Essex this morning. We won't be visiting Liverpool again any time soon.'

'Well, that's good to hear Jock. But, from what John tells me, I think you'll make a good successor for Alastair. And who knows what the future holds? Perhaps our paths will cross again?

'Perhaps?' Jock replied with a smile. 'But before I go, there's one thing that's been bothering me. I think I've figured out your whole game plan except for that copper. Was he working for you?'

'No. He was spying on you though. Unfortunately for him, his spying on you ended up being a happy coincidence for me,' Grace replied.

'So, what was that all about then? Kidnapping him? Just to set up Craig and Ged Johnson?'

'Partly, but I had a bigger end goal in mind. I knew that there was someone who would do anything for his safe return. He was leverage.'

Jock nodded appreciatively. 'You've certainly got more balls than any man I know.'

Grace laughed. 'I'm not entirely sure that's a compliment, but I'll take it.'

'It is,' Jock assured her.

'Well, John and I just wanted to make sure there were no hard feelings before you left. We hope this is the end of the whole incident.'

Jock nodded. 'You'll have no more trouble from us. You have my word.'

'Good,' Grace said as she stood up and John followed suit. 'Until we meet again, Jock,' she said as she extended her hand.

Jock shook her hand. 'Until then, Grace.'

John and Grace walked out of the Radisson and onto Old Hall Street.

John glanced at his watch. 'Not long now until you see your boy, Grace.'

Grace linked her arm through his and they walked towards the car park. 'I know. I can't wait. I hope he's okay. I hope they're both okay.'

'They'll be fine. They're big lads and they can most definitely take care of themselves. I bet they've had a ball these past few weeks – sitting on their arses drinking hooch all day.'

Grace laughed. 'I'm sure prison is not quite the pretty picture you paint there, John. Anyway, tell me, how did your date with Steph go the other night? With everything else going on, I forgot to ask.'

'Not that great, to be honest,' he replied with a sigh. 'I think I've been friend zoned.'

'I'm sure you haven't.'

'I have. I know the signs. It's the story of my life!'

'Oh, John. The two of you seemed to have some chemistry. It certainly looked that way to me. So what went wrong?'

'There's definitely an attraction there, but we've become such good mates over the years that I think neither of us wants to risk that. I've lost count of the number of times I've been her shoulder to cry on. I don't want to be another statistic. And I think Steph would rather we stayed friends than became exes.'

'Oh no, and I had such high hopes for you two. I was even planning my outfit for the wedding.'

'Oh fuck off, Grace.' He started to laugh. 'I think I'm destined to be an eternal bachelor.'

Grace laughed too. She was feeling lighter than she had done in weeks.

'Where are we off to now then?' John asked.

'I've got one more meeting, then I need to pick up some paperwork from Faye and then we can head to The Blue Rooms.'

'Right. Where's your meeting?'

'Leigh Moss's house.'

'Oh?' John said with a flash of his eyebrows.

Grace sat on the sofa of Leigh's house in Crosby with a glass of Diet Coke which Leigh had offered her after she'd reluctantly invited her in.

'I can't believe you came here, to my house,' Leigh said as she sat down. 'How do you even know where I live?'

'You'd be surprised by the things I know,' Grace replied. 'But don't worry, I don't intend to make a habit of this. I just thought that after last night, we should chat. Clear the air?'

'Clear the air?' Leigh asked.

Grace nodded. 'I know we haven't always seen eye to eye, but I've always had a lot of respect for you, Leigh. I admire your work ethic and the way you stick to your principles.'

'Except when it comes to your son and stepson?'

'Except when it comes to any of my family.'

Leigh rolled her eyes and Grace saw red. 'Let's not forget that you came to me the other night looking for help, Leigh. You were quick to ditch all of your principles when it came to saving your boyfriend. Someone you put in danger because you were too arrogant to do as you were told and leave Alastair McGrath alone. So, don't you dare sit here in judgement of me for doing the same thing. You think because you're an upstanding DI that you're better than me? That your reasons for breaking the law are better than mine?'

Leigh's cheeks turned pink. 'No, I don't. And I appreciate what you did for Nick last night.'

Grace nodded, satisfied that she had put DI Moss in her place. 'So, what's happening with those two who kidnapped him?'

'We have CCTV of them grabbing Nick outside of his gym and bundling them into a van. We can't see the driver and they say they don't know who he was – just some heavy of the person who hired them, who as we both know was Alastair McGrath, but they won't say who it was and are uncharacteristically keeping their mouths shut for a change.'

Grace was glad that the Johnson brothers were sticking to their agreement and showing some loyalty for once. She supposed they had little choice – they were going down for Nick's kidnap anyway, so they gained nothing from implicating John, but they would most assuredly lose any of Grace's protection in prison.

'You definitely think Alastair was behind it then?' Grace asked.

'Who else would it be? Not that I can convince my superiors of that without telling them Nick was illegally surveilling them anyway.'

Grace nodded sympathetically, relieved that Leigh had pinned the blame for Nick's kidnap squarely on Alastair.

'I can't believe they took him. When I think about what could have happened if your men hadn't got to him when they did,' Leigh said as she blinked back the tears.

Grace passed Leigh a tissue from the box on the coffee table in front of her. The truth was, nothing was ever going to happen to Nick. As she'd told Jock, he was quite simply leverage. The plan had always been to persuade Bradley to take the fall for Billy's murder, and make sure that his brothers had no choice but to go along with it. When John had seen Nick Bryce watching Alastair and Jock at the bar, it had struck Grace that he was the perfect backup plan. Tony Webster had already told Grace that Leigh and her team had been warned off Alastair, and she knew that if Nick disappeared, Leigh would suspect Alastair and quite probably her too, which she did. It was then inevitable that she would ask Grace for her help. The Johnson brothers had proved that they couldn't be trusted, and just in case they tried to stab her in the back at the last minute, Grace would have the very DI who had arrested Jake and Connor owing her a very big favour.

'Well, they did, and he's okay, and that's all that matters. I'm glad we could help you out,' Grace said with a smile.

Leigh nodded. 'I thought you should know I'm quitting the OCG task force today. I'm handing in my resignation later.'

'Oh? Why?' Grace asked.

'After what I did last night, I don't feel fit for the job any longer.'

'Where will you go?'

Leigh shrugged. 'High-volume crime, or traffic. Wherever they can fit me in.'

'I'm sure you'll be happy wherever you end up.'

'You're not annoyed with me then?' Leigh asked.

'No, why would I be?'

'I thought that would be quite the coup for you. To have the DI of the organised crime team in your pocket?'

Grace laughed. 'Not at all, Leigh,' she said as she stood up to leave.

Leigh blinked at her in surprise.

'I have much more important people than DIs in my pocket,' Grace said with a wink before she walked down the hallway and opened the front door.

Chapter Sixty-Three

G race stood near the bar in The Blue Rooms where she could keep an eye on the door, waiting for Jake, Connor and Michael to arrive.

It was Jake she saw first as he walked through the double doors. The sight of him made her feel like her heart had stopped for a moment.

John Brennan walked up beside her. 'Fucking hell, I thought I'd travelled back in time there for a minute,' he said in her ear. 'He's a dead ringer, isn't he?'

Grace nodded. 'I know,' she replied, staring at her son. John was exactly right. For a moment, she too had thought she was in some kind of time warp. It could almost be twenty years earlier and she was looking at Nathan Conlon walking through those doors. All charm, smiles and swagger. She took a deep breath and reminded herself that it wasn't. This was her son, Jake. Fresh out of prison, but looking better than she'd seen him in months. Yes, he looked exactly like his father, and unfortunately had been acting like him at times recently too, but Grace held on to the fact that she was the one who had raised him. If he had anything of Nathan in him, then he had her too.

While Michael and Connor got distracted talking to Murf, Jake made his way over.

'Hiya, Mum,' he said with a beaming smile and his arms outstretched. Michael had taken them home to get showered and changed before bringing them to the club and she could already see that Jake had put some weight on. He filled out his designer suit again perfectly, the way he used to.

She pulled him to her and wrapped her arms around him, and he responded in kind.

'Jake. It's so good to see you,' she said as she inhaled the smell of shampoo and aftershave. 'You look so bloody well.'

Jake started to laugh as he took a step back from her. 'Prison looks good on me then?'

'Yes. But don't be getting any ideas about going back there any time soon,' she said.

'I won't, Mum,' he said with a smile. 'And thank you for getting us out. I knew you would.'

Grace smiled back at him. He looked so well. Clean-shaven, fresh, groomed. God, it was almost as if she had the old Jake back.

'Good to have you back, kid,' John said as he stepped forward and put an arm around Jake's shoulder.

'Thanks, John. It's good to be back,' Jake replied. 'I heard you played quite the part in our release yourself?'

'You could say that. I thought your mum was crazy when she suggested it, but it all worked out for the best.'

'You were a legend, John. You put in an Oscar-worthy performance. For a minute, I actually thought you had decided to work for Alastair McGrath,' Grace said with a laugh.

'What? As if I would. You know me better than that, Boss,' John said and Grace thought she detected the hint of a blush creeping up his neck. 'Can I get either of you a drink?' John asked.

'A bottle of Bud for me, mate?' Jake replied.

'I'll have a brandy, thanks,' Grace said.

As John was walking away, Jake gave her a gentle nudge. 'You know he fancies you, don't you?' he said with a chuckle.

'Oh stop it, no, he doesn't,' she said as she saw Michael and Connor making their way over. 'Stop trying to get him into trouble.'

'My lips are sealed,' Jake replied with a grin.

'Hiya, Grace,' Connor said as he pulled Grace into a bear hug.

'Hello, Con,' she replied as she returned his hug. 'It's so lovely to see you.' She stepped back from him and appraised the two boys, who looked smart in their suits. 'It's lovely to see the both of you.'

'It's nice to be seen,' Connor replied. 'Walton nick is an absolute shithole! I don't fancy going back there any time soon.'

'Music to my ears,' Michael said as he slipped an arm around Grace's waist. 'Before you two go off celebrating, we want to talk to you about something.'

The two boys looked at each other. 'Sounds ominous,' Jake said.

'Is this to do with what you were talking about in the car, Dad? About what happens next?'

Michael looked at Grace. 'I told the boys what we'd decided,' he said.

Grace nodded. 'Then yes, I suppose it is.'

———————

Five minutes later, Grace, Michael, Jake and Connor were sitting in one the booths at The Blue Rooms with drinks in their hands. Grace was pleased to see that Jake had hardly touched his bottle of beer. John had only passed it to him a few minutes earlier, but a few weeks ago, he'd have sunk it in one and followed it with a shot of whisky.

'I'm on standby, by the way,' Connor said with a smile. 'Jazz is convinced the baby is going to arrive any time now that I'm out.'

'I'm not planning on hanging around either. I'm going to see Siobhan and Isla. I do appreciate this little get-together, Mum,' Jake said, 'but I've really missed Isla.'

Grace smiled. Her two boys seemed to have their priorities right for a change, and she wanted to make sure they stayed that way. 'No problem at all. We wanted to meet you here so we could all sign the contracts with Sable Securities, there's no need to hang around. But before Danny and Luke get here, there was something else we wanted to talk to you about.'

Connor and Jake looked at her, their eyes full of concern.

'It's nothing to worry about. It's just some advice, that's all. Some guidance we'd like you to live by.'

The boys shared a quizzical look at each other.

'You have no idea how hard it was for us to see you two arrested and thrown into prison,' Michael started. 'Not to mention Jazz. Can you imagine if you'd missed the birth of your first child, Con?'

Connor shook his head. 'I know, Dad,' he said. 'You don't need to remind me. I feel bad enough already.

'We're not trying to make you feel bad. But we're asking that you don't put yourselves in that position unnecessarily again.'

'What do you mean?' Jake asked.

'We know what happened to Billy was because you were angry about Paul, and we understand that better than anyone. But in future, you need to think smarter, boys. You both have children to think of. You own some very successful and lucrative businesses. You make more in a week than most people make in a year. It's time to start acting more like professional businessmen and less like mindless thugs,' Grace replied.

'But that's what we do…' Jake started.

'It is a part of what you do, and no one is saying that you can't give someone a bit of a slap now and then, but you can afford to pay people to do that sort of work for you now, and, more importantly, you should. One of the major perks of being in charge is that you never need to be at the scene of the crime,' Grace said.

Connor and Jake nodded. 'That makes sense, but what if people think we've gone soft?' Jake asked.

Michael started to laugh. 'Do you think me or your mum are soft?'

'Fair point,' Jake replied with a shrug.

'All we're asking is that you think about what you're doing before you do it,' Grace said. 'No more running into things head first. Use those brains you both clearly have, and let your hired muscle do their job.'

Jake and Connor nodded. 'Okay,' they said in unison.

They were interrupted by two burly men in suits approaching the table.

'Afternoon, gentlemen. Please have a seat,' Grace said as she indicated the two empty chairs.

Danny Alexander and Luke Sullivan were the owners of Sable Securities. They had been in business for four years and during that time had made a good name for themselves and a solid reputation. Grace and Michael had met with them a few times and Grace had been impressed by their business acumen and their fearlessness. They had taken over a number of doors in Merseyside, the ones that Cartel didn't run, and had approached Michael about a possible merger. Luke, in particular, was an asset, having completed a business degree, and he had presented them with a bulletproof business plan that was beneficial for all parties involved. In fact, Grace and Michael had been so impressed that they'd decided to agree to a merger with Sable Securities, a deal that would allow the Carter family, owning the much bigger Cartel firm, to maintain a seventy-five per cent share in the business but let Danny and Luke take over as managing directors. In turn, this would allow Grace and Michael to remain on as CEOs and take a step back from the day-to-day running and its headaches.

It was a deal that all parties were pleased with and one that Grace was sure they would all profit from.

Grace introduced Danny and Luke to the boys and soon everyone at the table had fallen into an easy conversation.

Jake looked at his watch and Grace remembered that he and Connor were itching to get going.

'Shall we get down to business then, gents? I have the paperwork here,' Grace said as she pulled the manila folder out of her handbag. 'I believe my solicitor sent you both a copy to look over before our meeting.'

'Yes, she sent it yesterday. I've had a good read of it and it all looks legit to me,' Luke answered, his brown eyes twinkling.

'Great, shall we all sign on the dotted line then?' Grace said as she produced her favourite Mont Blanc pen. It was the one she signed all of her most important deals with. She wasn't usually a superstitious person, but she had never signed a bad deal with her lucky pen.

Grace and Michael were enjoying a drink alone. Connor and Jake had left shortly after signing the paperwork, and Danny and Luke had stayed for one more drink before heading back to their office to start packing up for the move to their new premises.

'That was all easier than I thought it was going to be,' Grace said as she sipped her fifth brandy of the afternoon.

'The contracts?' Michael asked.

'No, I meant talking to Jake and Connor.'

'Hmm, I know what you mean,' he replied.

'The contracts went well too,' she laughed, feeling the alcohol going to her head all of a sudden.

'Am I going to have to carry you out of here?' Michael said with a smile and a raised eyebrow.

'Maybe?'

'Shall I get you another?'

Grace looked into her glass and saw there was nothing left. 'Are you going to have one with me?' she asked. He'd only had one beer earlier with the boys and had switched to lime and soda after that.

'Maybe?' he replied.

'We could ask your dad to keep hold of the kids for the night?'

'And stay out drinking?' he asked.

'And dancing?' she added with a grin.

Michael laughed. 'I'll ring my dad now then. Do you want another brandy?'

'I'd love one,' Grace replied. Then she watched her handsome husband walking over to the bar with his mobile phone against his ear. Grace smiled to herself. Jake and Connor were out of prison, and most importantly Jake seemed to be back to his usual self. She and Michael had made some plans for the future. Plans they had talked through and, crucially, plans that they were both in full agreement with – plans that would keep all of their family safe.

Life was good.

Chapter Sixty-Four

Luke looked across at his business partner and smiled as they drove along the Dock Road.

'Did we just fucking do that?' Danny asked, his eyes shining with excitement.

Luke nodded. 'Yep. We fucking did, mate. We're the new Managing Directors of the biggest security firm in the North West,' he replied.

'Fuck!' Danny said with a laugh. 'I think that deserves a celebration tonight, don't you?'

'Yeah. But we need to help pack up the offices first. There are some things in that safe that I'd rather nobody else saw.'

Danny nodded in agreement.

Luke Sullivan and Danny Alexander had been best mates since they'd met in a playground at the age of eight. They went to different schools but lived close by each other, albeit in very different conditions. Luke's father, who had died shortly before he was born, had left his mother a significant amount of money and she had used some of it to buy a semi-detached house in Aigburth. Maggie Sullivan had thought she'd never have children and was shocked and elated to have fallen pregnant at the age of thirty-eight. She'd also worked as a sales rep for a local brewery and had been good at her job, so she earned a good wage and together they had enjoyed a comfortable lifestyle. After she'd died, when Luke was twenty, he had inherited everything, including the substantial nest egg she had built up over the years. It was that money that had allowed him and Danny to set up Sable Securities.

Danny's childhood had been as far removed from Luke's as it could possibly be. He and his sister, Stacey, lived in a two-up, two-down in Dingle on the border of Aigburth. They were abandoned by their mother when Danny was thirteen and Stacey just nine. Left with their abusive, alcoholic stepfather, Danny had practically had to raise Stacey, at least until he was sent to a Young Offenders Institution at the age of seventeen after braining his stepfather with a toaster and killing him outright. For years, Danny had had to defend himself from the man's drunken outbursts, but when he'd started on Stacey too, it had been the tipping point and he'd got four years for manslaughter. Stacey had been sent to a children's home, and though Danny had got her out again as soon as he'd left prison and found himself a job, he'd never forgiven himself for what had happened to her there.

Despite being from very different backgrounds, Luke and Danny had become firm friends upon their first meeting and remained so ever since. Despite the fact that

Luke had gone to Liverpool University to study business while Danny had been learning how to fix bicycles in HMYOI Hindley, their differences had never come between them. Not that Luke was an angel, but he had always learned the fine art of not getting caught. Danny, on the other hand, had had no choice.

'Let's drop in and see our Stacey on the way. She said they've got a load of boxes left over from their office move we could have. Save us using Tesco bags?' Danny said with a laugh, interrupting Luke's train of thought.

'Okay,' Luke said, feigning uninterest. The truth was he welcomed any opportunity to see Danny's younger sister, who was currently working as a secretary in a small accountancy firm in Kirkdale. She had moved to Manchester when she was eighteen, but had recently returned to Liverpool for reasons which Danny and Luke knew something of, although they both suspected they didn't have the full story. Luke had always seen her as a little sister too –until about six months earlier, when she'd come back into his life and turned his world upside down. Not that either Danny or Stacey was aware of that fact. Stacey was off limits in more ways than one. She'd experienced more heartache in her twenty-four years than most people did in a lifetime.

Luke and Danny walked into Stacey's small office to see her chatting to two uniformed police officers. Luke felt Danny's uneasiness as he stood beside him and knew they were thinking exactly the same thing. What the hell were they doing here?

'We'll be in touch, Stacey,' one of them said as he

extended his hand to shake hers. 'Thank you for your co-operation.'

'No problem. Glad I could help,' Stacey said as she shook his hand.

Danny eyed the police officers suspiciously as they brushed past him on their way out.

'What's going on, Stacey? It's not that fucking prick again, is it? I'll fucking—' Danny shouted as soon as the officers were out of earshot.

'Danny!' she snapped. 'Calm down. It's nothing.'

'The police don't just visit you for nothing, Stacey. What the hell is going on?'

'Simon is in trouble again, that's all. The police are looking for him.'

'I knew it was something to do with that fucker,' Danny snarled. 'I told you to let me deal with him properly. Has he been in touch with you?'

Luke saw the colour rising up Stacey's neck and across her cheeks and felt for her. Simon was her ex-boyfriend, and a waste of fucking oxygen. He bought and sold women like they were cars and had been about to do the same to Stacey when Danny and Luke had got her out just in time. It was a source of hurt and embarrassment for her that she had been completely fooled by the nasty little prick and any mention of Simon's name made her visibly uncomfortable. Luke wished he could take her out of there and let her get some air, but Danny wouldn't leave it alone until he had some answers.

'Yes. He's found out I'm working here, and he's called a few times.'

'What? When?' Danny shouted.

'Can you just leave it ... For God's sake,' Stacey snapped. 'It's been dealt with.'

Danny continued to stare at his sister, waiting for some sort of explanation as to why she hadn't told him about this, while Luke looked at the floor and wished his best mate could be a little more tactful.

'Why the hell didn't you tell us about this?' Danny shouted.

'Because of this, Danny,' she hissed. 'Because I knew you'd overreact. You always do.'

'But, Stacey—'

'But nothing! I am a grown woman. I can take care of myself. He called here and when I finally spoke to him I told him I wanted nothing more to do with him. He hasn't phoned since last week and now he's disappeared anyway because the police are looking for him.'

'The police are fucking useless,' Danny snarled. 'Let me and Luke handle it.'

'There's nothing to handle, Danny! Besides, I know exactly how you and Luke would *handle* this, and I've told you before, I want no part of that,' she said quietly. 'Just leave it to the police.'

Danny started to shake his head and was about to argue with her when Luke placed a hand on his arm. 'Stacey's right. Let her deal with this her own way.'

Danny glared at Luke, the vein pulsing in his temple before he let out a long breath and sat down in a chair. 'Whatever,' he finally said.

It was another ten minutes before Stacey Alexander finally herded her brother and his best mate out of the small office she worked in. Sitting back in her chair, she closed her eyes and let out a long, slow breath that she felt like she'd been holding in for hours. Danny and Luke could never discover the truth of all she had endured at the hands of Simon Hughes. If they did, they would never let her out of their sight again, but even worse, Simon would end up chopped into pieces and dumped in the Mersey. Despite her assurances otherwise, Stacey was terrified that her ex-boyfriend had found her, and she knew that he wasn't the type to take no for an answer. But Danny had already given up enough of his life protecting her and she couldn't bear him going to prison because of that again.

Danny slammed the car door closed behind him and folded his arms across his chest. Luke glanced sideways at him as he started the ignition and noted the stark contrast to when they'd got into the car outside The Blue Rooms less than an hour earlier. He knew better than to poke the bear when he was in a mood and silently pulled the car away from the kerb.

'We should do something about this Simon cunt. I knew we should have fucking dealt with him when we had the chance,' Danny growled after a few moments silence.

Luke nodded. 'I know.'

'Then why did you tell me to leave it alone in there then?' he snapped. 'Why didn't you back me up?'

'Because,' Luke sighed, 'your sister is almost as stubborn as you are. She doesn't want our help, mate. And I understand why. We wouldn't exactly be acting within the parameters of the law, would we? She's finally getting her life back on track. And like it or not, Stacey is a grown woman. You can't keep trying to wrap her in cotton wool. You'll only end up pushing her away…'

'What? You mean like I did last time?' Danny snarled.

Luke shook his head. 'I never said that.'

'But that's what you were thinking, wasn't it?'

'For fuck's sake, Danny. Don't be putting none of your guilt on me. Nobody blames you for what happened to Stacey. Nobody except you anyway.'

Danny sank back into his seat. 'If I hadn't been so strict with her, Luke … If I'd just given her some leeway…' he said with a sigh. 'No wonder she fucked off as soon as she could.'

Luke put a hand on his best mate's shoulder. 'You did the best you could. You were a just a kid yourself, trying to bring up a teenager – and she wasn't exactly easy,' he reminded him.

'Well, who could blame her for that?' Danny shrugged before falling silent.

Luke was thankful that the rest of the journey was quiet. He understood Danny's instinct to help Stacey. It was his instinct too. But the way they usually handled their problems was to beat them into submission, and they couldn't do that this time. Stacey had just got back on her feet. She had just walked away from a life of violence and fear and Luke understood her need to distance herself from anything connected to that as much as possible. No, they had to let the police handle him, no matter how much it went against everything they believed in. The thought of Simon Hughes being anywhere near Stacey bothered Luke just as much as it did Danny. He wanted to protect her too, and that included hunting down that cunt and making him pay for every bit of pain he had ever caused her. But Luke was afraid that admitting that would make his feelings for his best mate's little sister all too obvious.

Chapter Sixty-Five

Jake stepped out of his car and walked along the leafy street towards Siobhan's house. He looked around at the large, beautifully maintained houses and thought what a nice place she had chosen to raise their daughter. He hated the fact that she was an hour's drive away, but he understood why Siobhan had made the move, and he could see how she and Isla could build a nice life for themselves here.

Siobhan was renting a three-bed semi-detached house a ten-minute walk away from Carter's Wine Bar, and she had put Isla into the small nursery nearby. His daughter seemed happy and settled and he knew that was all that really mattered, but it still hurt him not to have her close to him. He'd had an arrangement to have Isla for a couple of nights every fortnight before he'd gone to prison, but he'd never had a set routine and sometimes he'd cancel at the last minute. He realised now how unsettling that must have been for a young child, and in future he was going to make sure he made more of an effort to be a stable influence in her life.

Jake knocked on the door and waited for Siobhan to answer. She was expecting him, but he still wondered at the reception he'd get from her after the last time they'd met face to face. She had come to pick Isla up and had objected to the state that Jake was in. He'd called her a judgemental cow and they'd had a massive row. He was ashamed to admit it now, but she'd been right to have a go at him. He'd been drunk and on coke when he should have been looking after his daughter. Anything could have happened and he shuddered as he realised how lucky they had all been that nothing had.

Siobhan opened the door and gave him a quick look up and down. She obviously approved because her face broke into a huge smile. 'Jake. You look great,' she said.

'Daddy!' Isla shrieked as she came running down the hallway to the front door.

'Isla,' he said as he scooped her up into his arms. 'My little princess. I've missed you so much.'

'Missed you too, Daddy,' she said as she placed her two chubby little hands on either side of his face.

Jake felt a rush of love for her that had him blinking back the tears and he pressed his face into her hair, inhaling the scent of Johnson's baby shampoo.

'Come in,' Siobhan said as she ushered them both inside. 'I'll stick the kettle on.'

Ten minutes later, Jake was sitting on the sofa in Siobhan's living room with Isla on his knee. Siobhan placed a hot mug of tea on the table beside him.

'You look really good, Jake,' Siobhan said again as she sat down opposite him on the armchair.

He laughed. 'Don't sound so surprised.'

'I'm not,' she said as she blushed slightly. 'It's just…'

'I'm only kidding. I know I must have looked a bit rough the last time we met,' he said. 'And I'm sorry about that, Siobhan. I really am. I was completely out of order and you were right to have a go at me about it. It won't happen again.'

Siobhan stared at him, her mouth open slightly.

'Are you okay?' he asked her.

She shook her head and laughed. 'I don't think I've ever heard you admit you were wrong before. I've heard you say you were sorry dozens of times, but if I'm honest, Jake, I've never really believed you.'

'Well, I mean it,' he said in all seriousness, realising too that she was probably right. He wondered if he had ever truly meant it before, or if it was just something that he used to say to make himself feel better.

'I know,' she said with a smile.

'I'm sorry about everything, Siobhan,' he said, suddenly overwhelmed with a feeling of guilt that he'd been burying deep inside himself for years. 'About Paul, and the way I treated you. It was unfair and I should have told you the truth before we got married. But it was just so hard to admit it to myself, never mind to anyone else.'

Siobhan held up a hand as though to stop him talking.

'Jake,' she said as she blinked back the tears. 'Please, don't. I'm not exactly blameless here, am I?'

'Well, no,' he replied, remembering that she had slept with one of his best mates and then agreed to get married, despite not knowing whether Isla was Jake's child or not. But none of that changed the fact that he had lied to her from the outset.

'And I don't just mean about Connor,' she said, as though reading his mind.

Jake nodded and looked down at Isla, her long lashes resting against her pink cheeks. 'She's fallen asleep,' he whispered.

'She was so excited waiting for you that she wouldn't have her nap. She's exhausted.'

'She deserves better than me, Siobhan,' he said.

'Don't say that, Jake. She loves you. You're her father.'

'Well, she deserves better than what I've been offering for the past few months anyway.'

'You were grieving,' Siobhan said. 'I know how much you loved Paul. How much you must miss him.'

'I do, but plenty of people lose people they love and don't turn into a complete mess, do they? And Isla deserves better than that. Paul's memory deserves better.'

'Well, it's nice to see the Jake I knew back.'

'And I am back, Siobhan. I don't need drink or drugs to get through the day any more. So, when you're happy to, I'd like to start having Isla overnight again. I thought maybe every other weekend, and one night through the week?'

'That would be great, Jake,' she said with a smile. 'It

would help me out a lot, but more importantly, Isla would love it. She's really missed you.'

'Brilliant. Thanks.'

They sat in silence for a few moments, watching their sleeping daughter.

'Can I ask you something without us getting into an argument about it?' Jake said.

Siobhan nodded. 'Of course.'

'You knew about me and Paul before I asked you to marry me, so why did you say yes? And why didn't you tell me?' he asked with no hint of anger in his voice. He hoped that Siobhan wouldn't feel accused. It was just something he had always wondered about.

Siobhan looked at him, her cheeks pink and her eyes wet with tears. 'I thought … I hoped, that it was just a phase, Jake. I convinced myself that it was just an experiment or something you needed to get out of your system. I thought that being pregnant and us getting married would change everything for you. I thought that me and Isla would be enough…'

'Siobhan,' he said with a sigh. 'It wasn't that you weren't enough—'

'I know that now,' she interrupted him. 'I realise now how naïve and selfish I was being. I know that you can't help who you are, Jake. But I was so hurt, and I loved you so much. I couldn't accept that everything we had, all we'd been through together, had been a lie.'

'It wasn't a lie, Siobhan. I loved you too. I need you to know that. It wasn't until I met Paul…'

'Was he the only one?' she asked.

Jake nodded. 'Yes. There was never anyone else, I swear.'

'Good,' she said with a smile.

'I do love you, Siobhan. I always will, but not in the way you need me to.'

Siobhan nodded as a tear rolled down her cheek. 'Not the way you loved Paul.'

'No,' Jake said, the word catching in his throat.

'I was sorry about Paul. Despite everything that happened. I hope you know that?'

'Thanks.'

A few more moments of comfortable silence passed between them again before Jake spoke again. 'Are you happy here?'

Siobhan looked at him, tilting her head to one side. 'It's not Liverpool, it doesn't feel like home yet, but it's quiet and my neighbours are nice. I love managing the wine bar,' she said, a smile lighting up her face suddenly.

'I heard you're doing an amazing job, but of course you would, The Blue Rooms has never been the same since you left. You managed the place better than anyone.'

'I enjoyed it. I miss the place. There was always something going on,' she said with a laugh.

'Well, if you fancy coming home, I could do with a decent manager.' Jake grinned.

'Oh yeah, and what would I say to your mum? She's only just given me the job. Thanks for the opportunity, Grace, but now I'm off,' Siobhan said with a flash of her eyebrows.

'She'd understand. She'd just be happy to have you and Isla nearer home.'

Siobhan laughed. 'She probably would. She's quite the woman, your mum.'

'She certainly is. You know, I always thought it was my dad's reputation I had to live up to, but he was nothing compared to her.'

'Well, I couldn't think of a better person for you to live up to then.'

Jake nodded. 'I know.'

Jake was driving home down the M6 listening to the radio when he thought back to his conversation with Siobhan. They'd talked until Isla woke from her nap and then they'd all eaten dinner together. It had been one of the best afternoons he'd spent in a long time. As awful as it was to have been charged and remanded for murder, that short stretch inside had shaken him out of the pit of despair he'd been wallowing in. On his first night inside he'd taken some spice and it had almost killed him. That stuff was some nasty shit. He'd been hallucinating and had ended up shitting his pants. He'd woken up two days later in the hospital wing and vowed never to touch another drug again. He was only three weeks on, but he hadn't wavered and he had no desire to.

Jake thought about his mum too. Siobhan was right, she was quite the woman. She was fearless. From the moment he was born she had always put him first. She had always been there for him, and he knew that no matter what, she always would. She always came through for him, no matter what the cost to herself. She put her family above all else and she had shown him what true loyalty was. It was because of that that her reign had gone unchallenged for over a decade. Jake smiled as he thought about the conversation Michael had had with him and Connor earlier, outlining the plans for the future. It was the right thing for everyone and the timing couldn't have been better.

Chapter Sixty-Six

Connor Carter looked down at the face of his newborn son and smiled. His heart felt like it might burst, such was the love he felt for this little bundle, wrapped in a blanket, as he raised one of his chubby little fists in the air, as though in a gesture of triumph.

'Yeah, little man. You made it,' Connor said with tears in his eyes as he kissed his forehead.

He looked up to see Jasmine beaming at him and he crossed the room to sit on the bed beside her. She had been through the wringer but she had never looked more beautiful to him.

'I don't think I've ever seen you look more content,' she said to him as she laid her head on his arm.

'You have made me the happiest man in the world, Jazz,' he breathed. 'You were fucking amazing there, girl. Fucking amazing!'

He heard her laugh softly.

'He's incredible, isn't he?' Connor said.

'Hmm,' Jasmine answered sleepily.

Connor kissed the top of her head. 'Try and get some kip, babe. Me and Paul will be right here waiting for you when you wake up,' he said quietly as he shuffled off the bed, careful not to wake his girlfriend, who had already fallen asleep.

Connor sat in the large wing-backed chair of the private hospital room and stared down at the face of his sleeping son, with his thick dark hair and chubby cheeks – he was quite simply perfect in every way. It had been just after 1am when Jasmine's waters had broken. His dad and Grace had just been rolling in from a night out as Jasmine and Connor were rushing out the door, Connor holding Jasmine up with one arm and carrying her hospital bag in the other.

Grace and his dad had been hardly able to contain their excitement and had waved them off in a flurry of cheering and smiles. Two hours later, Paul Michael Carter made his very noisy entrance into the world. Jasmine had been an absolute star and Connor had been completely blown away by her strength and her dignity. He knew right then that he would never love any other woman as much as he loved her right then. Her blood pressure had shot through the roof during delivery, but they'd given her medication and it had returned to almost normal levels. They also had her hooked up to a monitor to keep an eye on her overnight as a precaution.

'You waited for me then, eh? I knew you would. I'll never leave you again, mate,' Connor said quietly to the tiny bundle in his arms. 'I love you, son.'

Then Connor leaned his head back in his chair and

closed his eyes as Paul junior snuggled into his chest. Connor listened to the shuffling of feet up and down the corridor outside the room, the beeping of medical machinery and the occasional alarm going off. He wondered how on earth anyone ever managed to get any sleep in the place.

He was woken with a start a short time later by the loud beeping of machinery and a flurry of doctors and nurses as they came rushing into the room, speaking in a language that sounded completely alien to him. He looked down at Paul, who was still nestled safely in his arms. They weren't here for Paul. They crowded around Jasmine's bed and all Connor could do was look on in horror.

Epilogue

TWO MONTHS LATER

Luke Sullivan leaned back in his chair and surveyed the room. At least two dozen men dressed in suits were sitting around a large table. It was almost like a boardroom. He supposed it was a board meeting of sorts – the respectable face of the Liverpool underworld, except that it wasn't just Liverpool any longer. Luke saw faces from Manchester, Newcastle, Scotland and beyond. Even Jerry Smith, Jock Stewart's right-hand man, was sitting patiently, waiting for his orders. Luke and Danny had been trusted to do some of the negotiating with the new Essex branch of the firm, and Luke had been impressed with their set-up. He'd got to know Jerry in particular over the past few weeks and he liked doing business with him. Jock Stewart had taken over Alastair McGrath's firm as expected, and Jerry had in turn been promoted. He'd always been Jock's go-to man, but now he was second in command of the whole firm. It had been a role he hadn't particularly been looking for – he said he was getting too old, for a start

– but Jock had managed to persuade him. The old Scot could be a smooth talker when he wanted to be.

Luke knew how much Jerry liked working for Jock. He said he was much more stable and rational than their previous boss, Alastair McGrath. Of course, questions had been asked about Alastair's whereabouts and his apparent disappearance. Jock and Jerry had stuck to their agreed script: after his humiliating defeat at the hands of Grace Carter, he had done a bunk to the Costa del Sol with his Liverpool mistress. No one gave a shit enough to probe any further, not even Alastair's wife, who seemed relieved to finally be free of her controlling, philandering husband.

When Jock had asked Jerry to come to Liverpool and explore a deal that would make them all a tonne of money, he'd been happy to. Jock Stewart didn't get involved with people unless he rated them, and he rated this Liverpool firm very highly indeed.

Suddenly the hum of chatter stopped as the door opened. Jake Conlon and Connor Carter stepped inside the room. They both gave a nod of acknowledgement to the men seated around the table before taking a seat themselves. The door they'd just walked through remained open and Luke heard Michael Carter's laugh before he saw him walking through the door. He was an imposing figure and his presence in the room was palpable, but it wasn't until he stepped aside and Grace Carter walked in behind him that every man pushed back his chair and stood up.

'Gentlemen,' she said with a nod. 'Please have a seat.'

Everyone did so, including Michael, who sat next to Connor and Jake.

Grace Carter took her seat at the head of the table. 'Right, shall we get down to business then?' she said with a smile.

Luke smiled too. In a short space of time, he and Danny had been welcomed into Grace Carter's inner circle and it was a place they both felt they belonged. They had made themselves indispensable, particularly to Jake and Connor, and were fast becoming their go-to men. While Luke and Danny's business was security, they were both open to other ways of making money – and Grace Carter provided them by the bucket-load. She and Michael were quite obviously taking a step back from the hands-on side of the business, but there was no doubt in anyone's mind that she was still the woman in charge. She managed to keep all of the various major factions on side and loyal to her, and Luke had no idea how she did it. The woman was a legend.

Luke's thoughts were interrupted by the vibration of his mobile phone in his inside pocket. He had three phones and this was the one only Danny, and a few select people in this room, had the number to. It was for emergencies only – the Bat-phone! Luke frowned. Danny knew he was in this meeting. Discreetly taking it out of his pocket, he glanced at the screen and saw the text message sent by his best mate and business partner. It sent a shudder down his spine.

'I've just had a visit from Joey Parnell. He's not a happy bunny.'

Luke slipped the phone back into his pocket and resisted the urge to get up and leave, knowing it would disturb the meeting. It would be over soon anyway and he needed to speak to Grace. If Joey Parnell was back on the scene, then it meant bad news for all of them.

On the other side of the city, the new head of Merseyside Police's vice unit, DI Leigh Moss, was removing her rubber gloves as she walked back towards her car. She wiped the beads of sweat from her forehead with the back of her hand and let out a long slow breath. Seeing dead bodies never got any easier, but seeing dead bodies that had been mutilated in some way was something that never left you. This was the third young working girl this month to have turned up dead in some alleyway. Despite the girls having a connection to each other and to the Sunnymeade Children's Home, the police were no closer to finding their killer. The last one, though, Nerys Sheehan, had a connection to someone else, one that couldn't be overlooked.

Taking her phone out of her pocket, Leigh dialled Grace Carter's phone number.

Acknowledgments

As always, I would like to thank the wonderful team at One More Chapter for believing in me and bringing this book to life, most especially Charlotte Ledger, whose support of the Bad Blood series has helped it go from strength to strength. I'd also love to thank my amazing editor, Emily Ruston, who continues to provide her expert insight and advice.

I'd like to give a mention to a wonderful book club on Facebook – formerly the Notrights, and now the Gangland Governor's. They are a great group of people who have given me so much support, not to mention introduced me to so many good books. I am always grateful for my good friend, Mary Torjussen, for her ongoing support and all her wise advice.

A huge thank-you to my family for their constant love and support, especially my mum and dad, and husband, Eric. And finally, but most especially, to my three incredible boys – who continue to inspire and amaze me every single day.

YOUR NUMBER ONE STOP

ONE MORE CHAPTER

FOR PAGETURNING BOOKS

One More Chapter is an
award-winning global
division of HarperCollins.

Sign up to our newsletter to get our
latest eBook deals and stay up to date
with our weekly Book Club!
<u>Subscribe here.</u>

Meet the team at
<u>www.onemorechapter.com</u>

Follow us!

 @OneMoreChapter_

 @OneMoreChapter

@onemorechapterhc

Do you write unputdownable fiction?
We love to hear from new voices.
Find out how to submit your novel at
<u>www.onemorechapter.com/submissions</u>